Game
On

Also by Calvin Slater

Lovers & Haters

Hold Me Down

Published by Dafina Books

Game On

A Coleman High Novel

Calvin Slater

Dafina
Books

KENSINGTON PUBLISHING CORP.
www.kensingtonbooks.com

DAFINA BOOKS are published by

Kensington Publishing Corp.
119 West 40th Street
New York, NY 10018

All Kensington titles, imprints, and distributed lines are available at special quantity discounts for bulk purchases for sales promotion, premiums, fund-raising, and educational or institutional use.

Special book excerpts or customized printings can also be created to fit specific needs. For details, write or phone the office of the Kensington Sales Manager: Kensington Publishing Corp., 119 West 40th Street, New York, NY 10018. Attn. Sales Department. Phone: 1-800-221-2647.

Dafina and the Dafina logo Reg. U.S. Pat. & TM Off.

ISBN-13: 978-1-61773-136-5
ISBN-10: 1-61773-136-6
First Kensington Trade Paperback Printing: September 2015

eISBN-13: 978-1-61773-137-2
eISBN-10: 1-61773-137-4
First Kensington Electronic Edition: September 2015

10 9 8 7 6 5 4 3 2 1

Printed in the United States of America

PROLOGUE

This was too early in the morning for him, and during his summer vacation. At a time when Xavier should've been in his bed with the covers pulled up to his chin and copping some serious z's, he was yawning while following a short correctional officer with no neck and a butt the size of a small Buick down a drab, dreary corridor.

Xavier still couldn't believe that in another month he would be entering his senior year of high school. Never in his wildest dreams when starting out as a freshman at Coleman High did he ever think he'd make it all the way, given all the drama he'd had to deal with in his personal life. But as much as he wanted to celebrate, he knew there were some real hard truths he hadn't overcome yet.

He was still a wanted man with an undisclosed bounty riding on his bald head, placed there by Slick Eddie, a pissed-off kingpin who'd at one time owned and operated a multimillion-dollar chop shop out of a huge junkyard on Detroit's Westside. Slick Eddie was now doing a life stretch in prison because Xavier had ratted him, and his former soldier Romello Anderson, out to the police. Since then Eddie had sworn revenge. Xavier was sure he would never live to see graduation, and Eddie almost made good on his promise with a couple of unsuccessful attempts. It didn't matter how many hitters Eddie sent Xavier's way. Xavier was focused, and he possessed a deep-rooted conviction that nothing, not even Eddie, was going to keep him from stepping across the stage at his graduation ceremony.

As he trailed behind the correctional officer, Xavier had to admit to himself that it took a lot of guts to get him to this point. This was the women's side of Portus Correctional Facility, a place where his mother Ne Ne had been cooling her heels for a little over a year now. There was once a time where he didn't care about ever seeing her again, especially after the crazy move she'd pulled at the end of his sophomore year. Ne Ne and her jailbird boyfriend Nate had breezed through Coleman High's back parking lot in an attempt to abduct Xavier's now ex-girlfriend Samantha during the last school dance. Ne Ne was the main reason his relationship with Samantha was no longer. But since then Xavier had had some time to think about mending fences with his mother. Although her selfish butt didn't deserve his forgiveness, Xavier's father Noah had been instrumental in convincing the boy that nobody was perfect and everybody deserved a second chance.

And that's why Xavier was now sitting down in a graffiti-riddled booth with a thick glass partition separating him from an empty chair, awaiting the arrival of his inmate mother. He hadn't been able to understand it. Through the first ten months of her sentence, Ne Ne didn't look like she gave a crap about her son.

No letters. No collect phone calls.

But Noah hadn't left her any room to bring the noise with some weak excuse. Even though Ne Ne hadn't passed along any of the letters Noah had sent to Xavier and his brother while Noah was in prison, he wasn't about to do the same to her. So he had gone online and found her inmate number and mailing address through OTIS (Offender Tracking Information System) and wrote to her, providing the address and phone numbers where she could reach her boys. But still there was nothing. Then all of a sudden, three weeks ago, it had been like a switch flipping when Ne Ne started calling collect and sending the boys letters like she'd lost her mind, each claiming that she was new and reformed from her old ways. She had found the Lord and became born again and whatnot. Just what Xavier needed—another highly religious nut running loose in the family. And just when he'd gotten his relationship tight with his Bible-thumping old man too. Now he had to deal with this junk. But she was his mother and he respected the title.

Nothing surprised him about his mother.

Even as she took her seat on the other side of the glass partition, seeing her, Xavier wondered if her newly acquired faith was some scheme she'd cooked up to weasel her way back into his life. To convince him by using King James scripture to aid in her clever disguise of a woman who'd truly seen the error of her ways.

Ne Ne's looks had changed a bit. Age seemed to set in overnight. Where her face once held the unmistakable arrogance of the ghetto, it now seemed to be home to traces of humility. Gray lived in the tangles of her hairline. There were bags underneath her hard eyes, and she looked to be down quite a few pounds from the last time he'd seen her.

Xavier kept his eyes focused on her face. He just wanted to see if her new way of life existed there. But he couldn't really tell because his mother looked to be anxious, shifting around in her seat and avoiding eye contact. It was wrong to judge her primarily on her emotions. This behavior could stem from shame. After all, the last time Xavier had laid eyes on her was when she and her knucklehead boyfriend Nate tried to kidnap Samantha. Xavier surmised that if he'd pulled something so desperate, lowdown, and despicable, he'd be ashamed to look that someone in the eyes too.

Xavier picked up the telephone and waited until she did the same. When he spoke, his voice seemed to be a little harsh. "You know you didn't have a soul back then . . . the letters you keep sending to the house. How can I believe any of it?"

His mother kept her eyes cast downward. "I didn't know God the way I do now, son."

"Excuse me for not really buying it, but when convicts go to prison, a lot of them come out claiming to be holier than thou, you feel me?"

Ne Ne's eyes kept darting from side to side like she was watching a tennis match when she tried to look at him. "You have a right to be angry. I put you and your brother through a lot with my own selfishness. All I can say is I'm sorry."

He had come to see her with the intention of burying the hatchet, per his father's request. But when he finally caught her eyes, something inside him snapped and he went nuclear. "Are you sorry about hiding my father's letters from us? Trying to kidnap my girlfriend—you doggone right you put us through a lot. Then you had that bum that you called a boyfriend over us. And don't let me get started on how you threatened to throw me out of the house if I didn't sell drugs to help you—what kind of mother would say such things to her son?"

Ne Ne couldn't answer. The only sign of remorse was the tears sliding down from her eyes, leaving trails along her cheeks.

Xavier dug deeper. "When I was getting money, you didn't even have the decency to express concern about where it was coming from. All you knew was that you were lining your pockets. You didn't care"—he stopped and looked around—"if I ended up in a place like this, just as long as I kept breaking you off with the ends."

Ne Ne still held the phone to her ear with her left hand as she covered her face and cried into the other, chest heaving.

Xavier knew it was wrong but he felt nothing for her. "But that's okay. You see, even with everything you put me through, I still managed to make it through to my senior year of high school. And I'm going to graduate too. Do something that you never believed in. Despite you telling me that education was useless, I made it. 'Member you told me the only ways that a black boy could make it out of the ghetto was by selling dope, going to prison, or death?"

Ne Ne finally looked up, and through tears, said to him, "I've made terrible mistakes and all I ask for is a chance to let me make good."

Xavier was on the blink. He didn't have any sympathy for her. As far as he was concerned his mother was someone who had profited off the love he had in his heart for his family and then busted up and stripped away the one decent thing in his life. Samantha was gone, and it was all Ne Ne's fault!

"Ne Ne—"

His mother interrupted by saying, "Please, son—I'm your mother, it's okay to call me mom."

Xavier sarcastically chuckled while shaking his head. "You can't be serious. Ne Ne, tell me this is a joke." With both hands he flared out his ears. "I'm listening. Is this a joke?"

Tears streamed down Ne Ne's face as she tightly held the phone.

"*Mom*—that's rich. Whatever happened to 'Don't y'all ever call me mama, it makes me sound old?'" Xavier ruthlessly laughed at her as if her tears were a joke.

"Son, that's not fair. You forgave your dad."

Xavier blazed, "Pop wasn't the one who withheld the letters from me and Alfonso, did he?"

Ne Ne wiped her eyes with the back of the right sleeve of her orange jumpsuit. "How's my baby?"

"You have some nerve."

"Why ain't your brother with you?"

"I'm not gonna let you play with his head. Alfonso is doing well. I came here today to see if you were on the level, and I don't know. I don't trust you. Do you know how you affected that boy with your foolishness?"

Ne Ne's eyes were red and puffy. She sniffled. "So now I'm on trial here, is that it? You brought your behind up here knowing damn well you weren't gonna forgive me," she yelled at him.

Xavier's face held a touch of animation. His smile said it all. "That's the old Ne Ne I know."

Ne Ne let loose on him. "Look at you sitting there looking like your daddy. How dare you look down your nose at me, you little car thief. Here I am trying to tell you that I changed, but all you care about is losing your little rich girlfriend. You think the people in her world were going to accept you? Let me tell you one thing: All those old snobbish people were going to do for you was put a chauffeur's cap on your head and a broom in your hand."

Xavier looked away and wiped his mouth. When he returned his gaze, there were tears welling up in his eyes. "My dad told me that anybody can change. But in your case, I don't think it's true. I did come to visit you with the hopes that you had changed." He tightened his grip on the phone handle. "But all you are and always will be . . . is bitter." With that Xavier got up and walked out.

1

XAVIER

SATURDAY, AUGUST 29
6:35 P.M.

It was a couple of days before the start of a brand-new school year, and Xavier was kicking back with a few friends who were over for a little backyard celebration. Today was his seventeenth birthday and Noah had given him the thumbs-up to have a birthday party. The good Lord had indeed blessed Noah and his small family over the last two months. With divine help Noah was now working at a top-tier manufacturing plant, making a killing at Dynamic Engines & Axles as a line janitor in Livonia, Michigan. A change of address immediately followed. Noah wanted to move closer to his job, so he packed up the family and rented a bungalow in the city of Redford. Xavier had aggressively fought the move because it would take him quite a few buses to get to school. And he still was holding on to an attitude until Noah had presented him with a car as a birthday gift a few hours ago: keys to a silver 2013 Ford Fusion.

Even though Noah was at work, he'd gotten up early this morning and pulled out the grill. Xavier's old man wasn't a five-star chef or anything, but he'd taken his time to grill his oldest some ribs, chicken, steaks, and seafood for the birthday gathering. The backyard was festive—streamers hanging from chain-link fences, colorful balloons, a few folding chairs, tables with lively tablecloths and an assortment of party favors on top. Platters of food sat covered up with tinfoil to discourage insects on the table by a well-manicured back lawn. The garage door held a Happy Birthday, Xavier sign in place.

Being that they had moved into a beautiful neighborhood populated by white folks, Noah warned Xavier of the rules: Keep the noise down, and absolutely no alcohol or loud music of any kind.

Xavier walked out the side door carrying a tinfoil-sealed pan of barbecue chicken. He was dressed in a pair of Levi's, a navy blue T-shirt with Captain America on the front, and dark blue Chuck Taylors. He and his father had finally arrived at a mutual understanding about the way the urban youth dressed in today's society. If Xavier could tone down the swag in his wardrobe, then they could have more normal father-son discussions without Noah going all television evangelist on his oldest.

Everybody was over—Xavier's closest homeboy, Dexter, his partner Linus Flip, Bigstick, Dexter's girlfriend, Marissa Steel, some chick named Amber Sculley and a few others.

Xavier placed the pan on the table and went to take a seat.

After he had finished eating, his homeboy Dexter stood amongst a small crowd of teenagers. He was an almond color, making his light freckle-sprinkled cheeks highly visible. Dressed in tight-fitting, colorful clothing, Dexter looked like a cockatoo with a plastic cup of fruit punch raised to the sky. "This toast is for my dog." He glanced at Xavier sitting in a reclining lawn chair by the garage. "Dude's been there for me since day one, and I'm proud to call him my friend." Dexter became a little misty-eyed. "X, as we enter into our final year of high school I want to tell you that I love you, homeboy." Dexter looked at the crowd of his peers. "Y'all, join in and help me sing happy birthday to my best friend, Xavier Hunter."

Xavier chuckled as he looked over at London Curry. London was a senior at Coleman High and was deliciously thick in all the right places. She was dressed in a hot outfit that showed off all her curves, and with her short hair and beautiful eyes, she was looking off the hook.

Dex said, "On a count of three let's start singing."

He counted by putting three fingers in the air. On cue everybody pitched in and did their best to hold a tune while belting out the ghettoed-out version of "Happy Birthday" to Xavier. But Linus Flip stood from his seat and shut down the singing before the song could get off the ground.

"Man," he said, addressing the crowd, "kill all that corny noise for my mans here. Many of us owe fam a lot more then this cheesy birthday song." Jeans, a T-shirt, a blue and orange Detroit Tigers baseball hat, the bib tilted slightly to the right, and some crispy Air Force 1s decorated his six-six, dark-complexioned frame. Linus appeared to be tipsy, which was one of the no-no's that Noah had outlined before he'd green-lighted the party. Linus Flip's eyes were red and tiny. "X," Linus said, swaying and slightly pounding his chest with his right fist, "is my people and I'm loyal to the bone for this cat. Would chop off my right arm to save his life. And if it wasn't for him, a lot of you here today would still be getting bullied at Coleman High."

There were quite a few honeys sitting around and a few of them were posted up around Calvin "Bigstick" Mack. The All State middle linebacker was one of the captains of the Coleman High football team and had become a close friend to Xavier. There was a cute, petite dark girl with a pixie haircut sitting to his right named Tina Wiggins.

Bigstick said to Linus, "Man, sit yo' big Renaissance Building–head self down somewhere. Ain't nobody got time for that."

Linus went back at Bigstick. "Cuz, why you trying to style on me? I ain't said nothing when that breezy you sitting with was all on my socks a couple weeks ago down at Hart Plaza."

Bigstick smiled at the chick next to him before saying to Linus, "What that mean? Me and Tina here are just cool. Stop sweating yourself, homeboy. Nobody owns anybody."

"Bigstick," Dexter said. "You know Flip is feeling left

behind because he's been at Coleman for four years and still carrying sophomore credits."

The backyard erupted with laughter. Linus Flip had been drinking and the alcohol had him feeling some kind of way.

He took offense. "Dexter, if you don't shut up I'm gonna knock all those colors out of that loud shirt of yours."

Bigstick stood from his seat. "Linus Flip, I don't know what's wrong with you, fam, but you know all of us are boys and we don't step to each other."

Linus asked Bigstick, "What? You gonna do something?"

The tension in the backyard was getting thick.

Something was bugging Linus, and Xavier had to step in before things got out of hand. "Linus, chill out, homeboy. You up at my crib with these shenanigans. What's up with you?"

Linus Flip shook his head and said to Xavier, "Yeah. It's probably what Dex said. The fact that this is y'all's last year at Coleman got me bugging, that's all."

Xavier was real good at peeping out the truth, and Linus was lying. Dude was far from being on the level and Xavier was hip to it. There was something cooking, pulling, and pushing at Flip's soul.

Xavier said, "Come on, man. Don't you see all of these pretty women around here? Go grab one and whisper sweet nothings in her ear, homeboy."

"I'd rather go for a walk to clear my head," was all Linus said before stumbling past Xavier's Ford Fusion parked in the driveway on the side of the house, headed toward the front.

Dexter walked up to Xavier. "Linus has been acting shady lately, X. What's up with that?"

Xavier shook it off. "I'm sure it's nothing major. Homeboy probably just got a few demons pulling at him."

Dexter said, "I saw him going to his car earlier and taking sips from a bottle in a paper bag. You know Flip don't usually drink. Those gotta be some hella demons on his shoulders, my dude."

Xavier stood there playing with the peach fuzz underneath his lip and wondering what had Linus Flip bugging.

Leave it to Dex to make light of the situation. He grinned and said, "Maybe he feels like he's been replaced because *we* got a car now and *we* might not need him anymore."

Xavier screwed up his face at Dexter. "What do you mean 'we' don't need him now, homeboy?"

Dexter tried to be funny, patting Xavier on the left shoulder. "You know—our car in the driveway right there—*we*."

Xavier couldn't do anything but smile at Dexter. The boy was a straight-up clown.

Xavier said, "But on the real, though. He'll be all right. Remember that dude saved us from Dylan Dallas and Dutch Westwood."

"I remember. How many years did Dylan and Westwood catch for murdering Felix Hoover anyway?"

"The judge threw final-game NBA scores at those clowns. Just put it like this, homeboy. They'll be old enough to apply for Social Security when they get paroled."

Dexter was still holding on to the red cup. He poured some fruit punch onto the ground. "Hey, man, it ain't liquor, but I gotta pour a little out for the homie Felix Hoover."

Dex's girlfriend Marissa Steel walked over to them.

She was seventeen years old with a caramel complexion and cute Asian eyes. She was wearing a white casual knit tank, some high-rise denim shorts, and gladiator sandals. Marissa draped an arm around Dexter's neck.

"Is Linus going to be all right?" she asked with a sweet smile that could light up a room.

Xavier told her, "Don't you see grown folks talking?"

Marissa was cute but she had a mouth on her. "Excuse me, 'grown people.' I'm sorry for interrupting, but if us youngsters had some music to jam to I wouldn't be all up in y'all's business."

Xavier was quick with the retort. "That's why you should have the Pandora app on your phone, you little crazy chick."

She playfully balled up her fist and whacked Dexter on the right shoulder. "Did you hear what he called your girlfriend?"

Dexter laughed. "Tell 'im that you may be crazy, but you're my type of crazy."

"Xavier," said Amber Sculley. The girl wore a short haircut and was rocking the hell out of some cream and brown tribal print shorts and a cream tank with two brown palm trees on the front. She was standing at the food table with an empty plastic plate in her hand. "Ain't no more chicken? Ain't nothing left but pork ribs."

Xavier told her, "You either eat what's left on the table

or take your hungry ass three blocks away to the KFC—all you want is there."

Amber said, "You're so rude, Xavier."

Bigstick said to her, "Homegirl, while you're up at the table why don't you slap a few bones on a plate for me?"

Amber put her hands on her hips and rolled her neck. "I ain't the help, Negro. You got me twisted"—she pointed—"you better tell Tina sitting next to you to fix your plate. Do I look like the one givin' it up to you?"

Dexter stepped in and said, "Yep. I heard anybody can get down with you for the price of a McDonald's kids' meal."

Everybody roared with laughter.

Amber blazed Dex. "Aww, fool, I know you ain't talking. If it weren't for Marissa over there giving you pity sex, you'd still be a virgin."

With everyone laughing, London took the chance to walk over to Xavier. Once she approached him, she put her arm around his shoulders.

"I'm so glad that you're not with Samantha anymore. Being that you're a senior now it gives another girl a chance"—she traced a finger over the strong line of his left jaw—"to see if the rumors are true."

Bigstick laughed as he said to London, "I wouldn't get too close to him if I was you—homeboy still taking penicillin pills, if you know what I mean."

Laughter divided the backyard between the clueless and those that were hip enough to understand the joke.

Xavier was quick on the draw. "Aww, nah. You know I don't have no STD. Anyway, if that were the case you should probably check on your moms."

Bigstick tried to smile off his embarrassment as the others cracked up. Even his friend Tina was almost on the ground rolling with laughter.

"Ha ha," Dex shouted at Bigstick, "that's what you get."

"I think you better stick to football and leave the jokes alone," Marissa said to Bigstick, still chuckling.

"Speaking of football," Xavier said, "when does practice start?"

Bigstick smirked. "Man, don't even try it. You just threw shade and had everybody laughing. Now you wanna be my friend."

Xavier walked over and playfully reached down to hug his boy, laughing. "Awww, sweetheart, are you mad at daddy," Xavier said.

"Get off me, sucka," Bigstick said, laughing. "We take the practice field Monday evening, and I'm not even looking forward to it."

"Xavier," London said, interrupting the two boys, "can I speak to you alone?"

Xavier knew what that meant. And it was about time he moved on with his life. It'd been a hot minute since he hollered at Samantha. The last time was before she went off to Disney World with her parents and that clown Sean Desmond about a month ago.

Realization had finally kicked some sense into Xavier. Although Ne Ne was twisted, there was a bit of truth to some of the garbage that had spilled out of her mouth during his visit. She was right. He didn't belong in Samantha's world. She was straight up out of his league.

In keeping it real with himself, Xavier had grown tired

of Samantha's father meddling in his relationship with her anyway. There was no way he could get the old man to see that he and Samantha were made for each other. Men like Mr. Fox only saw the world through facts and figures, and there was no way that some ghetto trash would be able to produce the lifestyle that he himself afforded for his precious daughter.

Sean Desmond, on the other hand, was a prime candidate. And he just so happened to be all over television these days, with him signing with the Detroit Tigers back in June during the Major League Baseball draft. It made Xavier queasy every time he'd thought about the news. *Hometown Boy Makes Good* had been newspaper headlines around town. Sports television shows like *Sports-Center*, *First Take*, *Pardon the Interruption*, and *Rome* were still showing the same friggin' news clip of Sean Desmond standing at the podium, smiling and wearing a Detroit Tigers baseball cap, while the general manager proudly stood beside him, displaying Sean's jersey with the number 7 below the punk's last name. The ink had barely been dry on the fool's healthy eight-figure contract when he'd gone out and copped a Rolls-Royce Phantom and some fancy-schmancy half-million-dollar crib off the water out in Orchard Lake, Michigan. He had been inserted in the Tigers lineup and was playing flat-out-of-his-mind baseball.

There was no way Xavier could compete. Samantha was gone and it was what it was.

Xavier excused himself and led London through the side door and downstairs into a nice, cool den in the basement. The furnishings were pretty basic, except the size of the flat screen. An enormous eighty-inch Samsung television sat on a sturdy entertainment system surrounded by an earth-tone leather sofa, love seat, and armchair.

"So what's so private that my friends couldn't hear?" Xavier asked her as the two took a seat on the sofa.

She smiled. "Must be cool to have a new ride. When are you going to take me for a ride in it?"

Xavier shook his head. "Is that all you wanted to ask me?"

"I wanted to ask you if you have your license yet."

Xavier knew the game. Had played it enough times to know that she was nervous about being alone with him. So he played along.

"Went to a private driver school in June—right after class let out at Coleman for the summer." Xavier pulled out his wallet, removed a small rectangular card, and shoved it up to baby girl's face. "Bam—my learner's permit. In three months I'll be able to get a driver's license, you dig?"

London looked around the room. "So you live here with your father, huh?"

"My father and my little brother Alfonso."

"Where's your little brother? I'd love to meet him."

" 'Fonso's over his homie's crib. Knuckleheads are probably playing PlayStation or some crap."

"So, you're ready to go back to school?"

"Yeah. I think I'm ready to get this school year over so I graduate and get the hell away from Coleman."

Having a conversation with this chick was like talking to a brick wall. London might've been a dime in the face, but she was a straight-up dud in the conversation department. She was no Samantha and that was for damn sure.

Xavier decided it was time to kick things up a notch by scooting right next to her and reaching for her hands.

London watched as Xavier ran the tip of an index finger across the French-manicured nails on her right hand. She nervously swallowed and her breathing became labored.

"So is it true that you used to be a Zulu shot caller?" she asked.

Xavier said flat out, "London, are you a virgin?"

The question caught London by surprise and a silly look registered on her face.

"What makes you say that?" she asked in a firm voice, obviously frontin'.

Xavier became a little frustrated with her. "Be truthful with me. Why did you want to talk to me in private?"

London looked like she was about to lie but thought better of it. Xavier had a way about him, and it seemed like his eyes were peering through her soul.

She smiled nervously. "To tell you the truth, I've never been with anybody before, especially nobody like you. But"—she started kicking off her sandals and pulling her top up—"I think I'm ready."

Xavier might've been a lot of things, but a bastard he wasn't. London was clearly not ready to give up the goods and he wasn't going to let her play herself. He was too much of a man for that. Besides, his heart still belonged to Samantha.

He stopped her. "Listen, you don't have to do that."

"But I am ready," she protested.

"London, look me in my eyes and tell me you're ready."

She tried to do just that, but she couldn't.

To make her feel more comfortable, Xavier tried to make her laugh and crossed his eyes. London started cracking up. "Xavier, you are so silly. That's why I like you. You make me feel so safe."

That last line jarred his memory. Sent it back to a time where Samantha had told him that very same thing. How being around him made her feel secure. Damn. How he'd missed her. Stood to reason why he wasn't trying to push up on London.

London slid back into her sandals and kissed Xavier on the cheek.

"I feel like such a fool," she confessed. "My friends told me to give you some and that way I would have a chance to be your new girlfriend."

"London, don't let anybody fill your head with any nonsense like that. You seem like such a cool girl, and those are the ones I like hanging around."

"You know you have a fan base of girls at that school that would go out with you in a heartbeat. Every girl wants a piece of Mr. Fabulous. You know, everybody at Coleman says you're a thug and take stuff from nobody. But what you just did for me makes you special in my book. Thank you for not"—she looked down at her lap—"you know, taking advantage of me."

"I don't get down like that. Those lames at school that are hard-pressed for girls might get it in like that, but definitely not me, you feel me?"

Relief relaxed her face. "Can you still take me for a ride?"

Xavier said, smiling, "I don't see any reason why I couldn't."

2

SAMANTHA

MONDAY, AUGUST 31
7:00 A.M.

Mr. Fox, Samantha's father, was dressed in an expensive black Armani business suit. He entered the exquisitely furnished grand dining room, the hard soles of his Gucci plain-toe oxfords clacking across the granite tile floor. Pulling and making last-minute adjustments to his tie, the man of the house approached his wife and daughter sitting at an exquisite, one-of-a-kind marble dining room table that had been set for breakfast.

Mr. Fox stopped and kissed his wife on the cheek.

"Sweetie," he said to her, "what's for breakfast? I'm starving." He sat and surveyed the beautifully decorated table—bowls of fruit, a gorgeous flowery centerpiece, extravagant dishware, and fine Blossom sterling silverware were placed before them. He took his place at the head of the table.

Mrs. Fox was dressed like she'd just stepped out of bed, a colorful floral print headscarf over her hair, a housecoat adorned with unique shapes and colors, and comfortable slippers on her feet.

She smiled. "Bentley said it was a surprise," Mrs. Fox told her husband. "Said he'd be done shortly."

Mr. Fox noticed his daughter staring absently out at the tennis court through one of the three enormous Roman patio doors overlooking an immaculate deck into the rich green acreage that made up their backyard.

As he picked up the *Wall Street Journal*, Mr. Fox asked his daughter concernedly, "Samantha, pumpkin, what's wrong with my baby?"

Samantha set her napkin on her lap and looked awkwardly at her father before returning her gaze back to the lush greenery offered by the backyard.

Mr. Fox turned his head away from his daughter and said to his wife, "I slept like a baby last night. Dear, how did you sleep?"

Mrs. Fox offered her husband a smile. "Sweetie, you didn't sleep like a baby, you slept and snored like some old drunken bum in an alley behind a Dumpster."

Mr. Fox chuckled. "Are you snapping on me? You have some nerve. As violently as you sleep sometimes, throwing elbows and closed fists, I could use a couple of stiff drinks before going to bed. That way I won't feel any pain in my sleep."

"Funny. Fitzgerald, why are you in such a good mood today?"

Mr. Fox opened his paper to the business section. "My partners and I have managed to acquire some prime river-front real estate downtown. And with all of the big businesses buying up property down there to set up shop, our investment can be worth millions."

"Fitzgerald, you know we don't have business discussions during family time."

Mr. Fox winked at his wife and smiled. He then looked at Samantha. The girl was still staring out at the backyard.

Mr. Fox already knew what was wrong with his daughter. "If it's that boy Xavier, sweetie, give it time, you'll be over him soon. Besides, Sean admires you. He treats you real nice—"

"You mean he's rich, Daddy, and could possibly be rookie of the year, not to mention the direct access to the team you'll have with him as your son-in-law," Samantha explained sarcastically.

"Fitzgerald," Mrs. Fox said, "stop being insensitive. Leave her alone."

Mr. Fox watched as their butler, a dark, average-size English fellow impeccably dressed in black servant's attire, wheeled out a cart of breakfast foods.

"Great, Bentley," said Mr. Fox, rubbing his hands pleasurably as the butler started serving the family. "Just in time because I'm famished. My favorites—buttermilk pancakes with fresh strawberries, turkey sausage and scrambled eggs."

After Bentley finished serving, he asked in a heavy English accent, "Sir, might there be anything else?"

Mr. Fox was placing a napkin in his lap when he said, "No, Bentley, that should be all." He waited on the butler to leave. "Pumpkin," he said to Samantha, "I'm sorry for being so insensitive, but I'm your father and I want what's best for you. Surely you can understand that."

Samantha wasn't hungry. Didn't even bother with her food. Just kept staring out at the tennis court with her arms folded, like an answer to her problem would magically appear out of thin air.

Her father smeared butter over the top of his pancakes before pouring on deliciously thick and rich syrup. "My God, can you imagine what it would be like marrying into Xavier's family, a family full of convicts?"

This was the week for counting calories, so Mrs. Fox left off the butter and sparingly applied the syrup. "Enough, Fitzgerald. Can we eat in peace, please?"

Mr. Fox was chewing his food when he told his wife, "You said yourself you feared for your daughter's safety in Xavier's company."

Mrs. Fox was a little thrown off by her husband blatantly tossing her underneath the bus. "That's not the way I put it, Fitzgerald," she said uncomfortably, shifting her gaze to Samantha. "Yes, I—because I did fear for your safety. Samantha, honey, his crazy mother and her uneducated boyfriend tried to kidnap you—"

"To say nothing about that deranged Heather Larkin girl that he was messing around with trying to kick you down the stairs," Mr. Fox interjected.

Samantha looked surprised. Shocked. She hadn't told her parents about that little situation with Xavier's crazy psycho ex Heather Larkin.

Mr. Fox swallowed some food and chased it with a little orange juice. "What? You didn't think that one would get back to us, huh?"

Samantha slowly unfolded her arms with a look of concern on her face. "How long have you guys known?"

Mr. Fox asked candidly, "Does it matter?"

"Fitzgerald," Mrs. Fox intervened. She said to Samantha, "Honey, don't you think you should've told us about the incident?"

Samantha just sat there, pouting like a five-year-old— something she'd done millions of times when put on blast by her parents.

Mr. Fox poured more syrup over what was left of his pancakes. "If this wasn't your last year I'd snatch you right out of that little ex-con-producing public high school penitentiary. I should've had my head examined for letting my precious baby girl attend such a polluted, crime-infested dump."

"Gee, Dad, tell us how you really feel," Samantha said sarcastically.

"That will be enough out of you, young lady," Mrs. Fox interrupted. "We should have punished you for telling Principal Skinner not to inform us of the incident. But we let it go because you weren't harmed."

"Stands to reason we don't want you hanging out with Xavier," Mr. Fox said sternly.

Samantha looked at both of her parents. "I'll be seventeen next month—you can't keep running my life forever.

Next year I'm off to college—I can't believe that you guys are still treating me like a little kid." She zeroed in on her mother. "Mom, of all people I can't believe that you don't understand."

Samantha stood up from her chair, letting the napkin fall from her lap to the floor.

Mrs. Fox looked confused. "What is that supposed to mean?"

"My first day of school is about to begin in an hour and I don't want to be late, so may I be excused?" Samantha politely asked with a straight face.

Mr. Fox said through a mouthful of food, "Stay away from that Xavier boy. I don't want you to blow your chance with Sean Desmond."

"Oh, Daddy," Samantha huffed, as she turned on the balls of her feet to leave. "You will never understand."

Samantha had made it through the expensively decorated great room and passed the exquisitely hand-carved railing of the double staircase underneath a stained-glass dome ceiling that suspended a beautiful chandelier over a marble foyer. She had opened one of two huge front doors when she heard her father's voice echo:

"Sean Desmond is a good thing for you. Please don't blow it."

Don't blow it, she thought. Right now, the only thing Samantha wished would blow away was her dad's meddling behind—right out of her life.

She saw her driver, black Lurch, standing at the back of the Cadillac Escalade with the door open in the circular driveway.

"Morning, young lady," he said to Samantha.

Samantha knew it was rude, but she slid into the backseat without offering a word. She was pissed and didn't feel like talking. Why didn't everybody just leave her alone? She'd given her parents what they wanted, especially her father. The stormy relationship she'd had with Xavier was over. And as far as she was concerned, he'd moved on. The boy had totally flipped after she'd told him about her parents inviting Sean Desmond to Disney World with them. Xavier had acted like it was all her fault, like she had personally extended Sean an invitation.

As the driver circled and started down the long driveway, snaking through a dense, tropical oasis of freshly manicured grass, tons of shrubbery, and Mrs. Fox's prized rosebush gardens, Samantha was trying to picture her life without Xavier. He hadn't called her since hearing about the trip. Didn't answer the birthday wish she'd sent via text message. Had his little birthday party Saturday and didn't even have the common decency to include her. But from what she gathered Xavier had had his hands full with London Curry, some dizzy little nobody who was apparently trying to become the new Samantha.

Oh well, Samantha thought.

She had come too far, and had gone through too much junk, to worry about something she couldn't control. This was her senior year, the last year of high school, and she wasn't going to let anything stop her from enjoying it . . . even if it wasn't going to be in the company of the one that she still held mad love for.

Samantha could tell that the day was shaping up to be a hot one. It wasn't even close to eight o'clock and the sun was a fireball in the clear blue morning sky. She went into her Louis Vuitton tote bag and removed a pair of Prada sunglasses. With them on her face, Samantha made herself comfortable on the supple leather and stared out at the world through the dark tint of the windows. Despite not having the only boy she'd ever cared about in her life this school year, Samantha had to find a way to push through it. Shake it off. She would be just fine. Besides, her two crazy BFFs were still riding with her. Tracy McIntyre and Jennifer Haywood were her road dogs and they would never bounce on her. They were the Three Musketeers—one for all and all for one.

Yeah, she thought, as she looked out into the face of morning rush hour. *My senior year is going to be a lot of fun.*

3

DAKOTA TAYLOR

MONDAY, AUGUST 31
6:50 A.M.

"**D**akota!" Evelyn Taylor yelled from the upstairs room of their three-bedroom bungalow. "Get your tail up this instant! You gonna be late for school!"

Fourteen-year-old Dakota Taylor was a little girl with a big imagination. She had to possess one in order to stay in the same house as her mother.

The young girl lazily opened her eyes and yawned. She wasn't given a chance to do anything else before her mother screamed again.

"Dakota Taylor, do you hear me, girl, get out of that bed before I come in there and beat you out of it, now!"

Dakota sluggishly rolled out of the sack wearing a short nightgown decorated with playful, colorful kittens. She was overwhelmed, but joyful of the spectacular possibilities that the day could deliver. This could actually be the day that her Prince Charming galloped through on a black stallion and rescued her from a life dominated by her mother's miseries.

She stretched and yawned once more. Dakota wiped at her eyes as she slowly stepped over to the full-length mirror standing in the corner by her bedroom closet.

Evelyn screamed again. "Dakota, I don't hear no water running in that bathroom. Chile, get yo' half-breed behind in the tub and take a shower. I ain't gonna tell you no mo'!"

Today was the first day of school. Dakota beamed with excitement. Yet she stood there, a little horrified, but ready to embark on the beginning of her freshman year at Coleman High. She told herself, *Anything beats the loneliness brought on by having to stay locked up in the house for the entire summer.*

Dakota's African American mother Evelyn had married a Native American man by the name of Bemossed Taylor. Bemossed was a skilled laborer and Evelyn worked as a waitress in an upscale downtown Detroit restaurant, but between their two paychecks, the couple barely made enough to breach the poverty line.

Not long after Dakota was born, Bemossed took a walk to the store around the corner for some chocolate chip ice cream and a pack of Camel Lights and never returned. Her mother was absolutely devastated. Evelyn couldn't quite get over the abandonment, so she often took out her verbal aggression on Dakota. At that tender age where most kids started to form bonds and make friends with others, Dakota wasn't allowed to have any, and it was always mandatory that she come right home after school. Dakota never asked why she couldn't have any friends. That question wasn't worth the slap in the mouth for stepping outside of a child's place.

To escape her loneliness, Dakota often fantasized about another life, a better place. Fairy tales. There was no pain in her perfect place, just love, peace, harmony, and tons of fun. This was the reason why she enjoyed school so much. It gave her a sense of freedom. Sure, there had always been girls who hated on her looks, but she'd rather be amongst them than be around her tortured soul of a mother.

At four-foot-ten Dakota might've had the height of a Smurfette, but her beauty was otherworldly. The biracial melting pot had pooled the richness of ebony flesh and layered it with the prideful red skin belonging to Native American people to produce Dakota's breathtaking, exotic copper complexion. Her fine, silky locks fell down her back, a snapshot of similarity to her Indian ancestors who once roamed the rich, vast North American wilderness before the European settlers. Her African American heritage shone through in Dakota's high cheekbones, thick lips, wide nose, and full hips, thighs, and butt.

Dakota puckered out her lips and then flared her nostrils—anything to make herself look ugly. God knew she'd heard it enough from her mother. But she continued staring in the mirror, as if not believing the image of perfection that stared back.

"This chile of mine—I swear she gonna bring out the devil in me, 'cause I don't hear no damn water," Dakota heard her mother grumble as she walked down the stairs from the upstairs bedroom.

The girl quickly went into her dresser drawers, grabbed what she needed, and bolted across the hallway and into the bathroom, closing the door.

One thing she didn't do was disobey her mother. Evelyn was quick-tempered and heavy-handed, sometimes not giving a crap where her open-hand slaps landed on the child.

Dakota wiggled out of her gown and panties. She didn't waste a single moment jumping into the tub, closing the shower curtain, and turning on the water. When the bathroom door opened Dakota almost peed herself. Not knowing if her mother would snatch open the curtain and get busy with that thick black belt caused her to tremble all over.

She could hear her mother open the door to the medicine cabinet. A few pill bottles rattled around. "Dakota, I have to work overtime tonight, so you have your butt in the house when you come home from school. You hear me?"

Dakota took too long to answer and her mother ripped back the curtain. The young girl almost jumped out of her skin at the sight of her short, full-figured, dark-skinned, chunky-faced mother.

Dakota defensively put up her hands and cowered in the corner as the water sprayed over her body. "Mama, please don't hit me!" she cried out.

Evelyn had meaty shoulders, flabby biceps, and a fat, blubbery stomach that left her looking like she was nine months pregnant. The belt of the black terrycloth house-

coat wrapped around her stomach looked to be struggling to keep Evelyn's bulge inside.

"When I call you at five o'clock today, you better be in
this house and getting your lesson," Evelyn said intensely
with a no-nonsense look on her face.

"Yes, ma'am," Dakota said, relieved.

Evelyn snatched the curtain closed and walked out of
the bathroom.

Dakota let out a sigh of relief. The girl didn't know how
much more she could take. As she soaped down her body,
Dakota magically slipped into her fantasy. She couldn't
wait for her big, strong, handsome, courageous knight to
come and whisk her far away from this place.

4

XAVIER

Xavier's world literature teacher was a true giant standing in front of the class. Over seven feet tall, Mr. Emerson Chase looked like he had been freakishly drawn up by some mad-scientist cartoonist. The man's legs were skinny and long, like there was no end to them, with a torso that surprisingly could've belonged to a dwarf. Mr. Chase was in his fifties, with striking blue eyes and the kind of sandy blond hair that male models would've traded their very souls for. He sure didn't dress like anything special; a pair of khakis, a button-down shirt, and some extra-long Minnetonka moosehide moccasins—that looked like it took an entire moose to produce—completed his ensemble.

"Welcome to the world of literature," the teacher said

to his students in a nasal voice. He picked up a piece of chalk off the ledge and wrote his name in cursive across the blackboard. "My name is Mr. Chase. Let me start out, good people, by addressing the rumors. Yes, I did play basketball professionally for the NBA. A badly torn ACL cut short my career. But thank God I had my degree in English to fall back on." Mr. Chase looked out at the young faces before him. He had their complete and undivided attention. "I can tell that there are a few hotshot NBA hoop dreamers in here. Don't mean to burst your bubble, but let my injury serve as a bleak reminder for you to take your education seriously."

Xavier was sitting there looking up at Mr. Chase, shaking his head. Another foot and the cat's coconut would be scraping the ceiling. Aside from the rumors about Chase playing pro ball, Xavier had the scoop on how the former hoopster was the hardest teacher in the building to pass. Many students had crashed and burned here, with some of the smartest just hoping to come away with obtaining a plain old C letter grade. That wasn't gonna fly with Xavier. He didn't do Cs. It was either A or bust. Nothing was going to drop his 4.0 GPA.

"This semester we will be exploring works from classical playwrights, complete numerous essays, and for you guys, learn how to write romantic poetry, compose a news article, and my very personal favorite, write a movie review. You will be required to write a complete research paper. No excuses. This paper will count as thirty percent of your grade. I can be pretty hard, but I'm fair."

Xavier couldn't believe his luck. Dexter was sitting right next to him in the same doggone English class. With the camaraderie between the two, they were both in trouble. And right on cue Dexter started cutting up.

"I ain't never heard of Chase in the NBA. What? Was he a ball boy?" he whispered to Xavier, laughing.

"Stop it, you idiot," Xavier whispered back, trying not to laugh.

Xavier simply shook his head at Dexter. The boy was a flat-out moron and Xavier wasn't about to get caught up in his foolishness. On top of Mr. Chase's no-nonsense policy for shenanigans, homeboy was known to send fools who thought they were comedians right to the main office to have a not-so-funny chat with Principal Skinner.

Xavier tried to ignore Dexter, but dude wasn't having any of it.

"Psst," Dexter persisted. "Homeboy wearing moccasins—who he think he is . . . a white Indian on the reservation back in the Old West?"

Xavier just placed a hand over his face to conceal his laughter.

Dexter kept it up. "Homeboy, homeboy," he whispered, "that's one big ol' Indian. He probably has a horse parked out in the teacher's parking lot."

A few other students in the area heard the joke and started giggling at Dexter.

Mr. Chase singled out Xavier. "Mr. Hunter—"

"Uh-oh," a couple of students muttered.

Chase continued, "You have quite the reputation at this school. Well, I think I might have one too about being a stickler for not allowing any monkey business in my classroom. Would you, perhaps, like to share your joke with the rest of us?"

Xavier looked around at the other students and made a face like Chase couldn't be chin-checking him.

"You couldn't be talking to me because I'm not the one telling jokes," Xavier harshly explained, rolling his eyes at Dexter. Xavier might've snitched on Slick Eddie and Romello in the past, but that was for something totally different. He wasn't gonna rat on his boy. So he stood in and took the heat.

"On the contrary, Mr. Hunter," Chase said, walking over to the row in which Xavier was sitting. "I am not at all impressed with your many extracurricular contributions outside of your schoolwork. You don't frighten me with your aggressive tone. You may have a 4.0 GPA, but, Mr. Hunter, you'll find in my class that that won't purchase you any favoritism. Despite how your former English teachers rave about you, I'm going to reserve judgment. It's going to be tough on you in my class, Mr. Hunter."

Xavier wasn't afraid to speak up. "Mr. Chase, it seems like you are singling me out for some reason. Don't know what it is, nor do I care. My concern is that you don't let what you think you may know about me influence my overall grade in this class, you feel me?"

Mr. Chase said in surprise, "Now that does impress me, Mr. Hunter. Didn't know if you thought that I was going to jump on the bandwagon and show favoritism because of your academic achievements. But we shall see what type of student you will be in my classroom."

The certain level of respect he possessed for educators

kept Xavier from voicing what was really on his mind. Instead he bit his tongue and looked away.

Mr. Chase added, "Of course, your work will give you ample time to respond."

When Xavier looked back at Dexter, the boy was wearing some dumb smirk on his grill.

"Let me tell you all something," the teacher went on explaining. "There will be no favoritism in my classroom. Absolutely no brown-nosing. I don't take kindly to teacher's pets." Mr. Chase moved over to his desk, gliding like he was walking on stilts, and grabbed an arm full of course syllabuses. He began at the head of each row. "Take one and pass the rest back. As you will see, I follow my syllabus tightly and I DO NOT give extra-credit work, so hand in your assignments on time."

A chorus of groans rose from the students.

"If you're late to my class more than two times, you'll be sent to the principal's office to be reprimanded," Chase grimly warned his students as he handed out syllabuses to the last row. "I expect you to handle yourselves like young adults. Abide by my rules and you will have no problems. Now does anyone have a question?"

Nobody said jack. Xavier could see clearly that his new English teacher was going to be a trip. He wasn't into trying to win over male teachers anyway, so the natural charm he'd used on past female English educators wouldn't begin to apply to this guy. Xavier would simply have to watch his behind in Chase's class because it was apparent that Mr. Chase had made his mission personal by purposefully gunning for Xavier.

As he fumbled with the three-page syllabus on his

desk, Xavier's mind was working overtime. His last year of high school, and he couldn't begin to figure out what he must've done to piss off the English curriculum gods and get stuck with a hater. The day had officially gotten off to a rotten start, but Xavier's Spidey senses were tingling, which left him to believe that more trouble was right around the corner, waiting on him, and probably bringing drama to his life.

At fourth-period lunch Xavier had spotted trouble right away.

Some silly little girl gang who called themselves the SNLGs, short for Show No Love Girls, was sitting at a back table trying to bring attention to themselves by talking real loud and slick. He hadn't heard too much noise about them other than they had just formed over the summer and were now looking to carve out some reputation at Coleman. They were a handful of freshman girls following a junior by the name of Stephanie Chadwick. She was the leader but everybody called her Bangs for some odd reason. Bangs was a thick, dark-skinned chick with a horrible case of acne, ty-zillion braids, a bad attitude, and a real foul mouth. Homegirl could scrap too— probably why she'd been broken off with the "Bangs" nickname. There were rumors still floating around the school about her pulverizing some sophomore cat who'd played on the baseball team during her freshman year. Whupped on homeboy so bad that it had taken two security officers to pull the girl off the dude.

Wannabe gangstas, Xavier thought. *Everybody wants to be a gangsta.*

Students were everywhere in the cafeteria. Seemed like everybody was trying to talk at once. The noise was damn near deafening, buzzing like a friggin' beehive. Xavier was chilling out, though, sitting alone at his favorite table by the south wall, off to the side and in the middle region of the cafeteria. Had an unobstructed view of all the access doors and people coming in and leaving. There were still concerns about his safety. He had survived some deadly moments at Coleman High, but the threat on his life was still out there somewhere, lurking around, probably still wearing that same old dingy dark Rocawear hoodie. The last time Xavier had seen Slick Eddie's hitman, Tall and Husky, was around the beginning of June. The brother was sitting back behind the wheel of a cargo van in the school parking lot, off in the distance, and menacingly staring at Xavier like he was a dead man walking. Xavier wasn't sweating it, though. Not even the phone call Tall and Husky had made to Xavier around the latter part of June, threatening him, promising that he wouldn't live to walk across the stage at graduation hadn't been enough to send Xavier scurrying away to another school like a punk. The boy was 100 percent G and wasn't afraid to get downright dirty in order to keep enjoying the healthy level of respect he'd built for himself.

But it was always funny to him when he saw freshmen eating in the cafeteria for their first time. There was this quietness about them. Like they were harmless gazelles, hoping to stay out of the predators' line of sight while timidly eating. No direct eye contact with anybody. A stark contradiction to his first year at Coleman. Xavier had walked into his freshman status with a chip on his shoulder, daring anybody to knock it off. Always direct eye contact with a fool. Never backing down from bustas and bullies. Having respect in a dangerous place like Coleman was a must. And it had to be established somewhere within that first year. Xavier had seen far too many kids get tried, punked, and ending up having to go through high school . . . tormented.

"What up, doe, teacher's pet?" Dexter asked with a stupid smile on his face, walking up to the table with Linus in tow. "Dang, homeboy, that dude Chase ain't no joke and it seems like he wants to be BFFs with you."

Xavier said to Dexter, "No thanks to your tight-pants-wearing self. Homeboy, you got lunch this hour too?"

"Yep," Dexter answered. "I thought I told you in Chase's class. Guess you were too busy getting your butt chewed by Mr. Chase to remember."

Xavier looked at Flip. "You get yo' eat on this hour too?"

Linus Flip was about to answer before Dexter broke in on some old sarcastic stuff.

"You know Linus don't go to class, homie," Dexter joked, "every hour of the school day is his lunch period."

"You Mr. Funny Man all of a sudden," Linus said to Dexter in an aggravated tone.

Flip definitely hadn't been himself lately. Grouchy. Angry all the time. Xavier knew he had to get control of this thing before something popped off. He jumped in to squash it. "Fam," he addressed Linus. "Don't let his tight-pants-wearing self kick up your blood pressure."

This school year Dexter had decided to take a page from Xavier's style of dress and also tone his wardrobe down, but the only difference was that his clothes fit extra tight. Like he'd stayed up all night struggling to get into them before first school bell. Dexter was flexing with a gray button-down, same color khakis, and white Polo boat shoes without socks.

Linus Flip sat down at the table wearing jeans, a dark shirt, and some black and gray suede Puma sneakers. He seemed the least bit interested, but he asked anyway, "What are y'all talking about anyway?"

Dexter laughed. "Old man Chase put X on blast for disrupting the classroom."

Xavier said, "Fool, that was your ratchet self in there thinking his class was a comedy club."

Dexter responded, laughing, "It *was* me, though. To keep it real with you I thought I was cold busted until he pointed the finger your way."

Flip asked, "You two clowns in the same English class?"

"My luck has got to be bad. My senior year and I get a class with that clown," Xavier replied.

Dexter said, grinning, "That's one tall white boy— talking about he used to play in the NBA. I didn't know they had a league back in the Stone Age."

"See, that's that bull junk that almost got me tossed out of class, man," said Xavier.

"Naw, for real, cuz," Dexter continued. "What team did he play for . . . the Cleveland Caveman?—naw, I got it . . . yo, bust this . . . the Los Angeles Triceratops—"

Linus had to ask, "What the hell is that?"

Xavier just shook his head.

"Man, don't you guys read," Dexter said, sensing that his punch line just crashed and burned to hell. "Dinosaur that walks on all fours, two horns on their head."

Xavier and Linus sat there with their arms folded. They both looked at Dexter like the boy had completely flipped his wig.

Dexter said, desperately, "Y'all get it?—nothing then. You two crackheads sure know how to mess up a joke."

"All I have to say is don't drop out of school to do comedy, fam," said Linus, finally cracking a smile.

"Hey, Xavier," said Dexter. "Have you applied to any colleges yet?"

"How did we go from your corny comedy routine, to you wanting to know about college enrollment?" asked Linus.

Dexter said to him, "Did I hurt your itty-bitty feelings, homeboy? Knowing that your future job will be pretty simple? All you gonna have to do is stand at the end of a grocery store counter and ask the customers if they want paper or plastic."

Everybody knew that Linus was incredibly sensitive about the fact that he wasn't going to graduate with the class because of his lack of credits. And sensing that things were about to get out of hand, Xavier jumped in.

"You know, Dex, after all that drama that happened to me in my junior year, it kind of threw me. I stopped wanting to go to college—I didn't know if I was gonna live to attend. So I didn't fill out any applications in my junior year. Sat on my hands until two months ago. That's when my father convinced me to fill out a college application—ain't like I don't have the grades." Xavier stared down at the table, and then back up to Dexter. "I filled out an application to go to Michigan State. Don't know what I'll be majoring in. But I have to make it out of my senior year alive, first."

Linus sarcastically popped his lips.

Dexter ignored him and said to Xavier, "I think I'm gonna go to junior college. Find out what I want to do."

Xavier might've been engaged in the conversation but he couldn't help notice the chick Bangs was all up in some cute little female's grill, aggressively pointing her finger. The noise in the lunchroom was so loud that, somehow, the fiery confrontation had managed to fly under the radar.

Xavier had never seen this girl before. The sweet piece looked to be mixed, with an exotic complexion, gorgeous shoulder-length hair, nice juicy lips—every curve in the right place. Xavier had to laugh because the girl was so short that she reminded him of a cute dwarf.

"You missed it, Flip," Dexter explained. "Chase looked like he was about to send Xavier packin'. Was all up in his grill, talking about X wasn't gonna receive any special privileges for being a 4.0 student."

"Really," said Flip.

Dexter told Xavier, "Dude, when I got my schedule this morning and saw that I had Chase for English, partna, I almost went number two in my pants."

The voices were becoming aggressively rowdy at that back table. When Xavier returned his gaze in the direction of the SNLGs, Bangs had disrespectfully knocked the girl's book bag to the floor and was pushing the chick toward her homegirls. Xavier knew what that meant. It was about to get real for baby girl without some help.

The girl wouldn't stand a chance if the entire SNLG crew got down on her head.

"Chase's class is going to be hard, but—"

Xavier hopped up and headed in the direction of the ruckus without saying a word.

"X, where are you headed?" Dexter tried to ask.

Bangs swung on the girl and would've solidly connected, if it wasn't for Xavier pulling her out of harm's way.

Standing there, bug-eyed with surprise, Bangs aggressively asked, "Why you all up in my Kool-Aid, Xavier?"

Xavier might've smiled at her recognition of him, but it was no surprise. He was the man up in this piece and every student was intensely aware.

"I'ma need you to cut baby girl some slack," Xavier said politely, but the look on his face told her that it was more of an order.

"I know who you are, Xavier—the school's savior," Bangs said, like she was trying to be funny. "I'm Bangs, by the way. Trust me, we don't want any beef with you, boss."

It took a minute for the rest of the students in the cafeteria to peep what was taking shape, and when they recognized Xavier's involvement, the immediate area quickly evacuated.

The rest of the SNLGs rushed to their leader's back. Bangs knew what time it was, though. She pointed to her crew as if to tell them to fall back. Bangs might've been a notorious hothead, but she wasn't stupid. Stepping to a big dog like Xavier wouldn't be a good look—it would be a damn near fatal decision. So she tried to smile it off and play up for the audience.

The Smurfette looked up at Xavier and managed a smile, as if to say, "Thank you."

Xavier asked Bangs, "What'd she do?"

"Oh, Supermodel looked at us the wrong way."

Xavier already knew what it was about. Jealousy. The little Smurfette chick did have it going on, though.

Dexter walked up. "Y'all real tough all right. Tryna put the smash on itty-bitty over here for staring?"

Offended, one of the girls in the clique yelled, "We SNLGs fo' life, fool!" at Dexter.

Some little dark-skinned chick with cornrows asked Dexter in a tough voice, "Who is you?"

It didn't take Dexter's smart mouth too long to respond. He told Cornrows, "If you spent more time in English class instead of running with these losers, you would know 'who is you' is grammatically incorrect. Watch my lips and say it with me: 'who are you?' "

Dexter's diss left Cornrows feeling some kind of way. She was about to go off.

Bangs said to her girl, "Mouse, chill out." She looked back to Xavier. "All right, boss. You got this." She nodded in the direction of the south door. Her girls understood what that meant and began filing in that direction.

"Baby girl," Xavier said to Bangs. "I can't tell you how to do you. But if you gonna be a gangsta, don't be a bully, you feel me?"

She smiled and said, "We don't want any beef with the great Xavier." Bangs gave Xavier a halfway slick look before following her gang.

Mouse was the last one. Before she started toward them, the thugged-out chick turned around to face the girl.

Xavier and Dexter looked on as Mouse made an execution sign at the girl by dragging a hand slowly across her throat.

"You see that?" Dexter asked Xavier, as Mouse finally followed the rest of her girls.

"Yo, girls are getting worse than the dudes," said Xavier. He looked down at the young girl.

The tension in the cafeteria seemed to ease up a bit with students going about their business.

"What's your name, little mama?" Xavier asked her.

"Dakota . . . Dakota Taylor," she timidly answered.

The girl had a soft-spoken demeanor about her. She was a little cutie too.

Fresh meat, Xavier thought. The moment she'd opened her mouth he already knew the scoop. Dakota was a freshman.

Dexter bent down and retrieved her book bag. "I guess this belongs to you," he said, handing it over. "By the way, my name is Dexter."

"Hi, Dexter," Dakota said, almost with childlike innocence.

"And just in case you didn't hear, my name is Xavier Hunter."

"Nice to meet you, Xavier Hunter. I can't thank you enough for coming to my rescue."

"It was no big deal," he said. Xavier already knew the answer but still had to ask, "Well, Dakota 'Lil' Mama' Taylor, is this your first year at Coleman?"

Her smile was beautiful—dimples, the whole shebang. " 'Lil' Mama'? I like that." She fumbled around with the strap on her book bag. "Yes, I am a freshman. Is it that obvious?"

Dexter suggested to her, "You might wanna stay away from the short yellow bus crew." He pointed in the direction where the SNLGs had made their exit. "Looks like they're thirsty to make a rep, so watch who you stare at around here."

Dakota rolled her shoulders. "I just glanced at them," she admitted.

"It seemed to be enough to set them off," Dexter explained. He turned to Xavier. "Do you realize Flip just sat there at the table like nothing was happening?"

Yep. Xavier had noticed it. But he didn't want to overreact. Besides, he didn't need anybody's help handling a bunch of girls. All the same, though, he was gonna have to keep an eye on Linus.

Xavier said to Dexter, "You worry too much. Flip's straight, man, you feel me?"

Dexter looked at Xavier like he wanted to say, "Dude, wake up," but thought better of it. He shook his head and walked away.

"So, Xavier," Dakota said, showing off those fantastic dimples. "What did Bangs mean when she mentioned you were the school's savior?"

"I don't know, the girl's probably on something," Xavier joked.

Dakota stared dreamily up into Xavier's eyes. "You have a nice sense of humor, Xavier," she complimented.

"Thank you," Xavier said. "If you don't mind me asking, what's your ethnicity?"

Dakota smiled. "My mother is black and my father is Native American."

"That explains your beautiful skin tone." Xavier touched her hair. "Ain't no tracks in that wig."

Dakota laughed. This conversation was fun for her and she was eating it up.

"So is that North or South Dakota?" Xavier asked, smirking.

Dakota giggled. "I see you have jokes."

"I know I'm an idiot when it comes to American native custom. But doesn't every American native name mean something?"

"Xavier, are you trying to ask me if my name means something?"

"I guess I am, Lil' Mama."

Dakota smiled, showing off her deep dimples. "My name means 'friends to my enemy.' "

Xavier laughed. "Is that right? I guess whoever named you didn't have little ghetto chicks like Bangs and her SNLG clowns in mind. You're definitely not on their Christmas card list."

"I still don't know how I offended them. It was just a glance in their direction."

"In this school, a glance is enough to get your eyebrows kicked in. Listen, Lil' Mama, I gotta bounce. But check this out: I'm gonna need you to please be careful up in this piece." He looked around the cafeteria. "I don't mean to scare you, but this school can be dangerous. So please watch where you're stepping, you feel me?"

"I'll make sure to take your advice to heart." Dakota

smiled flirtatiously. "I'm sure if I get in trouble again, my big strong knight will come and save me."

Xavier knew who she was talking about but he played it off. "Dakota, I'm gonna need you to take those little chicks seriously. I've been around their kind before. They just threatened you and they're not playing."

Xavier went to step away.

But not before Dakota could say, "Bye, my big strong knight."

What had he done? Nothing flared his nostrils more than the weak pretending to be strong by pushing around those they thought were weaker to boost their ego, gain self-respect, all while creating a reputation for themselves. Dakota, whether she accepted it or not, was in Bangs's crosshairs. The chick was so nonchalant about it. She seemed like a nice enough girl—a little naïve, but didn't deserve the beef she'd just stepped into. He couldn't just leave her for the sharks. Xavier had every intention of watching Dakota's back, but even he didn't possess the kinds of superpowers that would allow him to be everywhere at once. Plus, he still had to walk around the building with eyes in the back of his dome, never knowing which cracks of the school Slick Eddie's roaches would scurry from and try to snatch his life.

This was a trip. Xavier could've saved himself the heartache of trying to make paper with Zulu back in the day by hiring himself out as a bodyguard to the nerd population at Coleman. Homeboy would've been flexing with a legitimate fortune by now.

But outside of all the drama that seemed to be hugging

him as tightly as Dexter's skinny pants, Xavier was burdened by curiosity about what was up with his man Linus Flip. Homeboy wasn't right in the melon. Something was up. Xavier couldn't address it right now, though. Chase was heavy on his mind. The cat would be the only teacher who stood in the way of Xavier graduating with a perfect GPA. He hadn't decided on a college major yet. He liked to write—maybe journalism, Xavier didn't know. With all the dangerous drama he'd been through, he was just happy to still be alive and have an opportunity to graduate high school to go on to receive a higher education.

5

SAMANTHA

Samantha was chilling with her two girlfriends, grabbing a little bite to eat in the food court at Somerset Collection. It was an upscale, luxury shopping mall on Big Beaver Road, located in a very pristine area in Troy, Michigan.

The three had made up their minds to attend the school icebreaker held at Northland Roller Rink on West 8 Mile in Detroit. The set was due to jump off in two weeks on September nineteenth, and Coleman High students were hyped.

And of course they all needed new outfits. The only thing was that Tracy and Jennifer were flat broke as usual. But Samantha had saved the day by graciously allowing her girls to sponge off her as she effortlessly ripped up the stores, while her dad's Black Card absorbed all of the damages. Shopping bags were sitting on the floor and tucked in every available space inside the booth.

"Gurl," Tracy McIntyre said to Samantha, as the three sat eating Thai food, "thank you for tightening a sistah up with a trip to her favorite spot, bebe. Love the two nice, sexy outfits you treated me to."

Jennifer Haywood also joined in by raising her Styrofoam cup of soda. "Hear, hear, I second that. My mother doesn't get paid until Friday after next, so I would've been the only chica there not flexing any new gear at the skating rink next Friday. I appreciate the outfits from Forever 21." She held up her shopping bag. Jennifer looked like she just wanted to hop across the table and hug Samantha to show appreciation. But instead she said, "Thank you, girl!"

Samantha smiled. "We're like the Three Musketeers— all for one and one for all remember? Plus when we turn up together we have to have our game tight."

Tracy cracked up. "Listen to Ms. Fancy-pants trying to sound gangsta—'turn up—game tight?' " she joked.

"Sounds like bad boy Xavier's influence all right," Jennifer cosigned.

Tracy said to Jennifer, "Gurl, next thing you know she'll start referring to us as 'homeboy' and ending her sentences with 'you feel me?' "

Samantha laughed. "Tracy, you're talking out of the side of your neck. Don't get cute with me. Remember, I still have every one of those receipts for your outfits, heffa."

"No, you didn't threaten to take back my bebe, boo-

boo. Gurl, me and you will be rolling around up in here, pulling each other's tracks out if you tried to take my bags from me."

Jennifer was laughing so hard she burped. "Oops. Excuse me," she said, slightly embarrassed, with a hand up to her mouth.

Samantha told Tracy, "That's a fight you would lose." She turned her head sideways to show off her flawless mane. "See, I'm all naturaaal. Unlike you, Choo-Choo Charlie, with all those train tracks in your head."

Tracy bragged, "That's all right. I might have train tracks in my head"—she jumped up from her seat and started twerking while looking back at her booty going wild—"but I gots me a caboose that brings all the boys to the yard."

Jennifer was laughing to disguise her embarrassment at the attention Tracy was gaining. "We can't take her anywhere," she said to Samantha. She then looked up at Tracy. "Will you sit your hot butt down before you end up with a million hits on YouTube."

Samantha was giggling. "Girl, you're crazy. I don't know about it bringing boys to the yard, but if you don't put that thing away, somebody is liable to get hurt."

Tracy sat back down, laughing. "You two are haters. Just plain haters."

"Tracy, nobody is hating on you," said Jennifer. "Trust me, my sistah, I have more valuable things to do with my time."

Tracy asked, "Like what? Chase down Derek King?"

Samantha chuckled. She said to Tracy, "No, you didn't go there!"

Jennifer popped her lips and rolled her eyes at Tracy. "Girl, please. Derek King is yesterday's news. But some other people—I won't mention Tracy McIntyre's name—still sniffing like a bloodhound behind Michael Brenner after he sweet-talked her out of seventy bucks and bought that girl Jewel he shares lockers with some Nike sneakers."

Samantha was cracking up. "Tracy, no, she didn't put your business out there in the street."

"I don't like that boy no more," Tracy protested heatedly. "Besides, he told me that was his godsister."

Jennifer said, "I could tell by the way Michael was making out with her down in the south lobby the other day." She sipped a little of her soda. "But I ain't even mad at him. You let him get away with it—on the third floor all hugged up with him yesterday."

"Since you're putting me on blast," Tracy answered back, "Mr. Yesterday's News is all around the school, kissing and telling. Like I want to know about how big your granny panties were the night y'all smashed."

Samantha was laughing so hard that tears formed in her eyes.

Jennifer's light skin turned crimson from embarrassment. "Uh-uh—Derek is a stone-cold liar. I didn't give him *none*."

"Okay, let's recap," Samantha said to her friends, wiping away the water. She pointed to Tracy. "You got swindled out of seventy bucks and now some chick is probably smiling anytime she sees you around the school." She smiled at Jennifer. "And you, my dear—granny panties, I'm not trying to go there with you. You guys are pathetic."

Tracy and Jennifer gave each other puzzled looks. And then they stared back at Samantha.

Tracy was the first to respond. "Gurl, you got yo' nerves."

Jennifer picked up where Tracy left off. "Got a rich, fine ball-playing brotha chasing you around town like a little puppy dog, but all you can think about is Xavier."

" 'Fine' ain't the word, Jen," Tracy weighed in. "That dude is a muscle-bound god wearing baseball cleats. And you just told us he copped a phat crib off the lake, and pushing a Phantom—what are you waiting on? I hope it ain't Xavier Hunter?"

Tracy's question dried up any trace of a smile on Samantha's face.

Samantha said, "Tracy, now you're starting to sound like my dad."

"That's right. Your old man is holding bank. That's the reason you're not impressed by Desmond's ballin' lifestyle, huh, Miss Beverly Hills," Tracy said, smirking sarcastically.

Samantha corrected, "FYI, I live in Birmingham, Michigan."

"Beverly Hills, Birmingham, Greenfield Village, Ellis Island—"

Samantha smiled and said, "You do realize the last two you mentioned aren't affluent cities, right?"

"My point is do you understand what you have in Sean is a dream to girls like me and Jennifer?" Tracy explained, sounding a little bit more like she was jealous.

Samantha made it clear. "Tracy, I have my own dreams, like dancing—I wanna make my own mark in this world with my talent. I don't need Sean Desmond or his money to become a successful woman."

"I'm just saying, Sam, any other girl would love to flex in that car, get invited to all the slamming parties that those athletes be throwing in those huge mansions," Tracy argued.

Seeing that their *happy* conversation was headed in a different direction, Jennifer said to Tracy, "Why don't you leave Sam alone?"

"Jen, I'm just saying that she's gonna mess around and miss out on a good thing by still being hung up on that good-for-nothing thug rat Xavier," said Tracy.

"Jen, sweetie, thank you, but I don't need your help," said Samantha, becoming a little heated. She looked at Tracy. "Let me straighten you out: I'm not thirsty for a man like you. Last but not least, Miss Thang, Xavier has more charm, personality, swag, and intelligence than anything you've ever dated."

"Okay," said Jennifer, with a silly look on her face. She said to Samantha, "Guess you don't need my help."

"Don't get mad at me, boo-boo," Tracy said, trying to play it down with a smile. "I'm just keeping it one hundred. And for somebody who claims to be over her ex, you sure don't sound like it."

Jennifer tried to squash it. "Guys? What are we doing? Remember we're the Three Musketeers—all for one and one for all."

"No, Jen, we're still family, but I'm just trying to look out," Tracy reassured her. "Sam, did you know that London Curry is going around sneak dissin' you? Tellin' suckas that you're jealous of her because she's the new *it* girl in Xavier's life."

"Seriously, Tracy, do you think I care about the girl's insecurities?" asked Samantha. "If she thinks that she has to step on me to improve her chances with him, then God bless her."

"You mean you're not gonna step to her?" Tracy asked.

"Why should I? She's Dumpster diving for my left-overs."

Jennifer looked at Samantha. "Good point."

Tracy smacked her lips and rolled her eyes at Jennifer.

Jennifer said, changing the subject, "I can't wait until the icebreaker. It's going to be off the chain at the North-land Skating Rink with cute ballers all over the place."

As usual, Tracy jumped in with her negativity. " 'Ballers'? Those immature little high school boys don't have no money. Many of them will stand on a chair, put a noose around their necks, and jump off if you asked them for five dollars."

Jennifer had grown weary of Tracy's tired tirade. She held up a bebe shopping bag—"Just like you, and me, sponging off Sam, huh. We're just as flat busted as the rest of the students. I'm just saying: When you live in a glass house, don't start shooting at it, sweetie."

Samantha laughed and high-fived Jennifer.

"Forget you, Jen," said a bitter Tracy.

Samantha explained, "This is our senior year, ladies, and we're going to have the best time ever." She smiled at Tracy's direction. "If Miss Sour Puss over there can get her behind off her shoulders, she'd enjoy it with us."

Tracy said, "I just don't want you to make a mistake and let a good guy get away."

Samantha was up on her girl's game. "Girl, bye—Tracy, you know this is not about me. This is about you wanting to use me as a doorway to get into Sean's circle, so you can"—Samantha used finger quotes—"find a baller and get chauffeured around in his expensive car."

"So what's wrong with that?" she asked.

"For you . . . nothing," Samantha said. "Just don't make this all about me, you social climber."

"That was really low, Samantha," Tracy said, knowing that her card had been pulled.

This time Jennifer gave Samantha a high five.

Samantha grabbed her drink off the table and raised it in the air, inviting her girls to do the same.

She said, "This is for our last year of high school, ladies. We are going to have a fabulous time. The icebreaker at Northland Skating Rink will be the beginning of a great school year."

Jennifer added, "We're the Three Musketeers—all for one."

Samantha and Tracy smiled at each other and finished the other half of the credo in unison, "And one for all."

6

DAKOTA

Underneath a partly cloudy sky, Dakota had mixed in with a crowd of the students walking home from school. Aside from a few guys trying to holla at her for her digits, she hadn't made any new friends yet.

High school girls seemed to be even bigger haters than the little witches in her middle school class. It was ridiculous. The new school year was seven days old and not one single girl had spoken a few words to her—well, with the exception of a super weaved-up chick wearing false eyelashes who had the nerve to ask Dakota what was she doing off the Indian reservation. Dakota let the insult slide off her back and kept it moving.

These derogatory remarks didn't faze her. The girl had been dealing with racial ignorance since second grade, when some little white boy stared her in the eyes and called her Pocahontas. Years of cruel remarks had desensitized Dakota and given her the tough skin she would need to deal with racially insensitive fools.

As she continued her stride down the street, Dakota couldn't help but notice how name-brand crazy a lot of her fellow students were. The backs of the students at Coleman were used to advertise big-name designers. She had heard one chick in her algebra class mention that it was either brand name or she would have to drop out. The statement had floored Dakota. She didn't think it was that serious. Nothing but jeans, a cute top, and some white no-name sneakers completed Dakota's look. The girl had more serious issues to contend with than the latest fashion craze, like her mother falling into one of her bad moods. As she walked her taste buds reminded her of the Snickers bar she'd promised herself while taking notes in class. There was a small candy store five minutes from her crib. To shave a few minutes off the trip, Dakota broke away from the other students and turned down a side street. A quick left placed her on a street where the majority of the homes were abandoned with overgrown yards.

Dakota had to admit to herself, besides the slight dustup with that girl gang SNLGs, high school didn't seem like it was too bad. Not as rough as the students in her middle school classes had made it out to be. The rumors about the violence at Coleman had been legendary and horrifying amongst her eighth-grade classmates.

Dakota was walking past what remained of a stripped, burned-out minivan parked along the curb and sitting on blocks, thinking that Coleman High was nothing like the rumors. Of course it had only been a week since the start of the school year. But there hadn't been one fight on campus. Not one confrontation. Those SNLG girls were probably showing off that day when they'd stepped to her in the lunchroom and were popping off.

That boy Xavier sure had those SNL—whatever— gangsta girls shook, Dakota thought, with a smile on her face. The brother was absolutely fine too. Looking like a dark-skinned version of LL Cool J. And she just loved how he stepped in and took charge. Dude was massive, possessed mad swagger, and flexed with a look that said he didn't play. She couldn't help it. Smitten at first glance. He was like a superhero to her . . . yeah, that was it, a real-life fairy tale. Prince Charming rescuing the damsel in distress. The way Xavier had stepped in front of the little girl gang to rescue her had been something out of a fairy tale. For the first time in a long time, Dakota had felt like someone actually cared about her.

Xavier had waved and winked at her today in the lunch-room. Dakota smiled so hard that you would've thought that she had been on the receiving end of a Barack Obama handshake. Dakota didn't want to approach his table be-cause some girl was draped all over him like oversized clothing on a skinny, sagging hoodlum.

If she wasn't mistaken, London Curry was the name of the girl who was hogging all of Xavier's time. Dakota just wanted to share a little of his time, and she might've come up with a plan to do it. His boys at the lunch table had been loudly talking about attending the icebreaker at Northland Skating Rink this Friday at seven. Dakota had decided if Xavier was going to be there, then she'd also be in attendance. Her mother wouldn't create a problem. She worked the afternoon shift at some water treatment plant in Dearborn, Michigan. Evelyn didn't clock out until one in the morning. Dakota would have plenty of time to share a word or two with her hero.

She was scheming, hashing out the final details when a vintage rust bucket of a Pontiac Bonneville pulled up to the curb and slowly rolled beside her. The sight of SNLG gang member Mouse—red bandana tied around her cornrows—hanging from the back passenger window, her short torso leaning downward with what appeared to be a black tire iron clutched in her left fist, chilled Dakota to the bone. The angry snarl on the girl's grill filled Dakota with the urgency to run.

"What up now?" Mouse yelled at Dakota.

If it was gonna be a straight-up one-on-one scrap, Dakota was down with it. But the car was filled with SNLG girls looking like they couldn't wait for the car to come to a complete stop. Bangs was driving the bucket and shaking her head like she was going to enjoy the stomping they were about to put on Dakota.

Bangs laughed out the open driver's window. "Xavier ain't here to save that ass, Supermodel," she shouted. "You gonna have to take this ass whuppin' today."

"I still don't know what I did to offend you," Dakota said, trying to talk some sense into Bangs. "Whatever it was, I apologize."

"Naw," said Mouse. "The only way this is gonna end is you bleeding out."

Dakota tightened her right hand on the book bag strap

around her right shoulder. She had to keep her wits about her. The numbers weren't in her favor. If it came down to it, she could run. She had been known as the fastest runner in her middle school gym class. It wouldn't be a problem to leave these girls in the dust.

"Can we just talk this out?" asked Dakota, frantically looking around for help.

There were no more words to be spoken. Mouse popped open the back car door and ran up on Dakota, swinging the tire iron. The first attempt whistled past Dakota's left ear. She ducked it so fast she almost slipped and lost her balance. When the other girls started quickly unloading from the car, Dakota had to stay on her feet. Hitting the pavement would find her in even more trouble.

"Get her!" Dakota could hear one of them yell at Mouse. Dakota was backpedaling now and doing a good job at staying clear of the tire iron. Mouse stepped in to deliver a skull-crushing swing that, had it connected, would've relocated Dakota's lips to another zip code.

A pudgy, brown-skin girl thought that Mouse needed some help and ran behind Dakota to deliver a ferocious shot to the back of her head, just about the same time Mouse unloaded with a blow that finally found its mark, blasting Dakota on the left shoulder blade.

Dakota stumbled forward, yelping in pain but managing to keep her footing. She was seeing stars from the punch. The hot, streaking pain barreling through her shoulder was no joke.

"I've called the police. Y'all better leave that girl alone," warned a heavyset elderly black lady, dressed in a flowery house duster, raising her cell phone in full view and standing on her front porch. "They will be here in seconds—please believe me."

Bangs stood down her female soldiers and faced the old lady with a hard stare.

"Honey, I'm not afraid of you," the elderly woman let Bangs know. "And if the police need me to testify, I will."

Bangs looked over at Dakota with a menacing glance. "This ain't over."

The leader wisely ordered her girls back in the hooptie and drove off down the street.

Dakota was in pain and breathing heavy, holding her left shoulder. It was tender to the touch.

"Baby, are you all right?" the lady asked Dakota with a look of pure concern on her face.

While there hadn't been time for Dakota to cry before, tears were now sliding down both cheeks. Her pain was so immense and her emotions so overwhelming that she couldn't answer the lady's question with anything but a nod of the head.

The lady turned and called into the house. "Otis, come on out here."

A dark elderly gentleman with salt-and-pepper hair slowly hobbled onto the porch.

The lady said to him, "Go and fetch the car, Otis. We have to take this young lady home."

7

XAVIER

FRIDAY, SEPTEMBER 18
5:57 P.M.

"Yes, London," said Xavier, agitated and talking into his cell phone. "Soon as my dad gets here I'll be on my way to scoop you."

Xavier listened for a few irritating moments while putting on his clothes—black denim Levi's, a matching short-sleeve shirt, and some black and gray Puma boat shoes.

He said to her, "I promise you that I won't spend all my time hanging out with my fellas."

Xavier couldn't do anything but shake his head as London continued to get on his nerves.

"I'm gonna skate with you, but you're asking for a little bit too much," he explained. Xavier heard his dad and brother walk through the front door. "Listen, London, my old man just got in. I'll be over in a few."

Xavier was about to end the call but London kept on running off at the mouth. So he had to boss up, slightly raising his voice. "Listen, I can't be on my way if you keep on talking, feel me?"

London was a highly sensitive chick and couldn't stand being put on blast. She responded by hanging up in his face. Xavier never liked clocking out on babes like that, but the fact was that her clingy ass had been seriously getting on his nerves lately. Everywhere he turned, she was in his face, sweating 'im something awful, like a sauna. He absolutely *hated* when Samantha was somewhere in the vicinity and London would get jealous and grab his hand—ooh, how he didn't dig that about her insecure behind. Xavier could've better understood London's reactions if she was his boo. But they were nowhere near that status. The girl was still a virgin—meant he hadn't even smashed yet and she was tripping like this. He could only imagine how she'd act if he'd hit it one good time. Matter of fact, he'd already experienced a chick like that. The girl that came to his mind left him shook. Heather Larkin had turned out to be more terrifying than the dead coming back to life. That girl was just another horrifying chapter in Xavier's life that left him thanking God for that situation being behind him.

Xavier's father Noah was still dressed in his work blues. He had one strap of a backpack bearing a UAW logo around his right shoulder and a red and white Playmate Igloo cooler in his left hand.

"Pops," said Xavier, smiling as he walked into the living room and playfully slapped his brother Alfonso in the back of the head, "why are you home from work this early? Let me guess, the boss gave you some time off to go and heal the sick, probably go and feed thousands of homeless people with two loaves of bread and seven fish, right?"

Noah didn't look amused. Matter of fact, he looked exhausted. "Son, I'm really not in the mood for your jokes. At least get your biblical facts straight. Jesus fed the multitude with *five* loaves and *two* fish. Stop trying to turn our Lord and Savior into a punch line, would you."

Noah was nowhere near the hotheaded, Scriptures-slinging jailhouse preacher he was after he'd been released from prison a year ago, where he'd immediately tried to convert Xavier into being a devout Christian. The junk hadn't flown with Xavier, though. Homeboy was not about that life and wouldn't allow himself to be transformed into an altar boy. Thankfully the two had been able to put aside their differences and arrive at an understanding.

"Pops, what's up with the sour face?" Xavier asked.

Noah let out a frustrated sigh. "Why don't you ask your little brother?"

Xavier said, "Uh-huh, this can't be good." Alfonso looked like he was trying to bust a serious move to his bedroom before he got interrogated by his brother. "'Fonso, freeze. Don't go running to that room. Hop yourself on back here, you feel me?"

The boy was geared up in jeans and an orange short-sleeve Polo shirt with the huge royal blue horse logo featured on the chest. The kid's Florida Gators baseball hat matched his white Air Force 1s with the orange trim.

Noah went into the kitchen.

Xavier could hear the refrigerator door open and close. When Noah emerged he was holding a bottle of Sprite. A twist of the cap released a hissing sound. "Go ahead, Alfonso, and tell your brother why I had to leave work today," Noah ordered his youngest son.

Xavier copped a squat on a sofa arm and folded his arms across his chest in anticipation. There was a more serious look on his face now.

Alfonso muttered, "I-I-I—"

"No need of you trying to sing, homeboy," said Xavier. "Out with it."

The kid was sweating it and had an embarrassed look on his face. "See, there is this girl at school and . . ."

Xavier's face became animated and he started cracking up. "Oh shoot! My little brother has his nose open!"

Noah calmly took a swallow of soda. "Jesus, Mary, and Joseph—don't encourage the boy, Xavier."

"Come on, Pop, Alfonso has his first crush. How old were you when you started diggin' on the girlies?"

"I've long since confessed my sins and we don't need to go there," said Noah. "Alfonso hasn't told you everything. His little jug-headed butt almost got suspended for fighting."

"Over a girl?" Xavier asked, shocked. He looked at Alfonso. "You're about to lose a few stripes over this one, homeboy."

"Got into it with some little boy named Kevin in the lunchroom over a girl named Molly—"

Alfonso corrected his father. "That's Myla, Dad."

Xavier was almost coughing up a lung laughing. "'Fonso, you pieced up somebody? What was the beef about?" he asked, holding his stomach from laughing so hard and trying to keep his composure.

Alfonso cast his eyes to the floor. "Well, Kevin was calling her names and pulling her hair. She told him to stop but he just kept on. I was only doing what I knew you would've done."

Alfonso was right. Xavier was known for smacking respect into bullies. Those who considered themselves beast always fell hard to monsters like him.

Noah pushed, "Go on. Finish telling him."

Xavier rubbed his hands together in anticipation of drama. "You mean there's more to the story?"

Alfonso kept his eyes glued to the floor. "Myla kissed me after I beat up Kevin. She said I was her hero."

"I don't get it," said Xavier. "Why did you get in trouble for defending the little girl?"

Noah stepped in. "Xavier, he should've gone and told a teacher. Not taken things into his hands."

"I guess you're right."

"I knew I shouldn't have given in and bought him those name-brand clothes—nothing but Satan."

Xavier couldn't do anything but shake his head. "Pop, no disrespect, but please don't go there. Clothes don't have anything to do with bullies."

Noah had been on that trip tip when he'd come home

from prison, insanely preaching that Satan launched attacks on the young through name-brand clothing. Said that young people were easy targets to commit unspeakable acts of evil in order to obtain big-name labels that were driven solely by their reckless thirst to become bigger than life. It had been one of the issues that pitted father and son against each other and almost ripped the family apart.

"Are you still going skating tonight?" Noah asked Xavier.

"Yup. 'Bout to leave right now."

"Be careful, son. It's dangerous out in those streets. And Satan is roaring like a lion, looking for someone to devour."

Xavier wasn't feeling like hearing a sermon. Dude had the keys to his ride and he'd made it to the side door. "All right, Pop, I'll be careful."

Before Xavier could close the door all the way, his old man said, "Make it back home at a decent time, huh, son?"

It was close to seven when Xavier made it over to Dexter's spot.

Dex jumped into Xavier's new ride and the silver Ford Fusion started down the street.

Xavier shook his head at how tight Dex was sporting his clothes. The boy had on a pair of Army green cargo shorts, a military T-shirt, and some pretty nice boat shoes to match.

"Dude, I hope you don't plan on walking by any jails looking like that," said Xavier.

Dex asked from the passenger seat, "Looking like what?"

"Wearing your gear so bootyliciously tight might get you some unwanted attention," Xavier said in a joking manner as he made a right hand turn onto a main street. He hunched his shoulders and said, "I'm just saying."

Dex laughed good-naturedly. "Oh, you got jokes. Home-boy, why you trying to clown on me, you know daddy got his clothing game on lock. I'm a trendsetter, baby. If anybody should know better it's you, my dude. You know my style got all the ladies smiling."

"And a lot of dudes too if five-o lock you up in the county jail with that I-need-love-in-the-worst-way out-fit on."

"Funny."

Xavier was cracking up. He drove a mile before jumping on the freeway.

Dex said to Xavier, "Since you talking about jail, what you gonna do about the warden? I swear I ain't never seen somebody needier than London."

Dex's question had Xavier scratching his head. He hadn't the slightest idea on the issue.

Xavier adjusted his rearview mirror and drove at a moderate speed in the thick traffic.

Dex switched the subject. "All day, the only thing I've been thinking about is how I'm gonna fare on those roller skates. It's been a minute since I was on some. Man, I am not trying to bust my ass out there."

Xavier didn't respond to Dexter's anxiety. Instead he said, "Flip wasn't at school today. Homeboy ain't even answering his cell joint. Fam been tripping lately."

"I've been telling you that. Don't know what that fool is on—walking around the school all quiet and junk."

"Cat has been drinking like crazy lately too."

"You think he's gonna show up tonight?"

Xavier peeked into his driver-side mirror before signaling and jumping into the far left lane. "The last time I hollered at him he said he was with it."

It was some real-life stuff jumping off with Linus Flip, and to keep it real, Xavier was worried about him. He didn't make a habit out of prying into the affairs of his fellas, but a sit-down with Flip was inevitable.

"X, I know you might not want to hear this, but I heard that Samantha's girl Tracy McIntyre is going around putting the badmouth on your name. Telling people that Samantha could've done better than going with a loser like you."

Xavier wasn't sweating Tracy. He'd heard the same thing. And the funny thing about it was that the girl had no reason to be spitting dirty on him.

Xavier said, "Homeboy, you'll know when I start worrying about something said by some ghetto heffa carrying close to a lousy 2.0 GPA."

Dexter laughed. "I'm hip. She probably can't even spell GPA, homie."

The two boys were in tears as they laughed and kicked it back and forth the rest of the way to London Curry's crib.

8

XAVIER

Xavier made it to the skating rink and maneuvered through the crowded parking lot. He whipped the Ford into one of two open spaces in the back next to a lamppost. Girls were everywhere, and as soon as they started walking toward the rink's entrance, London was all up on Xavier, like homeboy had put a ring on it.

Dexter didn't say anything, just shook his head and kept his laughter to himself. Lately everything London had been doing was starting to deeply irritate Xavier. The girl was trying too hard to replace Samantha when just being herself would carry more weight with him. She was so lost in Samantha's shadow it was pathetic. To keep it one hundred, nobody could replace a jewel like Sam. She was legitimately one-of-a-kind. The good Lord had indeed treated the world with an angel when he created a girl like her. And now she was in the company of a multi-million-dollar Major League Baseball–playing weasel who probably didn't recognize a good girl from the millions of thirsty groupies that were open to do what it took to be down with him.

Judging from the long line of young people waiting to get into the rink, you would've assumed that they were giving away free Air Jordans up in that camp. The show was on, with scores of teenagers looking to one-up each other on the brand-name-label tip. Cats with their pants sagging turned out in droves. The unusually warm weather for the end of September seemed like it had girls in competition to see who could get away with flexing the most uncovered body parts.

There was a car parked by the entrance, a huge crowd milling around it—a few knucklehead girls had their phones out taking selfies in front. The closer Xavier got, the more he could see the white Rolls-Royce Phantom coupe convertible with the brushed stainless steel hood. He couldn't remember the number of times he'd drooled as he watched the high-profile whip appear on the set of music videos. The friggin' thing was the ultimate status symbol of success. And someday, when he had enough cheese, Xavier had movie-star plans on cashing one of these bad boys out.

"OMG!" shouted London, like Sean "Puffy" Combs or somebody was getting out of the rear. She handed Dexter a cell phone and her small butt surprisingly bulldozed enough people away so she could get to the front of the crowd.

Dexter and Xavier exchanged knowing glances. If London was tripping hard like this over a car, then they knew the little chick was destined to have a gold-digging reputation amongst the future baller crews in the D.

Dex had a look of concern on his face. As he snapped off pictures of London doing everything but kissing the car's grill, he said to Xavier, "If Samantha's in there, then you-know-who probably won't be too far behind."

Xavier looked over at the car and scratched his chin. "You think this is that clown's ride?"

Dexter rolled his shoulders. "Wouldn't surprise me none. This icebreaker is only for Coleman High students. Do you know anybody else at the school who knows somebody styling with this much cheese?"

"Good point."

"That is a beautiful car," said London. "I wonder who owns it."

Dexter handed London back the phone. He completely ignored her and asked Xavier, "You good?"

Xavier brimmed with confidence. "Homeboy, she gotta make it do what it do. I'm not the type of cat to lose sleep over an ex, you feel me?"

Xavier could miss Dexter with that nonsense. He definitely wasn't buying it. At one time Xavier would've done anything to protect Samantha. Love like that just didn't fade away so quickly. Dexter knew better. He also knew that emotions were like lighting the wick on a single stick of dynamite. It would be just a matter of time before the stuff exploded.

"Samantha, Samantha," London jealously repeated, like the name was an awful taste in her mouth. "I'm so sick and tired of hearing that girl's name. Excuse me." She angrily stomped away and went to stand in line.

Xavier could lie to Dexter but not himself. He still had mad love for Samantha, a deep, bottomless love that would never fade. But Samantha had made her decision and it wasn't to stay with him. This was Xavier's last year of high school, and he wasn't about to get in any trouble by slugging it out with a hotshot MLB rookie sensation over a girl—although he wouldn't have minded smashing that fool for the flagrant disrespect he'd shown behind the school at the beginning of Xavier's junior year.

Inside, the music exploded over the skating rink as the floor teemed with activity. The lights were down low and the disco ball slowly spun like the earth on its axis, covering the walls, ceiling, and floor with silvery flakes. Tons of skaters were rocking, getting it in, roll-bouncing around on the floor to Bruno Mars's "Uptown Funk." The middle of the floor belonged to the elite, those who had no problem artistically expressing themselves by shooting clever tricks and ridiculously breaking it down with off-the-hook dance moves on skates.

As the three of them made their way through the dense crowd, Dexter started clowning around.

He had a hand over his nose, not to mention the task of trying to talk over the music. "Every time I come in this joint it smells like corn chips, stank sweat socks, and funky feet."

"There you go," said Xavier, laughing. He looked over Dex's shoulder and saw Samantha and her entire crew sitting in seats around the concession stand. He'd spat that craziness out of his mouth to Dexter earlier about not tripping if he saw her—that was until he saw Sean all up in her face.

Oh yeah, he was boiling. Jealousy swelled inside Xavier, like homeboy was about to go all Dr. Bruce Banner with it and rip through his clothes to turn into the ghetto version of the Incredible Hulk.

Things just got real.

9

SAMANTHA

FRIDAY, SEPTEMBER 18
8:41 P.M.

Sean Desmond was everything Xavier wasn't—he had a huge ego, was super arrogant, and also had loads of cash to burn. And though those things weren't super appealing to her, Samantha had to admit that it was refreshing to be out with somebody she didn't have to worry would be riddled by bullets. It was so much unlike an outing with Xavier. Her father had been on her case hard about giving Sean Desmond an opportunity. His constant badgering was wearing her down. So she was happy to be out and enjoying time with friends.

Of course Samantha would check her girl Tracy for meddling in her affairs later. The nosy heffa had seen Sean at Oakland Mall and invited him to the icebreaker. Sure, the event was for students only, but nobody could turn down a guy like Sean Desmond. He played for the hometown team, the Detroit Tigers, so he had no problem getting in. He was a rookie phenom and Detroit's newest media darling who had been given the key to the city.

Samantha and Sean were sitting at a booth by themselves. Tracy and Jennifer were all up on two of Sean's boys at the booth behind them. To keep autograph-hounding fans away from them, Sean had positioned four huge bodyguards around their area who looked like muscle-bound giant rock creatures. Sean's two boys, Ozzie and Cash, sitting with her friends looked grimy, thuggish— just the kind of men Tracy admired. They looked hot and a little gangsta with their expensive clothing and the tons of jewelry they were rocking.

"So tell me, baby," Sean said, smiling devilishly, staring into her eyes from across the booth. "Why aren't you skating?"

The music was tough to talk over, but Samantha smiled and answered, "Too crowded on the floor, just look out there."

The sheer volume of people on the floor was making it difficult for some to negotiate the curves, and as a result, a lot of skaters were left on the seats of their pants.

Sean's wardrobe was devoid of flair—nothing extravagant, a basic cotton Detroit Tigers short-sleeve shirt, cargo pants, sneakers. The only thing of value on his person was an expensive jewel-encrusted custom Rolex watch and Gucci sunglasses.

He smiled. "Thanks for the invitation, though. Glad to see you coming out of your shell, baby."

"Sean, I didn't invite you. Tracy did."

"I know that, but you wanted me to come. I could see that in your eyes. I'm the man of your dreams, Samantha—a good-looking stud who just so happens to play shortstop for the Detroit Tigers, and one day, I'll be a Hall of Famer."

Samantha didn't look impressed. "Congratulations on all your success, Sean. I'm happy for you."

"Baby, let's stop playing games. I want you to be a part of my team."

"Your team?"

"I've had an amazing season—I'm a shoo-in for rookie of the year. The Tigers are at the top of our division and we're headed to the playoffs. Sportswriters are saying that we can win it all. Just signed a multimillion-dollar deal with an energy drink company and my agent is in negotiations to use my face to sell sandwiches. With the right lady behind me, there's no stopping me."

"By your side?"

"Huh?" Sean asked, dumbfounded.

Samantha repeated, "*The right lady* should be by your side. Not standing behind you."

Sean totally ignored her. "Didn't we have fun at Disney World?"

Samantha folded her arms. "My father invited you."

"But answer the question. Didn't we have fun?"

"One: you were too busy signing autographs, and two: you were on the phone talking to your agent the majority of the time."

"Only securing the future for us, baby. I don't want

you to have to do anything once we're married except raise our family."

"So my wanting to be a professional dancer would be out the door with you, huh?"

"Like I said, I'm gonna get my grind on so that you won't have to do anything, baby."

Samantha already knew how Xavier had felt about her dancing professionally. He was encouraging and support-ive, and she loved that about him. Sean seemed to be the complete opposite. Selfish. Everything was about him. There was no way she could commit to somebody with this level of arrogance.

Samantha said with attitude, "Who says I'm marry-ing you?"

The question caught Sean by surprise. He sat back in his seat with a stupid little look on his face.

Samantha was about to say something else when her attention was diverted by a girl with a gorgeous com-plexion who looked vaguely familiar. All of a sudden, with a look of terror on her face, she bolted, like some-one was hot on her tail.

10

DAKOTA

FRIDAY, SEPTEMBER 18
9:00 P.M.

The skating rink was jammed tight with people. It was the perfect setup for a little person like Dakota to hide in plain sight. When she'd gotten off the bus, Dakota had every intention of renting a pair of skates and having some fun. Her plans had gotten kicked to the curve because she spotted Bangs and Mouse lurking around. If those two were at the rink, then the other clowns couldn't be too far behind. The grim looks on their faces suggested that they were here for more destructive reasons. Until Xavier arrived, Dakota would keep a low profile.

Since her attack, Dakota's instinct for survival had kept her out of her regularly scheduled lunch period. The library had become her new sanctuary. Inside, amongst the shelves and dusty hardback books, Dakota had found peace. She was merely staying out of the way. Doing what Xavier had suggested. Keeping low-key. Watching where she stepped. Sticking close to well-populated areas inside the school building. Taking other avenues home to avoid further conflict with the SNLG goons. A few times the gang members had come painfully close to nabbing her ass, but somehow, she'd managed to juke them and scurry away. But the efforts to stay safe had consequences, like adding space between her and the man she desired.

And that's why she was here today, checking for her strong, handsome knight. The SNLG girls were dispersed throughout the crowd. So she kept herself mixed into large groups. That was until Dakota saw Mouse glance in her direction. Not knowing if she'd been spotted by the little tire-iron-wielding lunatic pushed Dakota to seek out higher grounds. As she weaved her way through bodies, her heart pounded ferociously against her chest like it was competing with the powerful bass pumping from the surrounding speakers for the title of loudest sound. Dakota was so short that all she could see was a forest of legs in front of her and the same thing when she glanced back to see if she was being followed.

As she swiftly moved past the concession area, Dakota saw four enormous statue-looking brothas standing around a couple of tables like they were protecting the president or somebody. She was moving too fast to be sure, but the person that the men were huddled around looked like that new young rookie from the Detroit Tigers. His face had been all over TV and the newspapers.

Spotting Bangs in a crowd about fifteen feet away caused Dakota to dip into the ladies' restroom. Of course it was clichéd, but it was her only move. She took refuge in the last of five stalls, closed the door behind her, put the lid down on the toilet, and stood in a crouched position, facing forward. As she stood shivering, Dakota couldn't come up with one solid reason why God would allow her to be terrorized like this. She'd always been a good girl. Never hurt a soul. Did what she was supposed to do in school. Brought home straight As. All she wanted to do was make friends and have a normal teenage life. But after the beating she'd taken from the SNLGs, there was no way she was going out like that again without putting up a fight. Although the sleepless nights she'd endured from being clubbed in the shoulder by the iron were gone, a bruise remained, like she would be scarred for life.

When the restroom door opened Dakota's blood ran cold.

Damn!

That's when she'd realized that in her haste to retreat she'd forgotten to lock the stall door. It was too late for that now. There was a small canister nestled in her right pants pocket. She retrieved it and readied it for action. Dakota wasn't sure if whoever was in the restroom was there for relief or drama. It didn't matter, though. She was prepared to take it *there* if necessary. But once the first stall door was kicked in, Dakota wished that she could've turned invisible. They were here for her all right because the second door was kicked in the exact same manner—bam!

The third door sounded—boom!

The fourth one seemed like it had been kicked off its hinges. Dakota drew in a deep, nervous breath, expecting that at any moment her door would be next. Her mind was made up. All she needed to see was the whites of their eyes. The image of her badly beaten body lying helplessly on the restroom floor raced through her head. Butterflies danced around inside her stomach. Because of the weight they were supporting, Dakota's legs began to tremble. But homegirl held tight.

Not this time, she told herself. *Somebody is about to catch a beat-down at the hands of this little mosquito.*

She looked down at the floor, and on the other side of the door, there they were: toes belonging to a badly beaten pair of ladies' Air Jordans. Dakota said a silent prayer.

And then boom! The stall door came crashing in. Dakota didn't hesitate. She raised her right arm and sprayed Mace in Bangs's eyes. Everything happened in a blur. Bangs fell to her knees, screaming like she was losing her mind and intensely rubbing her eyes. Fortunately for Dakota, the SNLG leader had ventured into the restroom without the rest of her girls. Bangs probably wasn't sure if it was Dakota creeping into the restroom or not, so she'd walked in to just scope out the joint. And now she was rolling around on the floor, comically screaming because the Mace had her eyeballs on fire.

Dakota yelled, "Now leave me alone!"

She hurried out of the restroom and left Bangs rolling around on the floor.

11

XAVIER

FRIDAY, SEPTEMBER 18
9:35 P.M.

Xavier and Dex were posted up by a set of lockers near some video games. Through the crowd the two had a clear vantage point of Samantha and her little entourage.

Dex was monitoring his boy closely. Xavier wasn't fooling him. He knew that jealousy was coursing through his homeboy's bloodstream. The faces, biting of his lip, and every now and again, pacing in circles—all signs that could lead to an emotional explosion. Dexter just hoped and prayed that Sean Desmond didn't try to step to them with no noise.

"Damn, those are some big bodyguards," Dexter said to Xavier. "You straight, man?"

Xavier couldn't enjoy the three cats dancing a routine on skates because he was too busy watching Sam and Sean.

Xavier casually replied, "I'm tight, homeboy. And they're not big enough to stop me if Sean tries to style on me up in here."

"I see Samantha didn't waste any time trying to get you out of her system."

London rolled around with other skaters on the floor, and when she caught sight of Xavier, she frowned at him.

Xavier pointed to her. "I'm running around with that, so I don't have any room to be pointing fingers."

"True dat," said Dex. "But you ain't hittin' that. Can you say that about—"

"Dude, I'm not even trying to go there with you, you feel me?"

Apparently Xavier was feeling some kind of way about seeing Sam out with that clown. But there was nothing he could do about it. She was entitled to date whoever she wanted. He wasn't weak, and he definitely was no sucka. There was no punk in his game, because at the end of the day he understood that it was all about the number of zeros on a check. It seemed like six or seven figures was the only thing that could earn a potential mate Mr. Fox's seal of approval on dating his daughter.

"Okay, my dude, it's cool," said Dex. "It's a virtual honey oasis up in this piece. And they're all over your socks, playboy, you dig?"

Xavier had been aware of the attention the moment he entered the rink. Chicks were loving his flavor, his swag, the confidence—and the banging fact that he had a dangerous reputation in the school of being the wrong G to step to.

Xavier asked Dexter something totally out of the way. "You ever get the feeling that something bad was about to happen?"

Dexter's eyebrows knitted together in concern. "X, talk to me, guy. Give me the rundown on what's going on through that dome of yours, fam."

Xavier started to chop it up when he spotted Linus Flip headed toward them, stumbling, bumbling through the crowd and getting heated with anybody who tried to check him.

Dexter just shook his head. "Twenty dollars says he's been drinking, X."

Flip was wearing a pair of jeans sagging off his ass, a black Adidas shirt with the huge old-school flower, Detroit Tigers baseball cap slightly tilted to the side, and a pair of black on white shell-toe Adidas sneakers.

"My people," Flip said, clumsily grabbing Dexter around the back of his neck and pulling him so close to his mouth that Dexter made a stink face.

He twisted out of Flip's grasp, waving a hand in front of his nose. "Damn, fool, you smell nasty!" Xavier wasn't holding him up. He was blunt. "You've been drinking, homeboy?"

Linus casually leaned over into Xavier's space, bringing his funky breath closer. "Naw, fam, just a little cough syrup"—he put a fist to his mouth and started fake-coughing—"got a cold."

Dude's breath was on bump and the scent of alcohol leaked from his pores. The boy smelled worse than a drunken bum sleeping behind an alley Dumpster.

Dexter went hard at Linus. "Didn't know the makers of Patrón made cough syrup."

Linus pointed an unsteady index finger at Dexter and was about to clock out when drama jumped off on the other side of the rink. The DJ instantly stopped the music, causing an eerie silence before panic erupted, pushing and shoving started, and screams saturated the atmosphere.

Dakota was the cause of the disturbance. The girl was literally running for her life, weaving her way through bodies, with the SNLG girls right behind her.

"Damn . . . Lil' Mama," was all Xavier could say before jumping over the guardrail and heading in that direction. Xavier had to be quick because up ahead and over by the pro shop, Dakota had run out of real estate. The female gangsters had her cornered and were closing in around her for the beat-down.

Pandemonium had completely broken loose. People were running and screaming. Xavier had to dodge a couple of skaters who were trying to get out of his way.

Over the rail and spilling out into the carpeted aisle, Xavier pushed his way toward Dakota. When he finally made it, he couldn't see her because they had packed in on her, a vicious cloud of punches and kicks. At this point Xavier didn't care if they were females. He started peeling away girls. Whoever he grabbed went sailing through the air until Dakota was visible—Mouse being the first one bounced.

Once they saw Xavier the other gangsta chicks stood down.

Xavier went to help Dakota up when Mouse recovered and tried to blindside him.

"Where you going?" Dexter said to Mouse, grabbing her and swinging her around.

Xavier pushed Dakota behind Dexter and himself with a set of lockers at their backs.

Bangs had managed to pull herself from the floor. Her eyes were red and swollen. Didn't matter how many times she blinked or rubbed them, tears continued to roll.

She explained to Xavier, "Supermodel there Maced me."

"Nice work," Dexter said to Dakota. "Homegirl, Mace is cool, but next time use a Taser. Preferably one that will leave her smelling like bacon when you're done."

The crowd had thinned, leaving a clear area around Xavier and Dexter as they stood their ground against Bangs and her SNLG mob.

Xavier told Bangs, "Baby girl"—he nodded at Dakota— "what part of 'cut her loose' didn't you understand that day in the lunchroom?"

Mouse was back on her feet. "We SNLG!" she screamed and went to lunge for Dakota, but Bangs grabbed and restrained her. Mouse was struggling and trying to get loose from her homegirls. "SNLG until we die! Xavier, yo' name ain't stopping nothing. My chest don't beat no fear."

Xavier ignored the little chick. He focused his attention solely on Bangs.

He said to her, "If you were dudes, you'd be smashed by now. Baby girl, don't go taking my kindness for weakness. Consider this your last warning." He nodded back at Dakota. "This one here is off-limits. Understand?"

Bangs looked like she wanted to say something cute but thought better of it. "I get it, boss." She wiped away a few tears. "Anything else, boss? I mean, can we go?"

Dex had had about enough of Bangs trying to be slick, so he checked her. "Quit trying to be cute and stop with the 'boss' crap."

Bangs looked Dexter from head to toe, popped her lips, and ordered her soldiers out. Mouse wasn't buying anything. It took their entire crew to drag her tiny butt away, kicking, screaming, and cursing.

"The smallest one in the set seems to have the biggest fight," said Xavier as he watched them disappear into the crowd.

Dexter said, "Ol' girl is the only one of those cowards that seems like she's about that life. That's the one we might have a problem with."

A few pathetic-looking security guards finally arrived on the scene and were now directing traffic.

Dexter pointed at them. "Why is it that security always shows up when the drama's over?"

Xavier said, "You can't be mad at 'em, homeboy. I wouldn't put my butt on the line for minimum wage either." He looked at Dakota. "Lil' Mama, you tight?"

She might've been shaking her head as to indicate that she was straight, but the tears, minor bruising, and cuts on her face suggested that she was pretty freaking far from being okay.

Dakota was trying hard to keep herself together. She asked Xavier, "Can you please take me home?"

"Ain't nothing to talk about," answered Xavier.

Somehow, amidst the ruckus, London had managed to return her rental skates and emerge from the crowd wearing street shoes.

While Xavier was busy with Dakota, Dexter tapped him on the shoulder and pointed as London was approaching.

"Psycho chick coming up behind you, X," said Dexter.

London rolled her eyes at Dakota and instantly started in on Xavier. "Thanks a lot, Xavier. Everybody was having a good time until you decided to play Superman and save Lois Lane over there. Now they're closing down the skating rink."

"Kill all that noise," Xavier scolded. "Do you have your stuff, because we about to bounce."

"This night is busted," said Dex. "X, it's still kind of early. I think I can salvage the evening if you drop me off at the crib before London and Dakota. Maybe I can get over to my girl Marissa's house before she jets with her girlfriends."

London went off. "You're taking her home too? It's not enough that you had to go and spoil it for everybody by taking on"—she pointed at Dakota—"her battle, now you're offering cab services. Let her troublemaking behind get back home the same way she got here!"

Xavier said, "I got a better idea. Why don't you take out your cell, scroll through your contacts, and find somebody who could stand to be in the same car with you for more than two seconds, to take *you* home."

"So now you're picking this little skank freshman over me?"

Dexter couldn't resist a chance at a cheap shot. "Knowing what I know about your little naughty secrets, Ms. I'm a Virgin, I probably wouldn't be calling somebody else a skank."

London quickly crossed her arms and raised her right brow. "So tell me what you *think* you might know."

"You don't want to go down that road with me," Dexter said, smiling devilishly. "Because I personally know a line of brothers longer than the one on Air Jordan shoe release date that you told that same lie to before giving up the cookie to 'em."

"Ouch," was all Xavier could say, playing it off by looking down at the floor and scratching the back of his head.

Dexter's right jab of the truth had even managed to put a smile on Dakota's face.

London calmly rolled her neck in Xavier's direction, choosing to ignore Dexter's scalding-hot snap.

"So what's it going to be, Xavier?" asked London.

Xavier had made up his mind a long time ago. He looked at Dex and Dakota. "Y'all ready to bounce?"

The two fell in behind Xavier as the three of them started making their way through the crowd toward the exit. London was heated, and she wasn't the type to get rejected and go someplace quietly to cry. Instead, she trailed them, screaming, cursing, and yelling hot-mouth insults at the top of her lungs.

Xavier and crew had finally made it outside into the night air and were walking past the Rolls-Royce Phantom when London yelled, "The great Xavier, reduced to putting hands on females. Ain't enough that you got all the dudes in school shaking at the sound of your name, now you're trying to send a message to the girls at Coleman by throwing around a bunch of young girl thug wannabes?"

"What do you expect from an insecure little gangsta wannabe?" said a familiar male voice rising from a crowd of people standing to the rear of the Phantom, beside the highly polished chrome grill of a black Yukon Denali with the headlights on.

Just what Xavier needed right now, another punk looking to style in front of his homeboys. When the crowd of people suddenly opened up, standing there in the middle, was Samantha, her two girlfriends, four monstrous-looking fools dressed in black, that MLB-playing, multimillion-dollar jerk Sean Desmond, with two of his goons standing behind him.

Dexter quickly assessed the threat. "Fam, these fools rolling heavy. This could get ugly, X." He desperately scanned the crowd for any trace of an ally, somebody from Coleman flexing the moxie to stand united in the pocket with fellow classmates and bang out against outsiders. "Looks like Linus dipped on us again."

Xavier looked at Dexter. "Keep cool, my dude. This clown stands to lose a lot more than we do if he starts tripping, you feel me?" He glanced back at Dakota and instructed her, "Beat it if this thing breaks down."

Girlfriend nodded. The terror in her eyes had taken on a life of its own as she witnessed the entourage of muscle and swag approaching them.

London was playing the part of the cheerleading instigator. "Uh-oh, Xavier. Your woman-beating behind isn't messing with ponytails and cornrows this time. These cats are real men and they're about to take you on."

With his entourage at his back, Sean Desmond walked up on Xavier. "If it isn't the police department's favorite criminal," Sean arrogantly joked. "I thought you'd be dead or in jail by now. Black folks, I tell you—don't know how to go anywhere without starting trouble. We all were having such a good time too, until you and your little ghetto friend decided to smack up a bunch of girls. Now look at where we're at."

Xavier wasn't falling for the okey-doke. This fool was just speaking his mind—and even though he was worth a few million, there was no way junk was about to pop off.

Geesh, Xavier thought. Even with the look of concern on her face Samantha was still gorgeous.

"Is there a point to all of this?" Xavier asked Sean.

"You got the whole city open, playboy," Dexter added. "Why don't you go somewhere and celebrate your millions by buying a brand-new personality."

Xavier gave Dexter a "what part of be cool don't you understand?" look.

Sean Desmond pompously laughed like he had the whole world in the palm of his hand. "Good one," he said to Dexter, still laughing. Sean looked over at his bodyguards. "You know . . . a simple order from me and they would make it hard for your mother to identify your remains, little boy."

Xavier had to play this thing just right, because it had the potential to ignite into a swinging free-for-all of knuckles, caved-in teeth, and broken jaws.

"Come on, cuzzo," said the goon standing to Sean's right, dressed in black Gucci sneakers, tan cargo shorts, and a matching top. "Let me smash these two cowards."

Cash stood to Sean's left. "Sean, you and the body-guards can fall back. No need to get y'all's hands dirty." This one was wearing the opposite—tan sneakers, some black cargo shorts, and a top to match. "That's what you got us for. Taking care of that light work."

The crowd around was pumped and seemed ready to get this potential crime scene on the road.

Xavier said to Sean, "Homeboy, outside of Samantha we haven't had any real beef." He glanced at her. "You seem like you got that all sewed up now. So what's this really about?"

Before Sean could open his mouth, Samantha blasted Xavier. " 'Sewed up'? Let me tell you something, Xavier. I'm not a 'that' or a piece of property. Maybe if you were a lot more goal-oriented and a little less ghetto we prob-ably could've had a future."

Samantha's words sliced through Xavier like a power saw through wood. He hadn't meant any disrespect. But Samantha's shot was vicious. Cut right through to the bone.

"Nah, you got it wrong, Ms. Fox. It was your father that was up in arms when he found out I was feeling you," Xavier said before he knew it. "Dude is so intelli-gent when it comes to business, but I can't believe that he sucks so badly at being a good judge of character."

Samantha yelled with tears in her eyes, "I should've had my head examined messing around with you, ghetto trash."

Jennifer grabbed Samantha and tried to comfort her.

Tracy went off, though. "Better treasure those memories, boo," she said to Xavier. "This will probably be the last time that your little hood rat behind comes anywhere near somebody like her again."

A few minutes ago Xavier was thinking that Linus had jumped ship, like he'd done that day in the lunchroom when Bangs and her crew of scalawags had tried Dakota for the first time. He shook his head as Linus staggered through the crowd, pushing people out of the way.

At the sight of Linus Flip's bumbling approach, Sean Desmond's bodyguards became animated, like humongous stone statues springing to life.

"What's this?" Linus asked Xavier, stopping right next to him, swaying—his every clumsy movement screaming out, "I'm drunk as hell!" to everybody.

Sean Desmond laughed. "This supposed to be backup?" he asked Xavier with a hand up to his mouth, smirking. Then he turned to look at his entourage, waving his thumb in Linus's direction. "This is their backup, y'all."

One of Sean's bodyguards yelled out, "Somebody get him to an AA class, and quick!"

Everybody was laughing, except Linus, Dexter, and Xavier. Linus Flip might've been hammered but he wasn't too smashed to steal on Sean, clocking him in the right eye with a straight jab. Nothing but pure chaos ensued.

Dakota bolted like she'd been instructed to, but not before witnessing Linus being knocked to the ground and disappearing behind sneakers and Timbs. Dex wasn't faring too well either. While two bodyguards were stomping, trying to make Linus a permanent fixture in the asphalt,

Sean Desmond's two henchmen were wiping the floor with Dexter. Xavier was trying to hold his own against the biggest bodyguard—it wasn't happening, though. The punk's chin seemed like it had been made from titanium, the thing was so tough. Xavier's right and left combination would've been enough to put anybody else to sleep. Not this mug, though. Dude walked right through Xavier's punches. Immediately following, he delivered a straight right of his own and sent Xavier stumbling backward.

As bystanders scrambled across the parking lot, running for cover, the two security guards from earlier stayed out of the way. The only thing they could do was dial 911 and wait for the arrival of the Detroit police.

But Xavier didn't have too long to wait for reinforcements. His homeboy Bigstick showed up with the entire football team. They jumped into the skirmish, knuckles swinging.

The appearance of the first police cruiser was enough to stop the brawl and send everyone fleeing.

Working off pure adrenaline, Xavier staggered over to Dexter and helped his homie up from the ground. They ran, blending in with the others, all the way back to the silver Ford Fusion. Dakota was waiting by the car, trembling and shaking. The three of them jumped in and Xavier backed up and drove off, carefully maneuvering his way through frantic pedestrians. The parking lot was in complete chaos. But Xavier managed to stay calm and fought his way through car traffic. As soon as he hit open road, homeboy floored it.

*   *   *

Dakota's crib had been Xavier's first stop. He was now waiting on Dexter to get into the front door of his house. Xavier pulled away once his friend was safely inside. On the way back from the skating rink, the car had been silent. Nobody discussed any details. The soft hum of acceleration had been the only noise.

Ten thirty p.m. was the time on the digital clock in the dash. As he drove through the streets, Xavier struggled to put what happened into perspective. All it probably would've taken to dead the whole situation was he and Samantha leading by example and talking some sense into their friends. But instead they'd allowed themselves to get sucked up into the craziness. Truths had been spoken in anger. Words that couldn't be taken back. As a result, feelings were hurt. Physical damage had been done. The blood on the Kleenex Xavier was holding up to his left nostril was proof. And poor Dexter would probably have to disguise his black eye with sunglasses for the next week. There was no way of knowing what type of injuries Flip had sustained. And it was no better for him. The whole thing was his fault anyway. They probably could've squashed the beef if Linus hadn't dotted Sean's eye. Flip would have some explaining to do tomorrow, like why he couldn't keep the liquor bottle away from his lips. Dude had a straight-up drinking problem, and Xavier was going to get to the bottom of it.

Xavier was stopped at a traffic light on a major street when a black car with dark tinted windows pulled up on his right-hand side. He was too mentally and physically spent to pay attention to anything else but the traffic light. Call it intuition, but whatever it was caused Xavier to look in that direction. If he hadn't, he wouldn't have seen the driver's window halfway down on the Mercury and the pistol pointed at his head.

The first shot exploded Xavier's front passenger glass. He wasn't sticking around to see if he was hit. He got low, cutting the steering wheel hard to the left and flooring the gas pedal. The Ford jerked and spun out of control, moments later hitting a parked car, throwing him forward. There was another loud explosion. Xavier couldn't tell if it was a second gunshot because of the noise made by the air bag deploying, blowing up in his face. As he slowly drifted into unconsciousness, the only thing he could hear was tires screeching and the sound of a car speeding off into the distance.

12

SAMANTHA

MONDAY, OCTOBER 5
4:15 P.M.

Dance had been Samantha's last class of the day. She was now hanging out in the back of the school with Tracy and Jennifer while waiting on her ride. Students were walking home in crowds.

The weather forecasters could be jerks sometimes in getting the weather report accurate, but when Samantha had stepped out to retrieve the *Detroit News* before breakfast early this morning, she found out that last night's weather prediction had been right on the money. Morning temps had been swimming around in the low 40s but gradually ascended throughout the day until reaching the chilly high of sixty-five.

The sudden drop in temperature had been Samantha's excuse to show off her new cute Gucci purchases. Between the three of them her ensemble leapt out and grabbed most of the spotlight. Samantha's hair hung in tight curls, stopping right at the shoulders of the black Gucci quilted leather biker jacket that hugged her ebony dimensions like the thing had been tailor-fitted. The same brand jeans firmly clung to her backside and snaked downward over the tops of black Gucci riding boots. The showstopper was her black Gucci swing leather tote, though. She'd been receiving mad props on the bag all day long.

An after-school job interview had Jennifer casually dressed in a black wrap pencil skirt, three-quarter-sleeve blazer, and three-inch heels. Tracy was chilling in a hooded jacket, stretch knit pants, and some kind of black futuristic sneakers that zipped up at the sides.

It'd been seventeen days since the skating rink brawl and it was still the hot topic around campus. But "Who shot Xavier?" was the million-dollar question that had staff and students chattering and trying to pick out an assailant from Xavier's long, steadily growing list of enemies.

"Gurl, you know the boy ain't nothing but a thug and he had it coming," said Tracy. "Besides, he's the one that started the whole mess at the skating rink."

Jennifer made that face at Tracy that girls make when a girlfriend stepped out of pocket to say something stupid.

"You don't own a heart, do you?" Jennifer asked Tracy. "You have a hole with an ice pump in it."

"Which skating rink were you at?" Samantha asked Tracy. "You know Linus was responsible for throwing the first punch."

"Y'all heffas are just soft," said Tracy. "I could care

one way or the other about a hood rat, especially when you have a man like Sean Desmond riding for you."

"Is that all you think about . . . your own self?" Jennifer asked Tracy.

"Gurl, bye," Tracy dismissively said, waving Jennifer off.

Since hearing the unfortunate news, Samantha had been crying on and off in secrecy. Tracy had been so negative about the incident that Samantha didn't want to let her know how the news had affected her. Plus, she didn't have the energy for an emotional tussle with her girl.

"Has anyone heard any updates on Xavier since this morning?" Samantha asked, trying to hide the emotion in her voice.

Tracy popped her lips sarcastically. "That's your old boo, gurl. Don't you still have his cell phone number?"

"When I heard about it I tried his cell a few times and it went straight to voice mail," Samantha answered, like she was fighting back the tears.

Jennifer asked, "Don't you know where he lives?"

Samantha answered, "They recently moved and I never got a chance to visit his new house."

"Dexter has been walking around campus looking like a sick puppy all day, why didn't either of you two geniuses ask him?" Tracy said. "He has to know something."

Samantha was in the dark—matter of fact, the entire school seemed to be in the same fix. Nobody knew anything. The only information that had been leaked was that somebody had pulled alongside his car Friday night and opened fire. Her ex, for all she knew, was laid up in a hospital bed somewhere with tubes, wires, and all types of machinery dispensing, draining, and beeping in sync with his heart.

Samantha told Tracy, "I asked Dexter."

"What did he say?" Jennifer wanted to know.

"Said he didn't know and walked away, like he was mad at me."

Tracy butted in. "Why's he tripping? You didn't twist Xavier out."

Jennifer shook her head at Tracy. "Samantha, do you think Sean had anything to do with it?"

"Of course not, Jen, don't be silly," said Samantha. "Sean wouldn't risk his dream to do something that heinous."

"He wouldn't, but what about the two bodyguards, Ozzie and Cash?" Jennifer asked.

"Don't go putting that sexy Ozzie on blast," said Tracy. "Y'all already know that everybody had it out for Mr. Zulu."

"That is true, Samantha," Jennifer said. "It could've been anybody from Xavier's long list of enemies."

Samantha was about to address Jennifer when a white Ferrari 599, top off, with red interior roared into the school parking lot. The students standing around stopped talking and let their eyes feast on the $200,000 whip as it maneuvered through traffic, high-performance engine revving, pulling neatly up to the curb alongside Samantha and her girls, skidding to a halt.

Sean Desmond looked up through the open roof at Samantha from behind high-priced designer shades. "Get in," he said in a voice that sounded more like an order.

Samantha just looked at him, like the boy was out of

his mind for speaking to her as if she was his property. She was about to check him until Tracy went all super groupie with it and started sweating the ride.

"Ooh-wee, this joint is on and poppin'," she raved, stepping off the curb and excitedly walking the length of the driver's side. "Sean, it looks like you just rolled right up off the set of a rap video, fam. This is straight beast mode."

The smile across Sean's face showed the appreciation for Tracy's worship of his Italian sled. "Just treating myself because I landed a seven-figure deal with Nike," Sean said with all the cockiness of a MLB rookie sensation.

"That's a nice car, Sean. Congratulations," Jennifer complimented.

He said to Jennifer, "Thank you, Ms. Haywood."

Tracy added, "Why don't you hook a sistah up with her own Ferrari, since you banking like that."

Sean laughed at Tracy and ignored the small crowd starting to gather around the car, students with cell phones out and snapping pictures.

He looked at Samantha. "I'm sorry. Where are my manners?" The driver's door flung upward at an angle, causing a symphony of oohs and aahs to play out as Sean slid from behind the wheel and stepped out like a true boss. He stood tall, impeccably dressed in an expensive black business suit and leather Italian shoes.

Tracy was having a fit. The girl had both hands up to her mouth like they were a megaphone. "This joint is out cold. Let the record show that Sean Desmond only rolls in the very best."

Sean walked around to the passenger door and opened

it up. He elegantly waved an arm in Samantha's direction. "Baby, we have to hurry along. There's a team meeting I have to attend, and from there, we have dinner reservations."

Samantha smiled and looked at Jennifer. "Looks like I'll be seeing you later, Jen." She leaned in and whispered, "Text me if you hear anything else about Xavier."

"You got it, girl," said Jennifer.

Samantha walked up to the door, pointed at Tracy, who was still making a fool of herself over the car, and glanced back at Jennifer. "And do something about the gold digger."

"Oh no, you didn't, boo-boo," Tracy said, waving an index finger back and forth. "I ain't no gold digger. I just appreciate finely dressed gentlemen driving nice cars."

Jennifer cracked up. She said, "Translation: gold digger."

Samantha laughed as Sean closed the door behind her. He signed autographs for a couple of students and slid back behind the wheel, reaching up and closing the door. Sean revved up the engine and slowly pulled away.

The sun was going down around seven p.m. when Sean pulled up to a crowded valet at the restaurant. He nosed the Ferrari behind a brand-new Chevy Silverado with a beautiful burgundy paint job and a set of sparkling twenty-two-inch rims. Being that they were four cars down from being attended, Sean took the time to inquire about Samantha's gloomy mood.

He asked, "What's up with you, babe? You've been quiet ever since leaving Comerica Park."

Xavier had been her first love. Of course she was quiet.

How could she think of anything else when his condition was a complete mystery? While she'd been waiting in a comfortable lounge area until the team had finished the meeting, Samantha hadn't been able to resist the urge to try Xavier's phone again. Butterflies were still fluttering around in her stomach as she thought about the call going straight to voice mail, text messages unanswered.

Samantha was never one for biting her tongue. And she wasn't about to start now.

She asked Sean straight up, "I know you heard about Xavier. Did you have anything to do with it?"

He didn't answer right away, which made Samantha suspicious. Sean was looking away, like he was trying to concentrate on his place in line.

The boy wasn't getting off that easy. Samantha pressed, "I asked you did you and your thugs Ozzie and Cash have anything to do with what happened to Xavier?"

Sean managed a smile. "Do you know how much trouble that gangbanger could've cost me? Thank God this city loves a winner and recognizes the fact that I can help the Tigers win a championship. One phone call from my manager made all of that drama at the skating rink vanish. No media coverage. Simply squashed the entire thing like it never happened."

She could remember the chaos of the night. Samantha and Xavier had traded painful insults. Up 'til that point there had been a tiny spot in her heart reserved with hopes of them getting back together. Not now, though. What had come out of his mouth seemed laced with hatred. It hadn't been what he said, but how he said it that pierced her soul. And it pained Samantha to recognize it, but for the very first time since meeting him, she thought maybe Xavier was just a common street thug.

"Sean, let's be real," Samantha said. "Xavier isn't a saint, but you started that entire fiasco when you went after his manhood."

Sean looked like he was disgusted with her. "How was I supposed to know that he didn't have a sense of humor?" He looked in the rearview and worked his lower jaw from side to side. "It was his boy the alcoholic who I want— fool snuck me."

"Well, you asked for it."

"Whose side are you on?"

"I'm not on anybody's side, Sean. All of you were acting like immature little children."

As Sean inched the car toward the valet attendants, Samantha couldn't help but think about Xavier. Not knowing what kind of shape he was in had her nerves twisted in knots.

Her door opened upward. Samantha was greeted by a smiling, clean-cut young dude who looked like Justin Bieber.

"Good evening, ma'am," the Justin Bieber look-alike said, as he politely stood off to the right.

Samantha stepped out into the night chill. It was pretty busy. The valet line stretched as far as the eye could see, with a colorful assortment of makes and models. Some folks stood around with valet tickets in hand waiting on their cars to be brought up. All marveled at the Ferrari while anticipating to see which high-profile figure would slide from behind the wheel.

The surprised looks on faces when Sean stepped out

confirmed that all knew his identity. He walked around and swept Samantha up in a rush.

He said, "I really don't feel like signing any autographs."

"This is the life you chose," Samantha said as they were herded through a spotless glass revolving door.

On the way up, the elevator ride provided spectacular scenery. The car was glass and looked out on the River-Walk and the darkness of the Detroit River. Samantha's hopes and prayers were with Xavier as the doors dinged open. The interior of the steakhouse was elegant, sophisticated. Proper attire only. When they stepped up to the maître d', Samantha couldn't help but feel slightly underdressed. Most of the guests, much like Sean, were dressed in pricey garments. Any other person not fully dressed to code would've immediately been rolled out of there. But since it was Sean Desmond, the Detroit Tigers' million-dollar baby, the distinguished maître d' dressed in blue looked the other way.

Tables covered in cheery white tablecloths with elaborate centerpieces sat throughout the restaurant. Servers moved around different tables attending to the needs of the guests. Almost every eye in the dining room was primarily focused on Sean Desmond. He and Samantha followed the maître d' to the back, a wall of floor-to-ceiling windows. There was a surprise sitting at the table behind a humongous pillar. It was Samantha's mother and father.

Mrs. Fox was wearing a pretty dress, and her husband, a dark business suit.

Her father stood from the table with a hand held out. "Well, if it isn't the rookie sensation."

As Samantha hugged her mother, Sean and Mr. Fox shook hands.

"Mr. Fox, you're too kind," said Sean, "and I appreciate you accepting my late dinner invitation." He flashed Mrs. Fox a charming smile. "My, my, my, Mrs. Fox, don't you look beautiful this evening. I tell Samantha all the time that this world was vastly improved when God blessed it with you and your daughter."

Mrs. Fox blushed, smiling. "Thank you, Sean. How's everything going for you?"

They sat down, with Sean unbuttoning his jacket. "The usual—practice, two-a-days, meetings with Nike, sandwich and soft drink companies. Business never stops."

Mrs. Fox asked innocently, "What are two-a-days?"

"Mother, that's when the team practices twice a day," answered Samantha.

Mr. Fox jumped in, "Congratulations, son. There's nothing sweeter than success. While you guys were on the way up I was explaining to my wife that with you on board the Tigers have a legitimate shot at a championship this season."

Samantha just sat there and watched how her star-struck dad was acting, the big goofy smile on his face as if he was sitting on Santa's lap and whispering his Christmas morning wishes into the ear of the white-bearded one. Her old man was worth at least $3 million and could easily hold a suite for every ball game at Comerica Park. But here he was behaving worse than a giddy teenage girl backstage at a Drake concert.

Sean said, "We have Oakland this Saturday in the first round of the playoffs. Should be a tough one." He squinted at Mr. Fox. "Say, how would you and Mrs. Fox like a suite at Comerica Park to see the first game this Saturday? You can bring anybody you want."

Samantha just shook her head. The look on her mother's face was priceless. Ever since she was a little girl Samantha's parents had always conferred with each other before making plans, but something was telling her that that wasn't going to be the case here.

Mr. Fox didn't even consider his wife when he said, "It'll be our pleasure."

"Maybe after the game, you can come into the locker room and meet some of the guys," Sean said to Mr. Fox.

Samantha was looking for a reaction from her mother. And there it was—the pursed lips, the gradual flaring of the nostrils. Mrs. Fox looked like she was about to go there with her husband when a sweet young waitress walked up just in time. The girl took their drink order and walked away, barely able to resist a backward glance at Sean Desmond.

Samantha had forgotten that her iPhone was on vibrate. She almost jumped out of her socks when it buzzed inside her right pocket. Tension stuck in her throat at the possibility that Xavier might be trying to contact her. Rats. It was Jennifer. Samantha sent the call to voice mail, trying not to let disappointment register on her face. But it was too late.

"Baby girl," Mr. Fox said, "why the long face?"

Samantha stared at Sean. He absently looked the other way, which made her even more suspicious.

"Samantha, honey," her mother said. "What's the matter, pumpkin?"

Samantha came right out with it. "Someone shot Xavier a few weeks ago."

"Oh my God," Mrs. Fox blurted out, with both hands up to her mouth.

"I hate to see anybody hurt, but I would be remiss if I didn't say that I saw it coming," Mr. Fox said.

Mrs. Fox said to her husband, "Fitzgerald, how could you be so cruel."

The waitress was back and placing drinks before her guests. White wine for Mrs. Fox, gin and tonic for Mr. Fox—Samantha had ordered sweet tea, and before Sean, the waitress set down a glass of water.

Mrs. Fox, due to the bad news that had been dropped, immediately took a sip of her beverage. She waited until the waitress collected all of their food orders and walked away. "Samantha, sweetie, how bad is it?"

"I really don't know, Mother. I can't get in touch with him to find out."

Her mother asked, "What about social media?"

"Xavier doesn't do social media."

Samantha couldn't miss Sean's lackluster reaction to Xavier's injury. The healthy yawn just about summed up his interests.

Mr. Fox wet his whistle with a sip from his drink. "Sweetheart," he said to his wife, "Xavier was born and bred to be violent."

"Daddy, not now. Not the psychological babble."

"Fitzgerald, please," Mrs. Fox said.

Mr. Fox persisted, "His mother has violent tendencies. Case in point: The ruckus her and her loser boyfriend caused almost two years ago. Xavier inherited her unstable behavior, probably what led to him being shot."

"Daddy, no disrespect, but that's silly. Xavier has been on the honor roll ever since I met him our sophomore year. He has his ways, but so does everybody else. He's done a lot of good at Coleman."

Mr. Fox argued, "You said yourself that his father had gone to jail for selling drugs. Samantha, Xavier might be intelligent, but somehow, some way, heredity is going to tap him on the shoulder, and I guarantee you the boy will get himself sent to prison for a violent crime."

Sean finally spoke up. "Mr. Fox, may I?"

Samantha's father extended his right hand. "By all means, son, you are a part of this discussion. I believe you have a testimony that's lodged in humble beginnings. Please share with us."

"I didn't have my father around," said Sean. "But unlike most kids without a male in the home, I invested my time with constructive activities, like the Boys and Girls Club. My mother struggled to raise me. So I felt obliged to help her by working hard. I would pay my dues, practice fundamentals, and listen to coaches. It all paid off and now I'm able to purchase my mother the home of her dreams."

Mr. Fox sat back, smiling, showing off a full set of healthy pearly whites, like Sean Desmond was the son he'd always wanted. "Sean has just eloquently proven my case. We know his mother, and she is not a violent person. Just look at how her son turned out."

Mrs. Fox couldn't do anything but shake her head at her husband.

"Daddy, there's no talking to you."

Sean stepped up his game. He reached into his jacket pocket and pulled out a small box.

Samantha's heart sped up. Her mother's eyes widened and Mr. Fox smiled even harder.

Samantha was hoping and praying that the boy wasn't getting ready to play himself. If he was, Sean was in for an embarrassing reaction. Marriage was nowhere in her immediate future.

When he opened the box Samantha was able to breathe a sigh of relief. The diamond studded earrings might've been the size of ice cubes, with a blinding sparkle that played out underneath low house lights, but at least it wasn't an engagement ring.

Sean said to Samantha, "Baby, I want you to have these. Samantha, I can't see my future without you."

Samantha said, "Aww, Sean, they are really beautiful. But I can't take them."

The outburst came out of nowhere. "You can and you will," Sean said, almost in a growl. His forceful behavior took everybody at the table by surprise. He quickly cleaned up his act as he looked at her parents' baffled faces. "I mean, Samantha, I really want you to have these. Please don't hurt my feelings by not accepting them."

Mr. Fox seemed to have ignored the tone and Sean's voice. He said to his daughter, "Samantha, baby girl, those are gorgeous. I'm sure Sean paid a lot of money for them."

Mrs. Fox cut her eyes at Sean and then back to Samantha. She noticed her daughter's uneasiness. "Fitzgerald, the money isn't the issue. I think your daughter is grown enough to make that decision."

"Nonsense," said Mr. Fox. "I think it's a very nice gesture, and once someone gives you something, you take it and say thank you."

The salads saved the day. The waitress was back with two clean-cut gentlemen dressed in khakis, donning aprons.

Samantha didn't have the energy to go there with her father. So she stayed quiet and allowed the servers to serve them. The one thing that was on her mind—other than the tone Sean had used—was Xavier.

13

XAVIER

MONDAY, OCTOBER 5
8:30 P.M.

The pain medication had Xavier feeling woozy and his body numb, like he'd gone on a forty-ounce malt-liquor-drinking bender. He was resting comfortably on his bed with his eyes closed, the door closed, the shade drawn, and the lights out. The room was in complete darkness.

The entire night kept playing over and over in Xavier's mind like those old grainy black-and-white gangster films he'd seen a time or two on the TCM channel.

Gangsta rappers, Xavier thought. A bunch of suckas. It took him getting shot to bring the understanding that most of those fools were a bunch of lying phonies, with some claiming that taking a bullet bumped up street cred. A few had even gone on record boasting that they were hard to kill after having survived an attack, their lyrical content rich with much respect for those homies in the game who'd gone out and gotten themselves blasted for doing something stupid. Had kids all jacked up thinking that the only way to be a tough guy was to catch a hot one.

Xavier knew better, though. Those studio gangstas were just blowing hot garbage. The only thing that getting shot in the right shoulder had proved to him was that the junk hurt like hell. He'd never had his fingernails ripped out with a pair of pliers at the hands of some sick psychopath before, but it had to feel better than his current situation. The pain meds were the only thing that made it tolerable. He had to watch his pill consumption. The boy had seen far too many of his fellow students strung out on painkillers.

Thanks to the exploding air bag, the only thing he could remember from the night of the shooting was coming to in the recovery room, gazing up at his father and the attending surgeon. First thing out of their mouths was how lucky he'd been. But at no time had he remembered *luck* being associated with a hole in the shoulder. The bullet had hit the clavicle and fragmented, shattering the bone. The surgical team had done all they could, but pieces of the slug remained lodged deep inside the bone. The surgeon warned that trying to remove the tiny shrapnel would've caused extensive damage. Postsurgical x-rays had revealed the fragments. He'd spent that Saturday in the hospital and was released Sunday. It had been seventeen days since the shooting. He'd turned off his cell phone and tossed the device in the bottom drawer of his chest. Xavier was so confused that he didn't know who to trust.

Until he could sort this matter out, dude didn't want any contact with the outside world, period!

"Ahem." Xavier could hear the sound of somebody clearing their throat and see light through his closed eyelids.

He slowly opened his eyes and saw his kid brother standing in silhouette with the door open. Xavier's good hand shaded his eyes from the bright hallway light that flooded his dark domain. Alfonso didn't look too concerned about his brother's well-being, just a stupid little look on his face.

He pointed to Xavier's wounded shoulder. "Does that hurt?"

Xavier was grouchy and wasn't in the mood. "Naw, it feels like a day at Cedar Point amusement park—Alfonso, what do you want?"

"My friend Keisha who's in my class said her brother got shot in the leg two months ago. He was supposed to be some big tough guy, but Keisha said he was nothing but a wimp that cried tears the whole time."

"Alfonso, I promise you that I won't cry tears the whole time."

"How long do you have to keep that thing on your arm?"

"Alfonso, it's called a sling, and I'll be wearing it until I heal up."

Alfonso paused for a moment. "Is that true that you could've been dead?"

"Alfonso, I'm not dead."

"But you could have been."

Xavier was trying to be patient with his little brother.

"Dad said that you been locked up in your room since it happened because you don't want anybody to look at your face."

The kid had a point. The air bag had done a number on Xavier's mug—two swollen black eyes, a severely bruised nose, and minor cuts and scrapes had left him looking like he'd been dragged into a dark alley and worked over by a two-by-four-wielding steroid freak of a bodybuilder. There was no way Xavier was leaving his bedroom, not with a face that looked like a slice of week-old pizza.

"Well, Pop says a lot about everything," Xavier said dryly.

"Dad's friend really wanted to meet you."

Xavier thought about it for a second. His dad did have some female company over yesterday, a smoker. Even behind the closed bedroom door the fumes were recognizable. The two had been carrying on, laughing and joking like they'd been cozy with one another for years. But his dad had been cooling his heels in the slammer for almost a decade, so she had to have been some new chick. Her high, raspy voice was irritating and her laugh was loud. The lady had wanted to meet Xavier. But the loud-laughing heffa must've been smoking catnip if she thought that he would make her acquaintance with his grill looking like mashed up raw hamburger.

Xavier grunted from the pain and asked, "Alfonso, who is this lady?"

Alfonso said, "Roxanne—Roxanne Hudson. She works with Daddy at his job."

His old man must've been serious about her, because

he was a die-hard Christian and didn't go for any of that smoking jazz in his crib. But the way that those smoke fumes had been seeping through the cracks of his bedroom door left Xavier to believe Roxanne was a chain smoker.

"I don't like her," Alfonso admitted.

Xavier didn't engage. Sometimes his baby brother didn't need a response from him in order to continue his thought.

"Roxanne looks sneaky. Besides, she smoked too much."

Xavier moved around, holding his slinged arm, grunting.

"You're lucky," Alfonso said out of nowhere.

Lucky—there goes that word again, Xavier thought. The next person who mentioned it would have their spine ripped out of their nostrils by Xavier's one good hand.

He adjusted the sling and slowly rolled more to the right. "Why am I lucky, Alfonso?"

The boy wasted no time with the response. "Because you don't have to go to school until you get better. Maybe I should get shot."

"Alfonso, get your little self out of my room and close the door behind you."

After the door closed Xavier was back in the dark. Just like his relationship with Samantha. He hadn't thought about her much. Last time he'd peeped her, she was real cozy with that rat-face rookie Sean Desmond. But that was before all the drama went down and Linus instigated that fight.

Something was going to have to be done about Linus, though. Homeboy was unraveling at a rapid rate. That drama at the skating rink could've easily been avoided if the boy had been in a sober mind.

A rap on the door killed Xavier's thought. He had never laid a glove on his little brother before, but if that was Alfonso, his little behind was about to be pushed in the closet and locked in.

Before Xavier could say anything, the door opened, but this time the bedroom lights washed over his face. And just when he was about ready to go the hell off on Alfonso—

"Ooh-wee," said Billy. "That air bag put a lickin' on you, youngster. You look like a raccoon about the face."

Xavier winced as pain ripped through his shoulder. "Now tell me how you really feel."

The old man smiled softly, walking in and wheeling Xavier's desk chair to the side of the bed. He didn't exactly know if the pain meds had him delirious, but Billy's face looked different.

Xavier wasn't feeling like company, especially not in his present condition. But there was no way that he was going to tell Billy to bounce. Xavier would not have gotten as far as he had if Billy hadn't had his back.

Xavier groaned in pain as he tried to adjust his pillow with his right hand to sit up a bit. He said, "What's up with all the facial hair, geezer? What are you, hiding out in witness protection?"

Billy smiled and said, "Let me help you with that, squid bait."

"I got it, Gramps. Not helpless, you know."

Despite Xavier's protest, Billy helped him anyway.

"Now you want to tell me why you're looking like Rick Ross's grandpappy?"

"Woman trouble," was all Billy said. He took a seat,

laughing. "Now tell me what in the Sam Hill happened to your face and shoulder." Billy was sporting a new look. Because of his military background Billy's hair was always high and tight. Always been clean shaven. But now tangled gray facial hair had overgrown the black strands, stretching down both jaws and hanging two inches off the chin. He was wearing his favorite hospital scrubs, some type of camouflage shirt, and combat boots laced up to the top.

Xavier grunted as he attempted to raise his torso to scoot himself up. "Don't know where to start."

"Try the part where you get shot."

"You want the CliffsNotes version?"

"Whatever you're comfortable with."

"Somebody shot me."

"I see you want to be a knucklehead. Who do you think shot you?"

All of Xavier's past good deeds at the school hadn't exactly earned him any nominations for the "best classmate of the year" award amongst the scumbags at Coleman. His past efforts to rid the campus of gangs, dope boys, and grimy thieves had left him a marked man. He'd pissed off a lot of folks. Stepped on a lot of toes—his old boss Slick Eddie and former BFF Romello included. Mix in Sean Desmond and his clowns, and the line of colorful characters waiting to whack him ran longer than the ones at Best Buy stores on the eve of the release of the new iPhone.

"Don't know. Had to get my *Fast and Furious* Vin Diesel on to keep hot lead out of my butt."

Billy looked the kid over. "Didn't appear to work, did it?"

Xavier grunted as he adjusted the sling. "You got jokes."

"Carjacking?"

"Got shot before I could ask the dude."

"Who has the jokes now?" Billy asked, scratching his hairy chin. "What do the police think?

"Dude just rolled up and started cappin'." Xavier shifted his gaze out of the bedroom window. "The police—those jokers think it was random."

He could lie to Billy easily. But the truth wasn't that easy for him to forget. Xavier knew damn well that the shooter could be linked to any one of his enemies. Yeah, the police had questioned him the moment he was released from the hospital. There was absolutely nothing he could tell five-o. He hadn't laid eyes on his assailant.

Besides, he still hadn't told his dad or Billy all the details about his fascinating little Coleman High criminal history—joining forces with one of the coldest gangs in the city, stealing cars to support his family, being shot at by rivals, brushes with the law, near-death experiences, almost becoming a baby daddy, being stalked by a deranged jump-off, not to mention his number of school and street fights that read like the rough-and-tumble makings of a highly decorated championship prize fighter.

"The next thing I remember was waking up in recovery," said Xavier.

"All I can say, youngster, was Jesus must've been sitting in your passenger seat. Do you know how lucky you were that the guy didn't get out of his car to make sure the job was done after you wrecked and were knocked unconscious by the air bag?"

Xavier smirked.

"What's so funny?"

"Folks have been telling me how lucky I am, so I said to myself the next person that utters the word, I would take my one good hand and rip their spinal column out through their nostrils."

Billy grinned, fumbling around in the right pocket of his scrubs. "My switchblade says you won't. You little gremlin, don't think because you took a bullet that you're man enough to whup up on me. You youngsters better stop listening and believing those stank rappers."

Xavier winced in pain as he situated himself. "And you old geezers better stop believing that y'all can live at home by yourselves without a Life Alert bracelet."

Billy laughed. "That was a good one. So I guess you can launch your rap career now."

"What do you mean by that?"

"You know how those rap artists get shot and go triple platinum. Better get started, you already got the bullet wound. All you need now is a record deal and tattoos."

"Whatever, old goat."

"So how's your car?"

"Totaled—thank God."

"Why? Didn't you want it?"

"I can't drive something the rest of my senior year that I almost got smoked in."

"Good point."

Xavier asked, "Now you know all of my business. Tell me what's up with the whiskers."

"New beginning. My baby mama left me. Now she's petitioning Wayne County Friend of the Court for a large sum of child support money."

"You have to kick out the cheese for making an old man baby." Xavier laughed a little. "You still didn't tell me why you're walking around here looking like you're about to audition for that reality show *Whisker Wars*."

"Would you get off my whiskers, please? I forgot to shave."

"Forgot to shave for how long? Two years?"

Billy rose up from the chair. "You just make sure you don't get shot any more before you graduate. Stay out of trouble, you young punk."

"And you make sure to be careful and chew denture-friendly gum with those fake choppers of yours, you two-hundred-year-old walking mummy."

Billy laughed good-naturedly. "Seriously, youngster. Take care of yourself. Be careful. And if you need me, just hit me up, you feel me?"

Billy was trying to be hip. Xavier cracked a smile. "I feel you, homeboy. Yeah, I feel you."

The two shook hands before Billy left.

14

XAVIER

SATURDAY, OCTOBER 10
6:00 P.M.

Xavier was sitting with his legs hanging over the side of his bed. The sling was getting on his damn nerves and his wound was itching like crazy. His dad told him that it was healing. Xavier couldn't tell because he was still experiencing shooting pains in the shoulder.

Seven days later and Xavier was still shut up in his bedroom, only stepping out briefly to attend to his bathroom needs. Despite the swelling subsiding around his nose and eyes, he avoided the bathroom mirror. He just couldn't bear the image of his mangled mug. Pounds were melting from his body like perspiration drops because of a lack of appetite. Stress was a factor, and paranoia kept him peeping out from the closed blinds of his bedroom window. He wore the same pajamas day after day, with the dressings of his wound being the only thing he changed.

His father had made many suggestions about Xavier talking to a psychiatrist, maybe getting on some meds to stop anxiety from ravaging his mind. The boy would always insist that he was "straight" and dropped the conversation. His bedroom had become more like a tomb. No light, no activity, the only thought on his mind was how close to death he'd come. Sometimes his emotions would go haywire, which always ended with him breaking down crying in the same corner between the chest and wall.

Sometimes Xavier would obsess over the list of suspects. That list was long and loaded with limitless possibilities of who could've put in the work on him. Was it Tall and Husky, the big-eared cat with the low-cut fade and wearing the dark Rocawear hoodie who had been sent by Slick Eddie? Dude had chased him through the school hallways, bustin' caps at him last year during a morning football game. And even though Xavier's old enemies Dylan Dallas and his boy Westwood were looking at twenty-year stretches in the pen, what would stop them from hiring somebody to put in the dirty? If Eddie possessed the capability to sanction hits from behind bars, so did those two player-hating morons. Was it Sean Desmond? Or was it the lunch aide who made the milkshakes in the cafeteria? His old health teacher? Even Principal Skinner could've been the trigger man for all Xavier knew.

Xavier kept running the events over and over until his head throbbed, but he was no closer to narrowing down the culprit.

Somewhere beyond his bedroom door, he could hear that Noah's friend Roxanne Hudson was back. She'd rung the doorbell a little while ago. Her irritating voice was loud and carried throughout the house as she laughed at his father's corny jokes. The stench of cigarette smoke was back too, seeping through the cracks of Xavier's bedroom door. The two sounded like they were sitting at the dining room table. Just from her laughter he could tell that she wasn't his father's type. Noah was humble, a real live Bible-thumper who stayed true to the Scriptures. Roxanne, even behind closed bedroom doors, chilled Xavier with bad vibes. There was nothing he could do about it, though. His old man was grown.

Xavier braced the sling and stood, grunting. He retrieved the cell phone from the drawer and was tempted to turn the thing on. There had to be tons of text messages and a crapload of voice mails on it. Some sincerely concerned about his welfare, others just plain nosy. Dexter had to be the most worried. He'd been Xavier's right-hand man, stood by his side when everybody else had turned their backs. He owed his homeboy a phone call. Xavier felt bad that he'd told his father to tell Dexter that he didn't want any company when the boy had shown up at his doorstep the day after Xavier had gotten out of the hospital.

Later, maybe later, Xavier thought, putting it off.

Roxanne ripped off with screeching laughter, almost sounding like a croup cough. He couldn't stand it. Xavier didn't want to hear the sound of her voice, so for the first time since being shot, he turned on the television, loud enough to drown her out. Sitting on the bed, he began to surf through the cable channels 'til he stumbled upon a sight worse than Roxanne's irritating butt. It was the bottom of the seventh inning and the Detroit Tigers were up to bat. The first game of the MLB playoffs was well under way, and that slimeball Sean Desmond stood at the plate, a cocky batting stance, with his eyes trained on the pitcher. It looked to be a straight fastball down the middle—Sean swung ferociously, solidly connecting, and the ball went bye-bye over the center-field fence of Comerica Park.

Xavier wasn't trying to be malicious, but he hoped that that bum tripped over third base and broke something as he looked on while Sean arrogantly trotted around the bases waving to the cheering fans. Xavier watched as the television cameras showed some close-ups of fans going nuts in the stands. He tried to convince himself that he didn't want to see a celebrating Samantha. That would be lying, though. What he felt for her was still inside his heart. Not an emotion that he could just turn off. But he kept the feeling under lock and key. Had to. The boy had too many things he was dealing with and didn't need any further distractions.

It was the moment where Sean crossed home plate and started high-fiving his teammates that an uncharacteristic feeling swept over Xavier. He really wanted to put the big ugly-hurt on homeboy. Never had he wanted to hurt somebody so badly. The million-dollar wimp had smoothly danced into their lives and cleverly waltzed out with

Samantha as his dance partner. Then at the roller skating rink that night, to sprinkle salt in the wounds, Sean tried to make Xavier look weak in front of her.

Xavier was getting too heated and had to check his anger before raw emotions led him to do something stupid and regrettable, like shattering the thirty-six-inch screen of his Sony by hurling the remote at it. The TV cost too much to be getting crazy like that, so instead, he quickly turned to HBO. *Game of Thrones* would do just fine.

15

SAMANTHA

That big solo homer Sean blasted in the seventh inning hadn't been enough, as the Oakland A's thumped the Detroit Tigers by eight runs. Sean was now at a private table, drowning his sorrows in drink, as an entourage of his peeps sat around. They were deep off up in Benihana too. Sean had learned the hard way that he couldn't be dropping the dogs in public on broke fools. The coach had called in some heavy favors to keep that little skating-rink scuffle from turning into a full-blown media frenzy. The rookie didn't escape punishment. His coach fined him fifteen thousand dollars, mere peanuts for somebody like Sean Desmond.

"Don't you think you've had enough?" Samantha asked Sean.

The loud clanking noise from the cook's spatulas striking the surface of the hibachi grill as he prepared the food was deafening.

Sean blew Samantha off like she was nothing and guzzled down another shot. "I'm twenty years old and I don't need your permission."

His entourage took up every seat of the private section. The hanger-ons were out in full force, scantily dressed women parading around ballers trying to get lucky. Financially tapped-out brothas were trying to run game on jump-offs with the hopes of getting their action on. Nobody was talking more smack than Sean Desmond's two goons, though. Ozzie and Cash were sitting to Samantha's right, kicking game with Tracy and Jennifer.

"Leave the man alone," Ozzie said to Samantha. "His team just got it handed to 'em, let 'im drink."

"Exactly why he shouldn't be drinking," said Jennifer. "Too much alcohol is a waste of a good mind. Besides, he shouldn't be drinking anyway."

Cash jumped in with his two cents. "Who are you? Mother Teresa?" he sarcastically asked Jennifer.

"So you're completely comfortable with him destroying his mind, right?" Jennifer asked Cash.

"Whatever," said Cash.

Jennifer wouldn't let up. "See, it's friends like you that can't say no to people like him. That's the main reason why young millionaires die fast and broke."

Sean was really starting to feel the alcohol. He yelled out, "Justin Bieber."

Jennifer said, "Justin's not dead—although the country

would love to deport him—but if he keeps a destructive lifestyle, there is no telling."

Ozzie said, "Who let Little Miss Buzzkill up in this piece?"

Samantha said, "Jen is right. Sean, don't you think that you've had enough? You have another game tomorrow. Why don't you go home and get some rest."

It didn't take Tracy long with her airhead opinion. "Samantha, you need to cut it out. Sean is a grown man. Anybody that lives in a phat crib in Orchard Lake and drives a Ferrari and a Phantom is considered a grown man in my book. And you should quit sweatin' him."

"Isn't there one time where you're not in gold-digger mode?" Jennifer asked Tracy.

Tracy quickly threw up the "talk to the hand" gesture at Jennifer. "Girl, bye."

Cash cracked everybody up when he started making the sound effects of two cats fighting to poke fun at the two girls—"Cat fight," he said, laughing.

Sean snapped out of his alcoholic coma long enough to yell, "Y'all, chill out. Y'all are giving me a headache."

"Don't stop them now, I want to see Tracy and Jennifer box," said Cash.

The cook was plating the food and passing them around to everybody sitting in front of his hibachi grill.

When Ozzie received his grub he looked over at Samantha. "Heard that loudmouth punk we mopped up in the parking lot of the skatin' rink got his ticket punched."

Cash laughed with food in his mouth.

Samantha shot Sean a cold look.

He said, "I only told it like it was—the punk better be glad that we didn't twist him."

"Sean, you forget that we grew up together," Samantha said, "you're not a gangsta."

"And Xavier is, right?" Sean said.

Samantha said, "That's not what I meant."

"Don't sleep on me," Sean said, growing angry.

Samantha looked at Cash and Ozzie. "You might hang around gangsters, but you're not one."

Cash and Ozzie slapped hands, laughing sinisterly.

In a fury Sean stood up too quickly from the stool, wobbling, and staggered off salty.

One of the bodyguards tried to follow him. "I don't need your help. I'm going to the bathroom and I don't have to be a gangsta in there to take care of my business."

"See what you did," Ozzie said to Samantha. "Why did you have to go and get inside his head for? He has a ball game tomorrow."

Samantha didn't comment.

Cash asked Samantha, "So how is ol' Xander anyway?"

"Xavier," Samantha corrected Cash.

"Whatever," said Cash.

"Nobody knows," Jennifer cut in. "It's like he just dropped off the face of the earth."

"Good riddance," said Tracy. "Samantha's better off without him. When you have a man like Sean Desmond, everything else is irrelevant."

Samantha stood, wearing a look of disgust. "You know, Tracy, you used to have a heart. I hope when you're standing before God one day, you'll be able to look inside that gutter you call a soul and explain to him how you traded in your integrity, lusting after material items."

Samantha walked off in the direction of Sean, with Xavier heavy on her mind. She hadn't been able to enjoy the game because she was worried sick about him. It was true that they were no longer together, but the fact that he was hurt wasn't sitting too well in her spirit.

She was in a long corridor where the restrooms were. Sean looked like he was being held up by the wall, his back to her, with his cell up to his ear. Sounded like he was talking business, so Samantha waited until he ended the call.

"Are you okay?" she asked.

He had a silly little smile on his face. "I'm okay now." Sean walked over and grabbed her roughly around the waist and tried to kiss her.

"What are you doing?" Samantha asked, pulling back.

He grabbed for her, letting locks of her hair fall from the palm of his hand. "Are you going home with me tonight?"

A frown fell across her face. "Sean, don't be ridiculous. It's already close to eleven, and my curfew is twelve. Besides, I told you before that nothing will happen."

Sean raised his voice. "What? I'm not gangsta enough for you? I'm da man up in this city. What I want I get!"

Samantha pulled away from his grasp. "That's the alcohol talking."

"Xavier was better, huh?"

"Now was that necessary?" Samantha said.

He pointed his finger. "You're going to learn that I am not that trash, high school gangbanger. Do you know how many women out there would love the opportunity that you have? Samantha, you better get it together." Sean stormed out.

Samantha folded her arms and pursed her lips. Sean was going to learn to respect her. She was pretty and had brains to match; she knew she was the perfect catch. If he didn't learn some manners quickly, Samantha would have no problem kicking him to the curb.

16

DAKOTA

Dakota couldn't ignore her growling stomach any more. She was starving. Hiding out in the library to avoid those SNLG headaches in the lunchroom wasn't cutting it. This was her regularly scheduled lunch hour, and here she was hiding in the back of the library like a scared little mouse.

She'd been hiding in the library during her lunch break ever since somebody tried to smoke Xavier. The last time she'd seen him was at the skating rink, when he and Dex had saved her. She'd been proud of herself that night. It took real guts to face her fears.

Her stomach growled again, but this time it was more like a roar. It wasn't fair that her tormentors were probably downstairs in the cafeteria stuffing their faces full of whatever, while she was stuck hiding out in the library.

Skip it, she thought. There was still twenty-five minutes left of her lunch break to grab a quick something. And she wasn't about to waste it sitting around nerds. She didn't mean any disrespect, but she had grown tired of sitting at a table in the company of these Coleman High rejects.

No more!

Dakota snapped closed the books she was reading and walked out into the empty hallways. Damn—she was hungry and nobody was going to deprive her of friggin' basic rights. But all the same, Dakota still had to be careful. As she took the back way down to the cafeteria, she wondered about Xavier. If he was doing all right. It had been twenty-five days since Xavier's shooting. There were so many rumors being blasted floating around the school that it was hard to know what to believe. Where she'd had a mad crush on Xavier before, Dakota was now looking at him in a whole different light. She'd never had a big brother. Someone who looked out for her the way he was doing. Besides, to keep it one-hundred, Xavier was a Coleman High celebrity, a cat who every girl wanted to get with and every dude wanted to be like.

Dakota was almost to the lunchroom when she saw one of those SNLG girls rambling around in a hallway locker. Whether the chick was getting her theft on or the locker had been assigned to her was none of Dakota's business. Hunger pangs were kicking her tail and she wasn't trying to scrap with anybody. Anyway, Bangs had put the word out after the skating-rink fiasco that it was open season on Dakota, even sweetening the pot by offering twenty-five bucks to the first SNLG girl who stomped out her lights. The restroom was off to her left, so she ducked inside until the coast was clear. The stench of cigarette smoke was strong inside, but Dakota didn't pay it any mind nor did she look around. With her back to the stalls Dakota kept the door cracked, peering out until the SNLG girl sporting the bad weave found whatever it was she was looking for, closed up, and left.

Phew. She let out a deep sigh of relief.

All this drama to get something to eat, Dakota thought.

Her plan was to get into the lunchroom, get her goodies, and get out unnoticed. Aside from the nervous pitter-patter of her heart, she was good. Dakota was about to step out into the hallway but was denied by somebody powerfully yanking her hair from behind, pulling so hard that she came up off her feet, flying backward and landing on her back with a sickening thud. The immense pain started at the base of her neck, traveling down her spine, stopping and pulsating in her behind. Stars were flying while a brilliant display of lights inside her dome blinked from bright to dull. When the blurriness finally subsided, it wasn't a surprise or shock for Dakota to look up and see Bangs standing over her head. The SNLG head ghoul was still tightly clutching Dakota's beautiful locks and grinning like the worst was yet to come.

Bangs said, "Look at what fell into a ninja's lap. Mouse, didn't I tell you good things come to those who wait. Baby girl, we've been lookin' for you."

Dakota's little heart was beating so fast from fear that she could hardly catch her breath.

Mouse stepped into view, holding a cigarette longer

than one of her legs between the index and middle fingers of her right hand. "Ooh-wee, we owe you big-time!" she said in a voice filled with excitement. The girl took another drag from the Newport, mashed it out on the floor with a shoe, and then blew smoke from her mouth.

Bangs let go of Dakota's hair. "Get her on her feet," Bangs ordered Mouse.

Dakota was still a little groggy but felt her body being hoisted from the floor by a dark, thick bald-headed chick.

Bangs nodded and Mouse moved into position.

"Xavier ain't here to save you from us," Bangs said. "You must've thought the junk was funny when you pepper-sprayed me in the bathroom at the skating rink—yo' little stunt had me in the emergency room that night tryin' to get back right."

The bald-headed chick wrestled and locked Dakota's arms behind her back, giving Mouse a perfectly exposed target. It was the first time Dakota had gotten a real good look at her surroundings. There were three SNLG girls here, and it appeared that they'd been using this time as a smoke break.

A hand gesture from Bangs set things into motion. Mouse was a short girl and carried a low center of gravity, perfect leverage she needed to deliver the first shot. It was a solid blow right on the belt line.

Dakota damn near folded as she gasped for air. The chick holding her from behind wasn't having any part of Dakota trying to fall. She kept her on her feet.

"That felt good!" Mouse exclaimed. "Bangs, homegirl, one more—let me give her one more."

Bangs pulled out a pack of Newports, shook one out,

and lit it. She nonchalantly took a drag, waited, and blew out the smoke. "Oh no, we have other plans for this chick. Don't we?"

Dakota shrieked, scared at what these girls had up their sleeves. But Bangs was quick to get a hand over Dakota's mouth. Again Dakota's legs wobbled, but the goon at her back refused to let her drop to the floor.

"You ain't going nowhere, sweetie," said the bald-headed chick as she reinforced her grip.

Tears started to slide down both of Dakota's cheeks.

"I'm feeling it," said Mouse, bouncing around with her hands raised high overhead like she was just declared the winner in an eight-round boxing match. "Bangs, this chick ain't feeling me—one more—I promise you this time I'll bring the real heat."

Dakota was doubled over and gasping.

Bangs thought the entire thing was funny; she was even laughing a bit. She took another hit from the cigarette, waited, and blew out smoke. "Mouse, you got another level? Thought that was your best, homegirl." She puffed on the cigarette. "This is your last one, you better make it good."

No sooner had the words left Bangs's mouth than Mouse cocked back and unloaded it. This punch came bringing the noise—right on the belly button.

"Let her go," Bangs instructed Baldhead.

Dakota dropped to the floor and balled up into the fetal position. There was no screaming this time. It was all about sucking in air. Dakota was a good girl—why was this happening to her?

"Yeah, that was the one right there," Mouse said, still

bouncing around on her toes. "Manny Pacquiao is in the house." She even started shuffling her feet like some big marquee professional boxer show off.

"Floyd Mayweather," Bangs said, dapping Mouse out. "That was the hammer right there." Bangs took out her cell and made a call. "Do me a favor," she said into the phone. "Bring me that ackrite, home girl."

As Dakota lay on the cold, dirty floor writhing in pain, her one question was, where was He? Where was God? He must've been busy helping somebody else because He sure wasn't with her right now.

"Too bad that snitch Xavier Hunter ain't here right now," bragged Mouse. "I'd have to put it on him too."

Bangs laughed. "That's because he's somewhere laying low, like the punk he is."

Mouse and Baldhead were cracking up until the door to the lavatory opened. In walked a girl with a soft caramel complexion, her hair shaped into a mohawk. She was carrying a medium-size brown paper bag.

"Welcome to the party, Missy," said Bangs.

"I know y'all saved me some," Missy said, looking down at a helpless Dakota and licking her chops. She handed the bag over to Bangs.

Bangs took it, putting out her cigarette with her heel. She went into the bag and pulled out a can of blue spray paint. "Let's give baby girl the blues," she said.

When Dakota woke up lying on her back, she was choking. The strange chemical smell was suffocating. Where was she? Everything was blurry. Her body throbbed in agony. It was only seeing the toilets through the open doors of the lavatory stalls that jogged her memory. She'd been attacked by SNLG. Not knowing how long she'd been out, Dakota tried to sit up. The pain in her side stopped her in her tracks. Dakota had to get up—but those fumes! Where were they coming from?

It took some effort and many tears, but Dakota managed to make it to her feet. The many voices outside the lavatory door meant that students were in the hallways during class change. Tunnel vision drove her past the huge bathroom mirrors, without looking, and zeroing in on the doorknob. She fumbled with the thing at first until she got it open. The moment she was out students gasped, some holding hands to their mouths. A tall, dark-skinned girl screamed like she was losing her mind. Dakota paid none of it any attention as she struggled to stay on her feet, not able to lose that friggin' smell. She couldn't understand why everybody was looking at her. The three cats up on the left standing around an open locker were pointing fingers and laughing at her like she was some kind of circus sideshow freak. It wasn't until she finally arrived in front of a set of double doors and gazed in the windowpane that she saw her face for the first time since awakening. Well, at least the mystery of the powerful chemical smell was solved.

The fact that her entire face had been spray-painted blue was too much to bear.

A crowd of students made up the background image in the glass she was still peering into. The looks on their faces ranged from concern to taunting.

All of it was blue—everything blue! Her hair was now a stringy blue mess, stuck together by clumps of paint.

"She looks like a Smurfette," a big-lipped guy said to his other two buddies who had been standing in front of the open hallway locker.

Students roared with laughter.

"I bet you her face ain't bluer than the marbles in your draws, my ninja," the shorter cat of the trio said to Big Lips.

The laughter was explosive, slicing through Dakota's spirit and cutting to her core. The girl took a deep breath and felt a surge of adrenaline rush to her head. It was lights out after that. The last thing Dakota heard was the tormenting laughter.

17

SAMANTHA

FRIDAY, OCTOBER 16
7:00 P.M.

"**O**kay, guys," the dance teacher, Ms. Doris Sinclair, said to the young ladies in her advanced dance class. "It's extremely important that we nail this dance routine. That's why I'm going to rehearse your butts off until Christmas Eve." A hip-hop dance program titled "Snowflakes in Wonderland" had been set for December twenty-fourth. "No matter how difficult these combinations are in this routine, we have to be flawless, people."

Ms. Sinclair was in her mid-fifties, with a dark complexion and closely cropped hair. Her grill wasn't all that, but what the dance teacher lacked in the beauty department, her muscular physique made up for. She was barefoot and wearing red and gray school colors in the form of a gray T-shirt and red spandex shorts.

The girls were spent from the workout. There were a few with the heel of their right foot resting on wall-mounted ballet barres, stretching hamstrings, while others sat around performing various muscle-stretching techniques as they listened to the teacher.

Ms. Sinclair said, "It's essential that you guys put everything into the performance. I have a surprise guest from Juilliard."

"So what you're saying, Ms. Sinclair," said a thick honey, with her weave wrapped up into a ponytail, "not only is this choreography hard to do, and we only have a little under three months to get the bugs out, but instead of being with our families, we will be spending our Christmas Eve dancing onstage in front of an audience."

Ms. Sinclair said, "Debbie, we go through this every rehearsal. Sweetie, this performance will be sixty percent of your final grade. It's simple: You don't show up, you don't pass my class."

"I guess she told you," said a tall, slender girl. "Besides, I didn't qualify what I just saw from you as dancing. You'll come out better by recording a video clip of you twerking that big butt and uploading it on to social media. At least that way, you'll get some cheap 'like' button love."

Ms. Sinclair didn't go for any foolishness in her class. The students giggled a little bit, but looked to peep her position. The smile across her face was a rare moment. She never laughed, but the slender chick's joke was just too funny.

"Dawn," said Debbie, "you got your nerves—those big feet of yours. I don't know if you dancing or stompin' out a forest fire."

The teacher even laughed at Debbie's joke. She seemed to be in good spirits.

"Okay, settle down, you two," said Ms. Sinclair. "Listen, people, you are my advanced class—you're seniors. That means, ladies, that you are to act professional and stand as role models to my underclassmen." Ms. Sinclair smiled at Debbie. "And not twerking on Facebook or Instagram."

The girls chuckled.

Even with sweat trickling down her face and breasts, causing the bone-colored cami underneath her royal blue tank top to cling to her soft, sticky skin, Samantha was a treasure chest of phenomenal gems. Her hair was matted to the sides of her face by perspiration and the exhausted, beat-down look was due largely to the fact they'd been going hard ever since her last class.

"Well, ladies," said the teacher, "we had a really good session. Let's keep up the good work. Class dismissed."

While the rest of the girls retreated to retrieve their belongings, Debbie looked like she couldn't wait to gossip. She strode over to Samantha and Jennifer Haywood.

"So the blue girl came back to school today," she said, snickering. "Don't think I could ever come back after getting my entire head spray-painted."

"You know you're foul," said Jennifer. "Where is the sensitivity?"

Debbie said, "What are you talking about? I was only telling you what everybody else is calling her."

Samantha stepped in. "If everybody else drank raw sewage out of an eight-ounce spring water bottle I guess you'd do the same."

"What are y'all tripping for?" Debbie asked. "Why y'all being so serious? The junk was funny. As far as I'm concerned, she's just a dumb freshman."

"That *dumb* freshman has a name, and it's *Dakota*," Samantha said, with a bit of attitude.

"Whatever, Samantha," Debbie said dismissively.

Samantha and Jennifer couldn't do anything but shake their heads.

Samantha walked across the highly polished floors over to an oversize monogram Gucci tote bag. She drew out a bath towel and bottled water.

Jennifer asked, "Anything from Xavier yet?"

The sadness in Samantha's eyes was clearly noticeable. "Nothing yet. I keep my head up and wish for the best. X is tough. If anybody can pull through something like this, I know he can."

Jennifer said, "Oh, I knew it was something I wanted to tell you, girl." She took a moment to get her thoughts together. "Why is Tracy going around school making your business her business?"

Samantha dabbed at her brow with the towel. "What is her problem now?"

"She's all over the building, telling anybody with a set of ears that you'd be a fool not to lock down Sean Desmond. She's also saying that she thinks that you are still hung up on Xavier. And if you don't get your head out of your butt, you're going to end up losing him to somebody that's willing to do everything that you won't."

Samantha twisted the top off her bottle and took a sip. She said, unfazed, "To somebody like her?"

"Exactly, girl."

"You know what they call that, don't you?" Jennifer started laughing before Samantha could even get the word out.

"You are so silly. What are we going to do with her?"

"We're going to let her be her. Jen, we've been sisters since I arrived here in my sophomore year. I love you like I love Tracy. The thing about friends is that we have to love them for who they are."

Jennifer offered a sneaky grin. "Even if that friend is triflin', huh?"

Samantha laughed. "Yup."

Jennifer fell out laughing. "You don't have any sense. By the way, what are you getting into tomorrow night?"

Samantha said, "The Tigers are playing game four tomorrow against Oakland. Why don't you come with me?"

"Chick, you know I give two farts in the wind about baseball. I only went with you to the restaurant last weekend when they lost to show support for my girl and her new boo-thang."

"Peep you. Ain't you fancy—*new boo-thang.*"

"And listen to you—'ain't.' Since when did Ms. High Society Good Grammar start kicking it like that?"

Tears were flowing down Samantha's cheeks, she was laughing so hard. "Stop it, you little bougie heffa."

"I believe we both are. The only difference between us is that I'm more lower-class *bougie* with it than you. My daddy doesn't own half of the city like yours does."

"Stop it. Your father makes a decent living as a foreman at Ford. You need to quit."

"Back to you and your new boo-thang."

Samantha thought about it for a second. Just the sound

of "new boo-thang" didn't vibe well with her. But the stress that her father was putting on her about having somebody like Sean was unbearable. Samantha didn't want any of her father's drama. So she went along with it, just to shut his mouth. Her old dude was pushy and apparently trying to drive her into the arms of someone she could never love like she did Xavier. And she didn't know if she still loved him like that—who was she trying to fool? Xavier still owned major real estate in her heart.

"Sean is a *good* friend. He's not my *boo-thang*."

"You know I'm just playing, right?"

"Anyway, Oakland is up two to one on Detroit. In if they lose tonight, series over, and if you think Sean was trippin' when his team lost the first game, sista-girl, boyfriend's mood will probably be pretty foul."

"So will this be a repeat of last weekend, you know, when your boy was tryna find his ego at the bottom of a bottle of Patrón?"

"Lawd, I hope not. You want to tag along?"

Jennifer made a stink face. "And have to deal with those Ozzie and Cash vermin—uh-uh, no way."

"Girl, come on. Don't leave me hanging."

"You got Tracy." Jennifer couldn't even say that with a straight face.

Samantha pursed her lips and folded her arms. "Do you want me to beg you?"

"Yeah. Can you?"

"We'll be through to pick you up around seven. Sean's plane should be in by then. Have your butt on the sidewalk in front of your home."

Jennifer cracked a mischievous grin. "You bossing me around? I ain't your slave!"

Samantha chuckled. "Just be there, okay?"

Samantha put a finger up to her temple. "Oh. I knew there was something I forgot to tell you, girl. In August I auditioned for Juilliard."

Jennifer smiled at her girlfriend. "And?"

Samantha could barely maintain her excitement. "They are considering me for a scholarship!"

Jennifer leaped in the air and hugged her girl with genuine joy. "I'm so happy for you, girl!"

Samantha broke the embrace and put a finger to her lips. "Shhhh. I haven't told a soul except my parents. So keep this a secret."

Jennifer giggled. "Cross my heart," she said, dragging a finger over her heart.

18

SAMANTHA

SATURDAY, OCTOBER 17
9:00 P.M.

Sean Desmond's big-money Orchard Lake bachelor pad sat beside an enormous body of water. At seven thousand square feet, the thing looked like something on the cover of one of those magazines that showcase ritzy cribs. Huge foyer, chandeliers, large great room, a kitchen with stainless steel appliances, a master bedroom the size of a small lunchroom, with his-and-her sinks and a pretty decent-sized Jacuzzi tub in the master bath. The walls of the long corridor to the bedrooms were decorated with memorabilia. Sean's high school and college jerseys hung in shiny glass frames. There was a very spacious deck off the back of the house overlooking the lake, where an expensive covered speedboat and pontoon were docked down by the water's edge. The deck was accessed from the dining area. A crowd of at least thirty people wandered in and out of the sliding glass doors. The music was high and the voices of those partying carried clear on out into the dark night.

"You would think that the Detroit Tigers won the game last night and were headed to the divisional finals how these fools are up in this place partying," Samantha said to Jennifer as the two sat at Monterey Bay bar-height chairs and table tops around an exquisite fire pit that dressed their surroundings in an amber glow. Some sat at identical tables, kicking game, while others stood peering out over a fiberglass railing into the dark lake.

Jennifer said, "Sean is taking it pretty hard."

"Well, it was *his* wild throw to first base that scored an Oakland Athletics player home from third at a critical time in the ninth inning that cost them their season. So, yeah, the brotha's trippin'."

"By the way, where is he? Shouldn't you be wherever he is to make sure that Mr. Super Rookie's not doing something stupid, like drinking his liver cripple?"

"Girl, he's up in his bedroom. Said he didn't want to be disturbed. Besides, he's with his homeboy Cash."

"That's exactly the reason you should have your little butt in there. Cash and that ghoul Ozzie are bad influences. Those two bums don't know how to say no to him."

"I can't really blame the poor thing from hiding out. Media has been all up in a brotha's stuff. All the sports shows have been dissecting the play and coming to the conclusion and saying that the rookie just couldn't handle the bright lights on the big stage."

Jennifer looked around. "Where is the garden tool?"

Samantha couldn't do anything but laugh. "Girl, you need to quit. Tracy ran off with that fool Ozzie somewhere around here."

"Like I said, a garden tool."

They were laughing until Sean burst through the door—wild, red eyes—staggering from side to side and whaling away with a golf club at anything in his vicinity. People ducked and got out of his way as he continued to swing the club. The music was instantly turned down and screaming could be heard.

CRASH echoed the glass of the sliding door as Sean slammed the head of the club into it. The deranged look on his grill was enough to make a few girls scream, while most watched in horror as Sean ran up on some cat dressed in a Detroit Tigers home jersey and matching ball cap and started flexing.

"Take that Tigers crap off!" Sean screamed at the dude, taking swipes at him. The guy was quick, though. He managed to avoid getting his wig split and ran through the door, glass crunching underneath his feet.

"Dawg, what are you doing?" Ozzie yelled at Sean, tackling him to the floor while Cash yanked the club out of his hands.

Sean struggled with Ozzie, yelling and slurring his words, "G-g-g-get the hell off me, m-m-man!"

"Calm down," Ozzie demanded.

Sean started sobbing. "I lost the damn game for us. We should be playing Boston in the championship, but I blew it. Do you know how it makes me feel?"

Jennifer leaned in and whispered to Samantha, "I seriously think that your boy might need Alcoholics Anonymous."

Unbelievably, Sean heard her. And just when Ozzie thought that he had calmed his homeboy down, the Detroit Tigers rookie exploded.

"Is that what you think?!" Sean screamed in Jennifer's direction. There was no amount of muscle that could hold him. From somewhere deep inside, he gathered the strength to flick Ozzie off like the boy was a cockroach. He ran over to Jennifer and got in her face. "You think I'm a drunk?! Is that it?"

Jennifer looked at Sean with fear in her eyes, trembling.

When Samantha saw her girlfriend all but fainting, she jumped into action. There was no fear in her as she shoved him out of Jennifer's face. "She has a point. You have had too much to drink, Sean."

He threw up his hands and backed away, smiling foolishly. "Oh. My bad. That's funny. Did my mother suddenly die and leave you as my surrogate?"

"That's not funny," Samantha said.

It was strange to see Ozzie stepping forward and trying to be the voice of reason. "She's right, my dude. You are seriously on the nut, my ninja. You lost the game and you hurt—I feel you. But there's always next year."

Sean looked around in amazement. "I can't believe this. Anybody else wanna tell this millionaire what to do and how to do it—huh, tell me—anybody?"

It was so dark out that nobody could accurately pinpoint from which direction the dry, sarcastic reply came.

"Yeah, buddy, just in case you weren't paying attention when you purchased your home, there are other millionaires around here that are trying to have a peaceful evening," said a short, chubby-faced white man, standing on the ground just below, dressed in a blue cardigan sweater, tan Dockers, and blue-and-white boat shoes.

The guests stood idly by, wondering if the white man's remarks would be enough to push Sean over the edge and end up with a clip of the two of them posted on TMZ's website with the Detroit Tigers rookie's mitts around the dude's throat.

Sean made some kind of an irritated drunk face. "Who are you? Oh, you must have watched Vince Vaughn and Ben Stiller in the movie *The Watch* and thought you could do it too, huh?"

The white man laughed sarcastically. "No, I'm Stanley Genesis from next door, and my wife and I are trying to have a romantic dinner. And we would like it if you could keep it down a little, please."

"What did you say your name was?" asked Sean.

"Stanley—"

"It doesn't matter what your name is, because"—Sean slowly spun around with his hands in the air—"I own all of this here. And you, *Stanley,* are trespassing. So what I would like for you to do, *Stanley,* is get off my property, now!"

Samantha thought that Stanley would turn and flee because of Sean's forcefulness. But instead, he did the opposite.

Stanley retrieved his cell phone from his pocket and started recording the back-and-forth with Sean. "Pal, I get that you are upset because the ball that you launched over the first baseman's head cost the Tigers the ball game. I sympathize with you. But carrying on like this isn't going to make that play not happen."

Sean became enraged. "If you don't take that camera out of my face, the next scene is gonna be me putting my foot up your—"

"Sean," Samantha said, "do you really have to go there?"

"Smart lady," Stanley said, now filming Samantha. "I respect you, Sean Desmond, and all that your greatness will do for our town. However, this display of bad behavior isn't tolerated out here on this side. The police chief is a poker buddy of mine, and I would hate to have to call him on a big-time celebrity like yourself."

Sean pointed down at Stanley. "I'm giving you five to get your white self off my property."

"And you, Mr. Desmond, I'm giving your black behind five to stop all of this silliness."

Sean looked around at his boys, like he needed some type of confirmation. "No, this fool didn't—did he just say what I think he said?"

"I believe you dropped the first racial slur," said Stanley, still recording the entire exchange. "What? Are you going to get mad at the whole city because you choked"—he giggled—"no pun intended, but you choked and literally and figuratively dropped the ball."

Sean started cursing. Overdosing on pure adrenaline, he made for the deck steps with the sole purpose of shoving Stanley's phone where the sun didn't shine. This time Ozzie and Cash rushed him before he could get to the first step.

Ozzie said to Stanley, "Fam, get ghost and be up out of here." He and Cash struggled with a raging Sean.

Stanley said, still filming, "You and the *homeboys* keep the music and the noise down and I won't send this footage to TMZ." After he spoke his piece, Stanley stopped filming and disappeared into the night.

Ozzie and Cash started dragging a cursing Sean toward the door, and before they could get over the threshold, Ozzie called out to Samantha, "We gon' need your assistance, breezy."

Samantha gave Jennifer that "uh-oh" look before following behind as the two boys continued to drag Sean, kicking, screaming, and offering up obscenities like it was his native language. Tracy had emerged from wherever she was, straightening up her clothes. Samantha looked at her and merely shook her head.

Upstairs in the master bedroom, they slammed the rookie on the right side of his California king.

Ozzie told him, "Stay up here and calm down while I go next door and try to smooth things over with the dude Stanley."

Sean went to say something, but the doors closed on his words. Ozzie and Cash were gone and Samantha was left standing there, not having the slightest idea what to do. First off, this wasn't where she wanted to be. Behind closed bedroom doors with a liquored-up hothead. She felt uncomfortable, but before she could say anything, Sean's eyes started looking cartoonish, like they were about to bulge from his head. He heaved. His jaws puffed out and he slammed a hand over his mouth and broke for the bathroom.

Samantha followed, covering her mouth, as she watched him bury his face deep in the toilet and puke his guts out.

The boy wrapped his arms around the toilet bowl and violently heaved, blowing chunks.

"Sean, are you all right?" Samantha asked.

He looked up with bloodshot eyes and took a deep breath. "I've seen better days," he said.

"Are you about done?"

"Yeah. I think so. Can't face my teammates, though."

"Sean, you have to work on you for now and understand that everybody makes mistakes." Samantha moved to his side, stooped down, placed his left arm around her neck, and helped him to his feet. "Phew. You need mouthwash and a shower—pronto!"

"You know you still in love with this superstar."

The statement stopped Samantha in her tracks. She had to straighten him out. "Sean, we're friends. That's all. We've been that since we were kids."

"*Friends*, huh?" He removed his arm from around her neck, smiling.

Samantha nervously smiled. "Just friends."

The action was so fast and quick that it seemed so surreal to Samantha that Sean had both of his hands around her throat. The look on his face was pure madness.

His face was so close to hers that Samantha could smell the raw vomit on his breath when he spoke.

"I think it would be wise for you to get this through your pretty head: Samantha, you are mine," he said. "And if you ever forget about it, Ozzie and Cash will pay a visit to your house. Need I say more?" With that he shoved his vomit-smelling tongue in her mouth and forced a kiss.

Samantha fought until he broke the connection. Hot tears fell from her eyes.

"And don't even think about telling anybody about what I said, or Ozzie and Cash will visit your folks. And don't bother telling your little ghetto friend Xavier about this. Not unless you want to go to a funeral." His smile was so malicious that it carried the promise of the threat. "Do you hear me?" Sean forcefully asked, dropping his hands around her shoulders and shaking her.

Samantha hesitantly shook her head. Xavier would've never put his hands on her. It was this moment when she truly admitted to herself how much she missed him. Where was he? Why wasn't he here to rescue her? Tears slid down her cheeks.

Sean said, pointing downward, "I'm not gonna keep waiting for that." The diabolical smile said it all. "Now get back down to the party, while I clean myself up."

The moment he released her, Samantha ran out of the bedroom and closed the door. She had her back against a hallway wall and was trying desperately to stop the tears and trying to spit the foul taste of bile out of her mouth. Had Sean just threatened her parents? How could he? Her folks had known the boy since he was a toddler. She had seen this sort of thing play out ugly on the news, an obsession that quickly turned violent and ended with death and grief.

But what could she do? Samantha was totally alone. Not even Jennifer could know anything about this. It would probably put her in danger too. Her soul ached while the water continued to fall. God forbid if something was to happen to her mother and father. She wouldn't be able to go on. As the tears rolled, the one question remained on her mind: Where was her Xavier?

19

XAVIER

WEDNESDAY, NOVEMBER 11
9:30 A.M.

Xavier arrived at school late and his timing couldn't have been more on point. Dude simply couldn't believe his eyes. It was thirty degrees out—cold! But the serious drop in temperature hadn't stopped any craziness from jumping off. The girl Dakota Taylor was in trouble. Ol' girl was literally running like her life depended on it, with five SNLG gang members hot on her behind. He stood at the far end of the student parking lot behind the building and they were chasing her back toward the school. Homeboy had his own problems and issues going on, but he couldn't stand there and let Dakota get stomped out.

Xavier started jogging at first and then broke into a full sprint toward the building. He was completely unaware of how stiff his injured shoulder was until he started pumping his arms to increase his speed. But the adrenaline flooding his body was enough to drown out the pain as he breezed through the back doors and headed toward a hallway on the other side of the gym. The last girl of the crew was kind of slow and he saw her turn into a woodshop classroom. This side of the building was usually vacant in the morning and didn't usually bustle to life with students until later in the day.

It was lucky for Dakota that Xavier had chosen this day to come back to school, because she looked like she was about to get broke off with some real nasty treatment. There was no time to catch his breath. Xavier rushed into the classroom, surprising everybody. Those holding Dakota recognized Xavier and instantly let go and held their hands in the air. There was a standing locker open next to a tool crib. Mouse wasn't given a chance to pop any junk. Xavier shoved her in, closed the door, placed the security latch over the loop, and secured it by shoving a screwdriver through it.

"It's not what you think," Bangs was quick to say. Fear washed over her face as her eyes quickly searched for a way to escape.

Dakota looked shaken. Tears welled and the look on her face depicted somebody that was tired of being bullied.

"Lil' Mama, you tight?" Xavier asked Dakota.

Mouse was loudly banging on the locker door and calling Xavier every curse name in the book.

Through quivering lips Dakota managed a smile. "I'm okay now that you're back."

Xavier slowly approached Bangs. His mind wasn't right. The trauma that he'd suffered the night of the shooting had left him looking at everybody suspiciously. And for all he knew, Bangs's hands could've been dirty behind the killer that tried to pop him out. Xavier snapped, and before he knew it, he grabbed Bangs up by the collar.

"Why you trippin'?" Bangs said, desperately trying to resist. Her eyes popped open with fear. "W-w-we were just playin' with the little chick."

When the other female gangbangers saw this, they broke and ran out of the door.

Mouse was insanely beating on the door, screaming, "Let me out!"

Xavier slowly lifted his right hand into the air and made a fist with it.

Dakota was worried. Not so much for Bangs's sake, but Xavier had a bright future ahead of him, and knocking the dust off this dirtbag would seriously put it in jeopardy.

"Xavier," Dakota said, calmly, "she's not worth it."

Bangs was almost peeing on herself. The girl was so shook that she said, "Yeah, Xavier, p-p-please listen to her. I'm not worth it."

"Mr. Hunter," Doug Banks said, stepping into the picture. "You know what happened the last time when you took the law into your own hands? Do the right thing, son, and release her. Those other girls ran out of here so scared that they told me everything." He glanced at Dakota. "You must be Ms. Taylor."

Dakota just nodded, too scared to take her eyes off Xavier.

Despite the pounding coming from inside the locker, Xavier had razor focus. He was mad, but there was no way he was going to hit a girl, no matter what she was doing. But Bangs and her crew didn't know that and he just wanted to scare them a little and get them to leave Dakota alone. Mr. Banks came right on time.

Doug slowly walked over to the two. "Let her go, Mr. Hunter. Let me do my job." As soon as Doug defused the situation, he addressed the locker by removing the screwdriver. The door burst open and Mouse came out swinging. She was quickly wrapped up by Doug. "Young lady, calm down." He stared at Bangs and Mouse. "I've been out of commission for a little while. Just in case you two young ladies are not familiar with me, my name is Doug Banks, head of Coleman High security."

Xavier was taking deep breaths in an attempt to calm himself. It was no easy task. All kinds of emotions had caught in his throat so tough that he was almost choking. Dakota walked over to offer her support.

Doug smiled at Xavier. "As soon as I take the girls to the front office I'm gonna need to speak with you in my office, Mr. Hunter." He looked at Dakota. "I believe it's time for you to get some justice. Follow me." Doug escorted Bangs and Mouse out of the classroom, with Dakota and Xavier in tow.

An hour later, Xavier was sitting in Doug's office. It'd been a quick minute since Xavier had been there. Didn't matter, though. The joint still looked the same, like a place that modern technology refused to touch. The doggone computer monitor on his desk was thick and bulky. The white keyboard was so old that the thing had turned a dirty yellow.

Xavier had beaten Doug to the office and was sitting there with his head resting in his hands when the guard walked through the door.

"I've been gone for a minute, so we have a lot of catching up to do," Doug said, tossing a ring of keys on his cluttered desk and heading over to the coffeemaker.

Since the shooting, Xavier's entire personality had changed. Jokes were no longer funny. Not when somebody was looking to roll his dead body up inside a carpet and haul it away. Xavier's face held an intense seriousness.

"Why were you out?" Xavier said in a low tone.

Doug worked with the coffeemaker until he brought the water in the pot to a boil. "Had a little back surgery. Kept me out for a couple months."

"You good now?"

Doug grabbed a cloth and started wiping out a dark blue coffee mug that had *Security* stenciled across the front in white lettering. "I'm good, but what about you?"

Xavier uncomfortably fidgeted around in his seat. "Me? It's all good, you feel me?"

Doug ignored Xavier's lies. "This SNLG crew, what do you know about them?"

"They formed over the summer, a bunch of low-budget nobodies."

"They sure been giving your little freshman friend Dakota, no pun intended, the blues."

"Yeah, I heard about that. That should be some type of criminal charge, shouldn't it?"

Doug poured himself a cup of piping-hot coffee. "This stuff is going to be the death of me. Love me some black coffee." He took a seat at his desk and sipped some coffee with his eyes closed, as if savoring the taste. "Mmm. Not the best, but it'll do." He slurped from the cup. "They spray-painted her entire head blue. We called the police a half hour ago, got them involved. Don't know if it would do much good because they're minors. Probably get off with a slap on the wrist. But Principal Skinner threw the book at them. They were all suspended."

"That's tight. Maybe now Dakota can actually concentrate on some schoolwork instead of running for her life."

"Do you know what started it?"

Xavier shook his head. "Something as simple as looking at them the wrong way."

"Today, kids are getting killed by other kids for less—ridiculous, but that's the world we live in now."

Xavier stood from his chair. "Well, I'm glad you're back, Mr. Banks. But my English class will be starting soon and I need to get out of your way."

Doug took another sip. "Cool your jets. You have a whole thirty minutes before your third hour class. Let's just address the pink elephant in the room, why don't we."

Xavier plopped back in his chair.

"How's the shoulder?"

Xavier looked at him suspiciously.

Doug smiled and slurped his coffee. "You know I'm resourceful. Might've been away but I kept tabs on all my favorite students."

Xavier slowly worked his shoulder around. "It's still a little tender, but I'm tight."

"Slick Eddie? Romello?" Doug asked.

"Don't know."

"That's the bad thing about making so many enemies, you never know who's gunning for you."

"Yeah, but I'm still standing," Xavier said with a bit of attitude.

Doug sipped some coffee and raised his eyebrows. "I admire your fortitude, young man. Despite me giving you the advice to change schools when this thing first jumped off with Slick Eddie and Romello, you ignored me.

"Now here you are a senior, and still carrying a 4.0 GPA—remarkable. I've become your biggest cheerleader. Now, I might not be able to offer you protection out there in the street, but for the next six months I will have heavy police presence inside the building. I'm gonna do my best to make sure you walk across the stage at graduation."

"That's whassup," Xavier said, offering a half smile and standing up.

Doug said, "You were shot. Are you going through therapy?"

"Nope," Xavier nonchalantly said. "Don't need it. I'm straight."

"Good, good for you, but you don't look straight. We've been talking for about twenty minutes now and you haven't cracked one stale joke on me."

"Too much on my mind."

"Don't let this steal your soul."

Xavier nodded, opened the door, and bounced.

* * *

"Is that you, homeboy!" Dex said, ecstatically as he walked into Mr. Chase's classroom. "You're a sight for sore eyes, my ninja."

Xavier still held that serious gaze as he offered up dap to his homeboy.

"Man, why you ain't call a brotha? I was worried sick, guy." Dexter sat down at the desk next to Xavier's.

Other students entered the classroom and crowded, sharing their concerns and expressing their happiness at his return.

"My bad, homeboy. We got some catching up to do at lunch next hour, you feel me?"

"Yeah. I feel you." Dex couldn't do anything but smile. "My brother's back."

Mr. Chase looked like he had to duck his head when he walked his tall frame through the doorway.

He said, "People, we have a whole lot of work ahead of us." The teacher retrieved a stack of papers from his desk and started passing them out. "Pop quiz time. Everybody clear your desk." Chase skipped Xavier's desk. He told him, "You are exempt from this quiz, Mr. Hunter, but you need to come and see me after class."

When the bell rang, ending the hour, Dex said to Xavier, "I'll see you at lunch, cuz," as he walked out into the hallway with the rest of the students.

Mr. Chase walked over and closed the classroom door. He seemed to be too long to sit behind his desk, so he leaned on the front of it. "Mr. Hunter, I'm glad to see you back in school. How are you feeling?"

Xavier took his time answering. He seemed to be sizing Chase up. His first interaction with this man had left him believing that Chase has some old personal vendetta against him. So he was cautious with the response. "It feels like I was shot, Mr. Chase. By the way, thank you for emailing my assignments to me."

"I believe we got off on the wrong foot, Mr. Hunter, a kind of misunderstanding, if you will. I've been doing some research and it shows that you have an exceptional writing talent."

Xavier was losing patience. "Mr. Chase, is there a point to all this? I mean, I'm hungry and it's my lunch hour."

Mr. Chase pursed his lips. "Okay. I'm going to lay it out for you. You know that my policy is strict on makeup work, but in light of your current circumstances, I will allow you to make up for time lost. But I have a proposition for you."

Xavier looked at him sideways.

"What I mean is that I have a friend who runs a publishing company in New York. They're starting a line of urban books. But to be considered as a potential writer, you must first win an essay contest."

Xavier frowned. "I don't know about this, Mr. Chase. I'm no writer."

"Not according to the papers that you wrote in your junior year for your English teacher. The one on the most venomous snakes in the world blew me away. You have a gift, Mr. Hunter. And I would like to grant you an opportunity to display your talent."

"Why me?"

"Because you have the gift. What do you say?"

"You have me curious."

"I won't kid you. There will be a lot of talented kids vying for the same opportunity. Your essay has to be original and it has to be compelling."

This opportunity had come out of nowhere. Was this God's way of trying to make it right for the bullet he took? Xavier didn't know. He took it as a blessing and ran with it.

Xavier shook Mr. Chase's hand. "Thank you. I got this."

When Xavier walked into the lunchroom, paranoia jumped all over him as tight as spandex, so many people in one tight area. Anybody could start trouble with him at any time. All eyes were on Xavier, though. His nerves were on edge and fear made his blood run cold. Trying not to show weakness was tough, but he had to put his big-boy Fruit of the Looms on and boss up. Judging by the silence that fell across the cafeteria, you would've thought that Principal Skinner had entered and announced the suspensions of everybody sitting in fourth period lunch.

The tension finally eased up with students patting Xavier on the back and congratulating him on his return as he headed to his favorite table. Dexter was sitting there by himself. Everything went back to normal once Xavier took his seat.

Dex said, "So why'd you ice out your boy?"

"Honestly, homeboy, I just wanted to be alone. Nothing personal. Had to get my thoughts together, you feel me?"

"These fools have been up here trippin'—rumors flying around left and right."

Xavier was having trouble coming clean with Dexter. Smack dab in the middle of a busy lunchroom was not how he wanted to bring his homeboy up to speed. The potential for cats ear-hustling on their conversation was real and could quite possibly put him at risk.

Xavier didn't know who he was looking for but he searched the crowd for faces that looked like they didn't belong. "Seems like every time I close my eyes I can see the flash from the barrel."

Dex asked the obvious. "Who do you think did the deed, homie?"

Xavier stared into space for a moment and then he turned his attention back to Dexter. "Didn't get a description. All I saw was the blast. For all I know it could've been you on the trigger."

"You think Slick Eddie is trying to keep his word?"

Xavier was inspecting his fingernails as if looking for dirt underneath. "Now you sound like Doug. Tell you the truth: I've stepped on so many toes, I couldn't even tell you. Might be that fool."

"Did you say Doug was back?"

"Yeah. Returned today from back surgery and it was a good thing too. Dakota was getting a beating again from those SNLG chicks and Doug stopped it."

"What happened?"

"That's a conversation for another day, homeboy." Xavier pinched the bridge of his nose, like he was mentally worn out. And on top of it, his shoulder was starting to ache. "You know my dad bought me another ride and I took the bus this morning."

Dexter had a frown on his face. "The bus?"

"Can't bring myself to get into another car after that night. Too closed in. Nowhere to run."

Dex couldn't do anything but shake his head and feel bad for his best friend. "Man, I wish I had been there."

"And you probably would've ended up with a slug in you"—Xavier looked at his shoulder and then back to his boy—"or worse."

"What now?"

"I'm gonna finish school, my dude, you feel me?"

Dexter said with an immense smile, "I hear you, cuz. That's what's up."

"That big fool Chase just hooked a brotha up. He wants me to enter some writing contest. First prize is a book deal with a major publishing house. Could be some college loot, you feel me?"

"That's what's up," said Dex. It was as if he were measuring his words to ask, "So, what's up with you and Samantha?"

Xavier shrugged. "I haven't talked to her since the night at the skating rink. Basically I've been busy, you know, trying to heal from a bullet wound."

"Was that a low-key diss?"

Xavier just shook his head.

"You know she's starring in that Christmas Eve dance program."

"How could I miss that info? The posters are nearly on every wall of the school. I'm happy for her."

"Are you planning on hollerin' at her?"

Xavier wasn't able to answer the question because Bigstick walked up.

"What up, fam," Bigstick elatedly said to Xavier. "Man, I'm glad to see you back."

Xavier stood and gave his friend the homeboy hug. "Good to be back. I thought I would never get back here, you feel me?"

Bigstick said, "You? Get out of here. You can't keep a good guy down. X, if you need anything, holla at yo' boy. I gotcha back, see what I'm saying?"

Xavier smiled and said, "That's good to know, family."

"Listen, X, the coach wants to see me so I'll holla at you later." Bigstick pushed Dex on the shoulder. "Now you're back, X, this scrub can stop looking so sad and trippin' over his bottom lip."

Xavier slapped Bigstick five. "Later, superstar."

Bigstick bounced and walked out of the south door of the cafeteria about the same time that Linus Flip staggered in.

Dexter looked on as Flip clumsily bumped into other students and rudely pushed them out of the way.

Dexter said to Xavier, "This ninja's been up here wildin', dude. Straight up out of control. It's a wonder that this fool hasn't been kicked out. I bet you he's smashed right now."

Xavier stayed cool. Ever since that skating rink scuffle Linus caused, Xavier had been leery of him. He didn't think that Flip had anything to do with the shooting, but he wasn't going to rush into ruling the clown out.

"X, my ninja," Linus said as he stepped up, "what up, doe?" He was so drunk that he didn't recognize his own strength when he grabbed the hand on the same arm as Xavier's wounded shoulder.

Xavier grimaced. "Watch what you doin', fool."

Linus's eyes were small and red. He got up in Dexter's grill. "What up, doe?"

Dexter was quick when he said, with a hand up to his nose, "Definitely not yo' breath, homeboy!" He took a step back. "What did you brush your teeth with this morning, horse doo-doo?"

Linus tried to laugh it off. "Nah, just finished kissing your mama. Tell her the next time I come over to take some time out and scrub her dentures with some bleach."

Dex went back at him strong. "I noticed you've been snuggled up with the bottle lately. What, are you depressed because we will be graduating and leaving you and your ninth-grade credits behind?"

At first Linus was snarling, but it simply faded into an inebriated smile. As tall as he was, Flip walked up on Dexter and looked down. "Don't make me have to come down there, little man." He laughed like the snap had a Kevin Hart flair to it. He looked at Xavier. "X, man, I really need to talk to you"—he cut his eyes at Dexter—"privately."

Dex went off. "So no 'how you doing, X?' or 'do you need anything?' Not even a simple 'X, can I kill somebody for you?' Nothin'? What's your deal, homeboy?"

Linus disrespectfully turned his back on Dexter and said to Xavier, "Like I said, boss man, can I get a minute?"

Dex was about to go off, until Xavier placed a hand on his shoulder and said no with a simple head gesture.

Xavier extended his hand toward the south entrance. "Let's do the thing." On the way out Xavier continued to study the faces in the crowd, thinking that he had to deal with Linus Flip carefully. The boy had turned into a stone-cold alcoholic over the last year and now he more than likely needed a favor.

When they stepped out the door, Linus asked directly, "I need your back, man. I need some cheese like ASAP. Kinda got myself into a little situation and I need like 3Gs to get back right."

Xavier said, "I'm not holding like that anymore, guy. You gonna have to find some other way up out of your dilemma, you feel me?"

Linus looked around and saw that they were all alone in the hallway. "I got a way to make some bread. Got this cat that's gonna put me down to deal some pills. I already got the spot, a few workers. All I need is a lookout."

The light bulb going off inside his head stopped Xavier from checking out on this clown. Linus was acting strange and Xavier needed to find out why. He was down for his crew like that. This would be the perfect opportunity to keep an eye on Linus and probably do a little research for his essay.

"Why me?" Xavier said, playing the role.

Linus made that "why not you?" face. "You'll be watching my back. And a guy's back is trusted to those he can count on. I promise you, the cake will be sweet, dog. What do you say?"

It wasn't about the money. Xavier was just looking out for his homie.

"Give me a little time to think about it and I'll give you my answer in a few days," Xavier said.

"All right, homie," Flip said excitedly. "By the way, I'm glad you're back. And anything you need throughout the day, get at me."

As Flip walked away, Xavier thought that Linus had been straight tripping and he was going to get to the bottom of it. The boy had been drinking heavy—something was stressing him. But to do this, Xavier would be putting himself right back in the eye of the hurricane. Sitting up inside one of those houses would be dangerous. If the police weren't trying to raid them, stick up kids were trying to get their action on. Anyway, Xavier was taking a big chance to research the origins of Linus's problems, and then try to solve them for his friend.

When he walked back into the cafeteria, Xavier asked himself one thing: Was Linus's life worth potentially going to jail for, or worse—possibly getting himself killed?

20

SAMANTHA

WEDNESDAY, NOVEMBER 11
3:15 P.M.

Under normal circumstances, Samantha would've been jumping up and down at seeing Xavier walking toward her on the wide sidewalk in front of the building near student parking. Those emotions were kept in check by Sean Desmond's threat. The maniac had promised that his two henchmen would give Xavier the *business* if she ever went near him again.

The boy was sick and possessed a whole storage unit of mental issues. After he'd threatened her parents, it was chilling for Samantha having to watch Sean bond with her dad. He was charming and clever at convincing Mr. Fox that his affection was sincere. The two had become real chummy lately too. They were even spotted sitting courtside at the Palace of Auburn Hills, taking in Detroit Pistons games—or in Sean's luxury suite at Ford Field on Sundays to watch the Detroit Lions. So of course Sean Desmond stepped in as a volunteer when Mr. Fox casually announced while they were out enjoying a game that Samantha's driver had put in for a week's worth of personal days. Samantha could've choked, but said nothing because she didn't want to hear the *Sean is husband material* speech.

It was real cold out and fluffy snowflakes had started to fall when Xavier stepped to Samantha. The two let the awkward silence between them settle in before speaking, with each one remembering the blazing insults that were traded before everything went bonkers the night at the skating rink.

Sean was due to arrive at any moment, so Samantha was keeping a sharp eye out. "How have you been, Xavier?"

He took a moment, letting his gaze fall up on the scores of students walking home. "Me? I'm good."

Samantha nervously looked around. "Funny, you don't look *good*."

Xavier went all LL Cool J on her by smoothly licking his lips. "This coming from a girl whose eyes are darting around like she's expecting the bogeyman to materialize from somewhere." Xavier rubbed his cold hands together, blowing on them at the same time. "Why you look so jittery?"

There was no hiding the truth from Xavier. The boy was a genius at seeing through lies. Samantha knew she didn't have anything coming if she went there with him. She ignored the question and asked, while fidgeting with the strap around her shoulder belonging to a Louis Vuitton Palk backpack, "So did they catch who did it?"

"Naw—honestly, though, with all this crime in Detroit, I don't think the police care."

Samantha shifted her weight to her left leg and anxiously peered at the traffic jam in front of the school. She was trying to carefully ask questions that wouldn't generate any long responses from Xavier because if she knew Sean, the boy probably was in the company of his two thugs, Ozzie and Cash. It wouldn't be a good look when they pulled up and saw Xavier in her face.

"Sam, what's up with you?"

"Nothing. Why do you think there's something wrong?"

"You look nervous."

Samantha tried to play everything down by smiling. "Long day in dance class, that's all. Hey, look, I'm glad you're okay."

Samantha wasn't the only one looking skittish. Xavier was watching his back too.

"So, I guess congratulations are in order," Xavier said. "Look at you, every poster around the school has you featured to perform a dance solo in that Christmas Eve program, 'Snowflakes in Wonderland.' That sounds like it's goin' be hot."

Samantha smiled.

Xavier cautiously looked around. Didn't want anybody sneaking up on him. "Sam, I'm happy for you, honestly. It took some time for me to get here, but I can truly say that you've been more of a friend to me than I've been to you." When he reached for her right hand, Samantha's jumpy self snatched it back.

She looked down, as if embarrassed and ashamed of her reaction.

Xavier stepped back like he was trying to get a wider angle on the situation. "Sam, I've been around you long enough to know when something's wrong. Now, out with it. What's up?"

Lord knew Samantha wanted to tell him everything, but what would she have to gain from it besides putting Xavier in more danger than he was already in? Matter of fact, Sean had also threatened to harm her parents if Samantha tried to get cute and reach out for help.

She quickly changed the subject. "How's your dad and baby brother Alfonso doing?"

"Sam, why are you avoiding the question?"

Her nerves had tightened into a ball inside her throat. Part of her wanted to grab and hold on to Xavier until the end of the earth, but it was that other part that wanted to see him get to steppin' before trouble erupted. The trifling thought hadn't materialized fully before she saw Sean recklessly weaving in and out of traffic until he pulled up into the parking lot in a black Range Rover with Ozzie and Cash tailing him tightly in the same color Chevrolet Silverado Z71. They were all trying to look hard, like they were about to jump out and beat the brakes off Xavier's monkey behind.

Sean didn't waste any time clowning. He rolled down the window and said to Samantha, "What did I tell you I would do if I saw you near"—he pointed at Xavier—"that little underprivileged ghetto bum?"

Ozzie boldly stepped down out of the passenger compartment and was in pure combat mode. Dude's black skinny jeans were sagging halfway off his butt. The laces on his wheat-colored Timbos were loosely tied, and the thick black leather jacket made his upper body look like the tiny man from the Powerhouse Gym logo.

"Hold tight. I got this," he said to Sean, trying to intimidate Xavier by cracking the knuckles on his right fist. "My ninja, I've been looking to get into a good scrap for a while."

Cash thought everything was funny. He just sat behind the wheel of the Chevy, chuckling arrogantly.

"Get 'im, my little Hercules-Hercules," Cash spurred Ozzie on.

Sean stayed in his vehicle, left arm resting on the windowsill and staring directly at Xavier through the open window. "You're about to pay for that disrespect at the skating rink, ghetto trash."

Xavier silently stood his ground, like he was sizing up the entire situation. His eyes were darting back and forth, to each face. Samantha was simply praying that her ex walked away. But she knew that that would never happen. As students started to catch on to this long-anticipated throw-down from the skating rink, Samantha was so shaken that she didn't know what to do. Xavier was a hard-nose bruiser who didn't give a damn one way or another about some dude's street cred or the size of his bank account; he was going to take the fight straight to 'im without flinching. And she knew from experience that it was hard to stop him once he got going. Ozzie was another nightmare. Samantha had heard tons of stories about how ruthlessly he dealt with his rivals, with a few of those tales ending in gunplay. The boy was nothing nice, but Cash was twice as violent. They both carried guns, the type of brothas you didn't play with. And the way it looked, Xavier and Ozzie were about to go heads-up.

Samantha stepped in the middle of the two hood gladiators. "Please, you two, calm down. Haven't we learned anything from the violence in this world today? It never solves anything."

"It ain't gotta solve anything, as long as it gets rid of fools like this," Ozzie said, pointing to Xavier.

Everybody outside was now hip to the drama that was going down in front of Coleman High. Students didn't crowd out of respect for the possibility of gunplay.

Samantha just shook her head at Ozzie. She was aware that it was only a matter of time before Xavier went Xavier. Although the smirk on his face indicated sarcasm, Samantha knew the boy would stop at nothing until the threat in front of him was neutralized.

Xavier said to Ozzie, "Don't remember your name, homeboy, but I never forget a face, especially one I put my knuckle prints on at the skating rink that night."

That did it, but before Ozzie could push Samantha out of the way to get to Xavier, security rushed out of the main door.

"Samantha, get in the car," Sean ordered.

She was so confused. Xavier didn't quite catch the helpless look on her face because he kept his eyes focused on Ozzie, who happened to be slowly backpedaling toward the Chevy when security finally stepped up.

Ozzie said before stepping up into the truck, "This ain't over, playboy."

This was a hot mess and Samantha felt that it was all her fault. She was in terrible trouble without means of escape. Oh, only if Xavier knew about her agony. Sean had literally hijacked her ability to choose him as a boyfriend by threatening to harm her loved ones. She didn't want to get into the Range Rover with him. If anything, Samantha wanted to walk over and stand with Xavier, and she hesitated, looking in her ex's direction. That was until Sean played dirty.

"Samantha, remember me and Pop are going to the Pistons game tonight," he said on the sly. Sean devilishly looked back at his two goons and then back to Samantha. "We don't want him to be *late,* now do we?"

There was no other play. She was his prisoner. She was scared because he was growing bolder, like this whole thing was a game to him. He could have any girl he wanted, but why was he torturing her?

"Tick, tock," Sean said to her, holding up his left wrist with the expensive, phat timepiece strapped around it.

Instead of security coming out and immediately dispersing the crowd, Samantha watched a few of them walk around to the driver's side of the Range Rover. They asked for an autograph. She had no choice but to play ball. Xavier looked like he was about to say something to her, and she wished he would. It probably wouldn't have stopped her from getting into Sean's SUV, but it sure would've been nice to hear the voice of an angel before going back to her own personal hell.

21

DAKOTA

WEDNESDAY, NOVEMBER 11
3:30 P.M.

"**Y**ou know he wasn't worth it, right?" Dakota Taylor said to Xavier as she made her way through the crowd to catch up to him.

Xavier was walking away from the school with a bunch of kids following and still gossiping about the confrontation.

"Munchkin, I'm not sweatin' the small stuff," said Xavier, looking around like he was searching for something. "I can't even remember the cat's name."

Dakota motioned to the kids who were following Xavier as if dude was some hot, up-and-coming young hip-hop star out for a stroll in the ghetto.

"Why are these students still following you?"

"I don't know."

"You do know."

Xavier kept his eyes peeled to the traffic as the cars sped by. "Munchkin, my guess would be that they've heard about my legendary skills for knocking cats senseless, and being that this is my last year, they want to see if my rep is well deserved." He even managed to smile at Dakota after that one.

"I think they just want to see if some more trouble is going to jump off."

Xavier looked back but kept on walking. "Why can't they just be fans?"

"Whatever. I just want to thank you again for pulling those girls off me."

"I don't know, judging from the way it looks, I'm going to have to start charging you bodyguard prices."

"I don't have money."

"Well, you don't have a bodyguard either, chump."

She laughed. It sure felt good to laugh too. Dakota hadn't been doing much of that lately. Though there was much garbage circulating around campus with students being warned not to be caught talking or standing near Xavier, Dakota felt safe. Since getting to Coleman, this was the only time she felt that way. Didn't matter to her about the rumors of Xavier having a price on his head. She couldn't care less about who they thought put it there. Xavier was her knight in shining armor—her big brother—and she was thankful for him.

The hangers-on started thinning out the farther they traveled away from school grounds until it was just her and him, sitting at a bus stop and gazing out into the heart of rush hour.

Dakota had to ask the one question on her mind. "You look great physically, but how do you really feel?"

Xavier had that look like he'd been expecting her question. "Don't know."

She said, "Xavier, I hope you don't get mad at me, but I don't think you should've come back to school so early."

"Now see, if you had been anybody else, I probably would be clocking out right now, but since you are a munchkin, you can have your say." Xavier was squinting, straining to see something that was happening two blocks away.

Dakota was still running her mouth. "I still can't believe that your dad bought you a brand-new car and you're not driving it."

"I don't feel safe in a car," Xavier said flatly.

Dakota was stumped. "Where did that come from?"

Xavier kept staring off down the street. "You're pretty intuitive. You will probably not ask me why I wasn't driving the new car. So I just saved you some time. I'm not driving my car because I don't feel safe in a little enclosed space." Xavier rubbed his eyes. He didn't seem like he was paying attention to her. The look on his face was like he'd seen a ghost.

"Don't you think you should go to therapy? I mean the whole 'not safe in a car' thing is not normal. I think what you have is called post-traumatic stress—I read about it in *The New York Times*. Happens to soldiers that return home from the war or anybody who's experienced some type of trauma."

Something down the street had Xavier's attention.

"Are you hearing me?"

"Yeah. Just thought I saw something."

"Seriously, don't you think you should go to therapy?"

"It's not that serious, super geek. I don't feel safe in a car right now, that's all."

Dakota looked around. "Yup. I can see how standing at a bus stop is a lot safer."

Xavier just shook his head. "Will you let me deal with my issues, please? Anyway, why don't you talk to the principal in bringing awareness about bullying to Coleman."

"I don't know about that."

"I'm not trying to be funny, but who better than you to help shed some light on the subject? You might even be able to counsel people."

Dakota look confused. "I wouldn't know how to get started."

"You know what, I'll talk to Doug for you and see if homeboy can get the ball rolling. Don't worry about it. I got this."

She trusted Xavier. And if he said that everything would be fine, then she believed him. Besides, he was responsible for getting the major players in the SNLG crew kicked out. They wouldn't be bothering her anytime soon. As Dakota peered out into traffic, she wrestled with the idea.

Xavier is right, she thought. There were more students being bullied. Dakota couldn't, and wouldn't, let them silently suffer. Xavier, whether he knew it or not, had influenced her to fight and to stand up for herself. What better way to champion a cause? Dakota had made up her mind at the bus stop to become the voice for the voiceless.

22

XAVIER

SATURDAY, NOVEMBER 14
6:30 P.M.

Xavier was seated at the dining room table outlining his paper. Alfonso was at the library with a friend, and Noah and his irritating girlfriend Roxanne Hudson were out enjoying a movie date. The house was all his. Nice. Quiet. Just like he liked it whenever he sat to unleash his thoughts upon the world. His concentration was fragmented, though, resulting in him writing in spurts. He kept on replaying the scene outside the school on Wednesday, when he had to seriously restrain himself from kicking in ol' boy's hairline. Sean Desmond was a big-shot MLB rookie, and those two were apparently his personal bodyguards. Just the kind of cats who packed heat and weren't afraid to bust caps. There was no doubt that he could've easily taken that lame in a one-on-one. But dudes

like that wouldn't hesitate to pull out and start letting off
if they lost the scuffle. Bullets hurt, and Xavier wasn't
trying to go down that road again. So he was more than
happy that nothing had gone down.

He was more worried about Samantha, though. Ol'
girl looked shook. Like she wanted to tell him something
but couldn't force herself to spill the beans. His love for
her was tattooed inside his chest and would live there as
long as his heart beat. There was no way he could turn a
blind eye to her situation. Her facial expression screamed
out help. And that rat Sean Desmond just sat in the truck,
smiling. Letting his minions conduct his dirty work. Until
Samantha asked for his help, Xavier's hands were totally
tied. But once she untied them, Xavier was going to enjoy
beating the crap out of Sean and whoever else stood at
his back.

As he wrote, Xavier felt like he was out of his mind.
Next weekend would be the start of his little investigation. Linus needed money in a major way and Xavier
wanted to know why. He'd already set the entire thing
up. Linus wholeheartedly agreed that Xavier would func-
tion as lookout, nothing else. He'd be sitting in one of the
windows of an upstairs bedroom inside a two-story rick-
ety old colonial. And since he was in the position, Xavier
figured he might as well take advantage of the situation.
To gather a bit of info on the workers. To see what made
them tick. There would be three workers he would be
able to talk to and get the scoop as to why they were willing to risk their freedom for a piece of the so-called
American dream. He would only have to put in two to
three hours of work after school. It would be just enough

time to spy on Flip. Also, it would provide him with enough time to interview all three boys, get what he needed, and quit.

As he wrote, Dakota slipped into his mind. It looked like Dakota would get the chance to put together an anti-bullying campaign. Doug had come through and Principal Skinner was on board. It was time to bring awareness to Coleman. The date had yet to be determined, but Dakota securing the principal's vote was major.

Xavier put a hand over his shoulder. Despite his wound being fully healed, the thing still throbbed on certain days, especially with the cold front that had dropped into Detroit and showed absolutely no signs of leaving anytime soon. Aside from all of that, Xavier was having trouble trying to digest what he thought he saw while hanging out at the bus stop with Dakota a couple of days ago. There had been a man driving a yellow taxicab who looked like his friend and mentor Billy Hawkins. Even though Billy had been acting weird since Xavier had gotten shot, a cab driver he wasn't. From a distance it sure did look like him, though.

Xavier was almost finishing up when he heard Noah's girlfriend walk her loud mouth into the house behind Noah.

"Man," said Roxanne in her usual throaty smoker's voice, "that damn Denzel Washington is such a cutie. And did you see the way he walks, Noah, in that one scene where it was in slow motion after the explosion—you talking about a bona fide phenom with the coolest strut in Hollywood." She snorted out a laugh and didn't give Noah a chance to answer. "Oh my God. The man is so sexy. Noah, I would leave you in a heartbeat if Denzel asked me." She put both her hands to her mouth and play-fainted onto the couch.

Xavier had seen just about enough. He couldn't stand her and didn't want any part of a conversation. He started packing up his things to move his work into his bedroom.

Noah walked in and threw his keys on a small table by the front door. "How's the writing coming?" he asked Xavier.

Xavier loved his father, but seeing Noah with Roxanne always put him in a bad mood. There was something about the chick that didn't sit too well with him.

"I thought you guys weren't coming back until later on," Xavier said to Noah.

Roxanne sat up on the sofa. "You must've had your-self a little hot tenderoni action droppin' through," said Roxanne, smiling and giggling.

"Seriously. You got all that from the question I asked my father?"

Noah said to Xavier, "Naw, son, I figured I'd come back and cook my lady a special dinner."

Roxanne stood up from the couch. Her attitude came out of nowhere. "Are you gonna let your son talk to you like he's the parent?"

The lady was bonkers and Xavier wasn't about to buy into it.

"I don't think he's talking like that. Jesus, Mary, and Joseph—you're overreacting."

She put her hands on her hips. "Spare the rod and spoil the child. That's what's wrong with him. You let him get away with too much. He just wanted us out of the house so he could have his young tenderoni all up in his bed-room. What does that Bible of yours say about ruling your household?"

"You don't know me," said Xavier to Roxanne. "You don't know anything about me."

Noah stepped in. "Xavier, I'll handle this. Just go to your room."

"My pleasure," said Xavier.

Roxanne smacked her lips. "You see his smart mouth? You need to check that gangsta attitude of his . . . before he gets shot again."

As much as Xavier wanted to go off, he took the high road and walked back to his bedroom. When he closed the door he heard:

"Sweetie, I really think you owe my son an apology." That was his father.

"So I have to apologize for stating the truth, and the truth is he'll be plugged again if you don't check him."

"You are completely out of line, Roxanne," Noah said, trying not to sound too intense. "I would never say any-thing like that about your fourteen- and seventeen-year-old sons."

Roxanne snapped, "That's because my boys have this little thing called manners. They're well-behaved and don't get into any trouble."

Xavier could tell that his father was becoming frus-trated.

Noah's religion totally opened up the front door and took a hike with his next response. "Manners are the only thing you can brag about. Those two boys of yours are dumber than frog turds."

Roxanne hit the roof. "No, you didn't go there. We'll see just how much intelligence your hoodlum has when you have to go identify his body—oh, yeah, since he's so good with numbers, see if he can figure out his casket measurements while he's on this side of the dirt."

Noah went biblical. "The tongue is a little member but in it lies great power."

"Sounds like you're trying to go to the Bible on me. Exactly what are you trying to say, Reverend?"

Noah didn't flinch. "Be careful that the curses that you speak on others don't come back to harm yours."

Xavier was laughing. His father had just scored points in a major way. It wasn't the way Xavier would've liked to have seen it handled, but the old man did it his way, with style and class.

However, it pissed Roxanne off. Sounded like the idiot was headed for the door when Xavier heard Noah stop her.

"Listen, baby, this entire thing has gotten way out of hand. I was gonna cook you dinner. But since we've been given this beautiful day off from the plant, let's go to a nice restaurant and discuss this thing like normal adults. What you say, kitten?"

There was a long silence at first. And then Xavier heard Roxanne say, "Okay, Daddy. You have to take me to the London Chop House if you want me to forgive you."

"It's done. Let's go." There was the sound of Noah snatching up his keys from the table. "Xavier, I'll be back. Make sure your little brother gets something to eat when he comes home from the library."

Xavier was left sitting on his bed with a *What just happened?* look on his face. That wasn't how it was supposed to end. Roxanne should've been on her way home by now, angry, screaming at the top of her lungs, insanely flipping off motorists, cussing and cursing the day Noah was born. But instead she had gotten what she wanted—not just to go out for a decent meal, but to dine at one of the most expensive restaurants in town. He wanted to call it like he saw it. The old man was whipped. And if it was like that, Xavier couldn't be happier that this was his last year of high school. Noah had been away and this was the first real relationship since Xavier's mother Ne Ne. And the way those two were carrying along, marriage didn't seem like it was too far behind. There was no way he could live in the same house with that woman and her boys. It just wasn't gonna fly.

Xavier tabled all of that drama and set to work to put the finishing touches on the outline.

23

SAMANTHA

Samantha's bedroom was bright and festive, warm and boasting a brilliant scheme of beautiful colors. Contemporary furnishings sat on top of light-colored hardwood floors. She was sitting in the middle of a queen-size bed with her favorite white fuzzy teddy bear named Mr. Fluffy nearby. Samantha's knees were pulled into her body, chin resting on top and arms wrapped around her legs, rocking back and forth. Her dance solo was a little over a month away, and here she was so worried about other things that it was hard to focus. Too much nervous energy had caused her eating habits to become irregular. It was true. She'd grown up with Sean, and yesterday's version was nowhere close to the monster that was now turning her senior year into some cheaply made horror flick.

Sleep had become a total stranger. Sometimes Samantha would wake up in cold sweats, arms flailing and feet kicking, fighting off an aggressive Sean in her nightmares. Her mother was aware of something going on with her daughter but couldn't figure it out. And Samantha was trying hard to stay one step ahead, even though the physical exertion was trying to give away her secret. She blamed the bags underneath her eyes on the demands placed on her by an overachieving instructor to perform a near-perfect dance solo in the upcoming Christmas Eve program.

Samantha rocked backward and forward until tears formed. She wiped them away, knowing that if Ozzie and Xavier would've tangled outside of school, somebody could've gotten hurt, or worse, killed. Her urge to talk to Xavier that day had put his life in jeopardy. This was something that she had to figure out on her own. Samantha sometimes felt like she was trapped inside a dark box with no way to escape and the walls were starting to close in around her. The sadness of being all alone was too much to bear. But she'd rather keep quiet than run the risk of that lunatic hurting one of her parents.

There were heavy footsteps approaching her door. She quickly dried her eyes, grabbed Mr. Fluffy, and fixed herself in the bed like she was sleeping.

Mr. Fox knocked on the door. "Is my little princess decent?"

Samantha lightly cleared her throat to chase away any signs of anxiety. "Yes, Daddy. You can come in."

Her father stepped in, casually dressed in dark slacks

and a cardigan sweater. "Pumpkin, how's my little girl doing?"

She didn't lift her head because her red eyes would give her away. "I'm all right. Just a little tired. We've been rehearsing pretty hard. Every day after school, you know."

"Sweetheart, I want to tell you that I'm supremely proud of you. You've grown up into a beautiful young lady right before our eyes. I still remember when you took your first steps. How you fell down and skinned your knee. I felt so bad that I picked you up and at that point I swore to protect you from anything."

Tears welled in her eyes. All she wanted was to come clean about Sean. Tell her father about everything. Let him be the one to chase away the bogeyman. But the thought of Ozzie and Cash creeping through the darkness of her home and snuffing out her parents stalled her efforts at rescue.

Her father continued on. "You may get mad at me meddling in your business, but your dad has your best interest at heart, sweetie. I want you to have a man somewhat like me. That's why I'm happy that you and Sean are spending time together. He's a good guy—protective, provider, an all-around inspiration to a lot of people. Besides, he's become my new buddy. I can never say no to him spending his money on treating me to watch NBA and NFL games from luxury suites."

If only you knew what your good buddy has planned for you if I reveal how the psycho is really treating me, Samantha thought as she clutched Mr. Fluffy closer to her chest.

Mr. Fox walked over and kissed his baby girl on the

jaw. "Dad's going to the Detroit Pistons game tonight. If you need me, just call my cell phone. I love you."

Samantha told him, "I love you too, Daddy."

Samantha was awakened from a much-needed sleep by her ringing cell phone. She'd been so tired that it felt like she had been asleep for hours. But it was only eight o'clock. Samantha was surprised to see that it had only been an hour since her father had left to go to the game.

"Hello," she groggily answered.

It was Jennifer. "Girl, get your lazy bones up."

"Girl, I need this sleep."

"I know, right, since our dance teacher enjoys whipping us like government mules."

Samantha laughed.

Jennifer said, "You made me forget what I called you for—oh yeah, I just saw your dad sitting courtside at the game with your boo on TV."

"Girl, please. He left with Sean about an hour ago."

"Well, I bet you that there's something you didn't know." Over the next five minutes Jennifer put her girl up on game.

All Samantha could manage to say afterward was, "Tracy's a garden tool."

Jennifer wanted to know, "You mean you're not even mad?"

Samantha let out a frustrated sigh. "Girl, no."

"Why not? If my best friend had slept with my man I'd be pissed."

"Jen, first off: Sean Desmond is not my man. I'm not giving him none so he went to the girl whose legs wouldn't say no. I have so much on my mind that Tracy's issues don't even matter."

"So I tell you that Cash called me trying to get into my pants and offered up information that he thought would get him in and you just act like you don't care. He told me that Sean went over to Tracy's house and picked her up and they went back to Sean's. Cash told me that the both of them were holed up in the bedroom all night eating lobster and getting busy."

Samantha let out another frustrated sigh.

"I wouldn't stop until I had two handfuls of that heffa's bad weave in my fist, is all I'm saying," said Jennifer.

"It's not that serious, Jen."

"Sam, are you all right? You've been acting different for a while. What's going on with you?"

Samantha gave her girl the same spiel she'd given everybody else. "Nervous energy about my dance solo. It has to be clean and flawless." She couldn't tell Jennifer the truth. It would put her in jeopardy.

"Aww, girl, you got this. It pains me to say it, but your butt is the best dancer in our troupe. And trust me, the teacher wouldn't have handed the most important solo routine to two left feet. With the exception of a few haters in our class, all the rest of us have faith in you. Now cut it out."

Samantha had been informed that a representative from Juilliard would be at the Christmas Eve program. She had no idea why they wanted to come down since she had already auditioned. It was November and the board hadn't made a decision on accepting her yet. Doubt had been eating away at her lately, but Samantha took the rep's visit as a good omen. And she wasn't about to trouble herself with Tracy. A lot was at stake. She wouldn't allow herself to be bothered with the fact that Tracy, one of her best friends, would go behind her back. Not that she cared one way or another about Tracy and Sean rolling around in the sack behind closed doors. That wasn't the point. But the fact that she ignored the "girlfriend" code and got her betrayal on was a punishable offense. She believed Jennifer. The girl had no reason to lie. But for right now, she had to put it out of her mind. Samantha could only deal with one problem at a time—Sean's psychotic butt was at the top of her list.

Samantha said to Jen, "Thank you for being such a good friend and a wonderful sister. I love you."

"Aw, girl, you're gonna make me cry—stop it. I love you too."

Samantha talked to Jennifer until the wee hours of the morning. She hung up when she heard her father's deep voice. Sounded like he was talking to somebody on his cell phone when he ascended the stairs. Probably Sean. But all she knew was that he was home safe . . . at least for tonight.

24

DAKOTA

The feeling that Dakota was experiencing couldn't compare to anything in the world. The boulder was lifted and her burden felt as light as air. Whoever said that a kid getting suspended from school wouldn't bring about a positive change in attitude was high off dollar-store wine. After her suspension, the SNLG head honcho Bangs had returned to school with a new outlook on life. After Principal Skinner had gone all fire and brimstone and tossed the little gangbangin' heffa and a few of her partners out on their cookies, Bangs had come back like she had some sense. Word around campus was that she had severed ties with the gang, devoted herself to her studies, and even started to attend every last class. Now,

Mouse was different. The little chick had dropped out, replaced Bangs, and started running the gang from the outside. It didn't matter, though. Those gang members who were still in school knew the drill. Xavier was back and Dakota was off-limits.

Dakota had been given special permission from Principal Skinner to walk around the school and pass out literature to students. The girl had stayed up half the night grabbing alarming stats and other information off the Internet about bullying and putting together her first flyer to promote awareness. A date had been agreed upon by the principal, Doug, and the majority of the teaching staff. March eighteenth was the date, a Friday. The campaign would kick off after the first bell and last until the last class. There would be lectures about bullying taking place in the small cafeteria and auditorium. Tables would be stationed throughout the school with free T-shirts, balloons, coffee mugs, and key chains in promotion of stopping bullying and raising awareness.

It filled her with absolute joy to walk around and pass out flyers for the event. Made her feel like she was making a difference. She wore a necklace with an odd-looking eagle charm, which in her Native American culture embodied courage, honor, and strength.

Dakota walked into the cafeteria, where Xavier and his crew were posted up at their usual table. She passed out a few flyers as she moved in his direction. Dakota walked up on the guys having a conversation.

"Ay, Xavier," Bigstick said. "Baby girl is gonna be doing her thing in that Christmas Eve dance program, huh?"

Dexter said, "I'll be there to show my support. Man,

they got poster boards up all over the place about it. 'Snowflakes in Wonderland' is going to be off the chain."

Xavier said, "That's wassup. We gonna be up in that piece deep to show Sam the support, you feel me?"

Dex was the first one to clown when he saw Dakota standing over Xavier. "If it ain't Harriet Tubman, the little woman who is trying to stop geek and nerd oppression," he said.

Bigstick was chilling. "Is there nobody off-limits to you, moron?" he asked Dexter. "She is standing up for what she believes in."

Xavier just smiled. He knew what was coming.

"Thank you, Bigstick." Dakota set her sights on Dexter. "I know you're trying to be funny, and Dexter, when I say 'trying to be,' that's a stretch." She stopped and looked at everybody sitting around the table. "You all know the story about Harriet Tubman leading slaves to their freedom by using the Underground Railroad, but did you know that she was famous for assisting in other worthy causes? One of which happens to deal with equality for women. Yup. She worked on the side of other female activists like Susan B. Anthony and Emily Howland to aid in the struggle for a woman to have the right to vote. So, Dexter, when you bring up our black heroes, or sheros, make sure you do so without being so disrespectful."

Dexter had this dumb look on his face, like he'd been walking outside in a horse corral and stepped in it.

All Bigstick could say to Dexter was, "I bet you feel silly."

Xavier's head was on a swivel, surveying the lunch-room crowd. Dakota hated to see him so uncomfortable.

It was almost to a point of Xavier showing vulnerability. She wasn't used to it. To her Xavier was a warrior, a lion that growled and roared to alert all that he was indeed king of this Coleman High jungle. He'd taught her a lot, like how not to be scared and to never let anybody punk her.

She said to Xavier, "Thank you, big brother, for helping me"—she brought the stack of flyers into view—"get started."

"You don't have to thank me, munchkin," said Xavier. "It's my pleasure. Besides, the one thing I hate and despise more than anything is a bully, you feel me?"

"Word 'em up," Bigstick said, dapping out Xavier.

Dexter was so embarrassed all he could do was nod in agreement.

Xavier asked Dakota, "Do you need anything?"

Bigstick looked over at Dexter and smiled. "Damn, Dexter D, this is the first time I ever saw you this quiet."

"Whatever," was Dexter's only reply.

"Well, people aren't exactly being helpful," Dakota said. "Some take the flyers and they end up on the floor. Others think that this serious issue is just a joke."

Xavier stood up from his seat and yelled, "Listen up!" He waited until the noise slowly tuned down and he had everybody's attention. "The students at Coleman High have an opportunity to do some good in this raggedy building. This girl right here"—he put an arm around Dakota—"is passing out flyers to bring awareness about bullying. Most of you know her. Her face was painted blue some time ago. Nothing like that will ever happen under this roof again, you feel me? March eighteenth will be the day we finally put an end to bullying. Let's all stand up to these weak punks."

Xavier nodded at Dakota. She went around the entire lunchroom and handed out leaflets to students.

Some cat wearing glasses with lenses so thick that his eyes looked like two raisins stood up and screamed, "I'm with you, Xavier! I'm tired of giving up my lunch money. 'Bout time somebody stood up to these bastards!"

Some short girl with a jacked-up weave said, "All of our faces might be painted blue one day if we don't all stand together to defeat these bullies."

The girl united the lunchroom as people cheered and whistled.

"Thank you," Xavier said to the crowd. "We appreciate your time and patience."

Dakota found that these students were a lot more receptive than the ones she'd encountered earlier. But Xavier had a powerful presence about him, one that she loved. Things were finally looking up for her, and she had him to thank for it.

25

XAVIER

The butterflies in Xavier's stomach felt like they were trying to fly up through his throat and right out of his mouth. His nerves tightened inside his chest. Every car door that opened and closed brought palpitations to his heart. Xavier was in front of a bedroom window of a shabby colonial on the grimiest side of town. Dude couldn't believe he had the stones to pull something like this off. It would be either the kindest thing he'd ever done or the dumbest. But Flip was family, and aside from that, the boy had saved Xavier's hide once. Xavier had to do this. Xavier had stayed up half the night trying to convince himself that this was, in fact, the right thing to do.

Linus Flip had just stepped out of the room after giving Xavier specific intel on what to look out for. The spot only sold designer drugs, nothing you would consider hard-core, but still highly illegal and could get a fool—if caught—sentenced to a healthy double-digit basketball score. Xavier's job was simple: identify and yell out anything suspicious. That went for five-o and stickup kids alike.

Of course this was going against everything he stood for, but he conveniently twisted the logic to make him comfortable in the house. While saving his boy, Xavier hoped to get the kind of info from the workers that would make a compelling essay that would win him the prize money. He would be able to use it at Michigan State. He could pool this whole experience into some slammin' street-lit novels with hard-hitting messages of morality. But he had to win the contest in order to make this dream come true.

Can I win this contest, though? he asked himself, as he sat on a stool looking out at a decaying street in a dying neighborhood. If he did win, would he have the chops to produce the kind of stories that could make him a phat living? Or was his big, long teacher Mr. Chase pulling his chain about him having that kind of talent?

Xavier wasn't able to give it another thought because some dude named Dark walked up in the piece.

He said to Xavier, "What up doe, pimpin'?"

Dark was actually light skinned. Not too tall. The boy must've weighed all of a hundred sixty pounds soaking wet, but his most distinguishing characteristic was his ears. Those things looked like smaller versions of coffee saucers.

Xavier had known the boy from the old neighborhood.

He'd moved from there about the same time Xavier and his family did. Dark was a quiet guy. Mostly kept to himself. Never caused trouble. Just a straight-up good dude, which puzzled Xavier. What was a boy like him doing in this house selling poison? It was worth getting to the bottom of. Xavier decided that Dark would be his first subject.

Xavier said, "You got it, homeboy. What's good?"

"Another day another dollar for me." He showed off an ivory smile. "Xavier, if you don't mind me saying, dude, you got too much street cred to be in the cut serving as lookout. What's up with you?"

So much thought had gone into the "why" aspect of him taking the gig that he'd plumb forgotten about the red flags that somebody like him, with his impeccable street pedigree, taking such a lowly position would raise.

He simply told the truth. "Just a favor for a friend."

Dark eased up and smiled. "I can dig it." He looked out a window as darkness settled over the city. "I know I'm only seventeen and I haven't been around for a long time, but I remember when this neighborhood looked better than this. Joint used to have green grass and trees. Now all you see is burned-out fools and run-down, vacant houses."

"Yeah. It definitely ain't gonna be winning any awards on beauty no time soon."

Xavier peeked at a car slowly rolling down the street. Even though the headlights were on, the vehicle was shrouded in darkness. Both boys breathed a sigh of relief as they watched the ride until it rolled out of sight.

Xavier looked at Dark. "Homeboy, what's your story?

I mean, back then you didn't seem like the type that would take this route."

Dark hunched his shoulders. "Not much to tell. It's the same old cliché: cracked-out mother. Dad jetted. Little brother and sister I have to look out for. Fast food jobs ain't gonna get it. Gotta be at home in the morning to get the two crumb snatchers ready for school."

"Sounds like you have to put yourself on the back burner, homeboy."

A sad look fell across his face. "This was supposed to be my last year of high school, but I doubt if I finish. The shorties need me, so I have to play big brother-daddy."

Xavier's heart went out to him. Ne Ne's behind might've been selfish, but at least she didn't have a crack addiction. Other than that, their stories were so similar. If there was one person who could feel homeboy's pain, it was Xavier.

Xavier wanted to know, "Dark, when will you turn eighteen?"

Dark eyed Xavier suspiciously. "A couple weeks. Why?"

"What if I can promise you a job with thirteen bucks an hour starting pay?"

"I'd say, have you been getting high off Linus Flip's supply?"

"Serious, dude. I can get you hooked up."

Dark looked cynical. "No disrespect, Xavier, but why are you trying to give me a job that it looks like you need?"

"Don't worry about me, homie. My game is tight. Plus I ain't tryin' to work in a car plant, you feel me?" Xavier peered out of the window. Nothing. The coast was clear.

"If you ain't full of it, I don't know how to repay you."

Xavier smiled and looked around. "You can repay me by taking good care of your family and staying the hell out of places like this."

For the next two hours Xavier and Dark kicked around. Unbeknownst to Dark, he'd supplied Xavier with a ton of valuable information. So far, this thing had all the makings of an explosive essay.

Xavier's first day in the spot was officially in the books and had been pretty pleasant. Dark seemed to be a down-to-earth brotha that life was trying hard to turn into a statistic. And Xavier wasn't about to let that happen.

It was one down, but there were two more days left in the house. Linus hadn't slipped up and shown his hand. He was giving himself two more days to find the answer, after that Flip would be on his own.

26

XAVIER

SUNDAY, NOVEMBER 22
7:02 P.M.

Xavier was able to get away from the crib with rela
tive ease today. Noah hadn't been there to ask his
usual million questions. He, Roxanne, and Alfonso had
gone to church early this morning and planned to stay
there until the end of the afternoon service. Before they
left, Roxanne had been on some old crazy stuff, all up in
Xavier's business, asking Noah why his oldest wasn't
going to church and making super-slick comments about
Xavier wouldn't have a hole in the shoulder if he had
Jesus in his life. And just to be slick, Xavier ignored his
father's pleading eyes and said to Roxanne, "Jesus was in
Jesus's life and He still came up with holes in His body, so
what's your point?"

You would've thought that the roof had caved in. Roxanne's ol' hypocritical behind did everything except bear a cross and douse the boy with holy oil. Xavier thought that his old man would lose his mind, though. He was almost late for church explaining to Xavier about his blasphemous statement. But it was all in fun. He didn't hate anyone, but exceptions were made for Roxanne Hudson.

He'd worry about her later. He had the strangest feeling that he was being tailed by a car on his way over to the spot. It looked like the same yellow cab he'd seen when he was chilling with Dakota at the bus stop not too long ago. And again the cabbie had made sure to keep a safe distance so as not to be identified. Xavier quickly filed it away as paranoia. Getting blasted in the shoulder would tend to have your mind spinning all different directions. But he needed to be focused.

Xavier had plans to be in the spot for a few hours today. Linus Flip had just stepped away to run an errand, leaving two other people in the house with Xavier: a cat that went by the street name Hustle, and an Xbox-playing fiend who rocked the handle Gameboy. The dude Dark had the day off.

Gameboy was a trip. He'd waited until Linus had left, then plugged in the system. He and the guy Hustle were down in the living room getting it in on a cheesy-looking flat screen, playing NBA 2K15. Judging by the sound being turned up so high, the two idiots were acting like they weren't sitting in a hotspot.

Xavier was sitting at his post in front of the bedroom window when he heard somebody pound on the door. It was funny because he hadn't remembered seeing anybody approach from the sidewalk. The streetlights could've been a factor. Every other one had been knocked out, giving darkness a slight edge over light. There weren't any alleys, so the visitor couldn't have come up from behind. Something wasn't feeling right to Xavier.

He got up and went downstairs where the bumping continued to grow louder. Xavier stood in front of the television until the two got the point and turned it down. That's when they heard somebody knocking.

He said to the pair, "I guess you boys can't hear the door."

Hustle was a pretty big dude. He was nineteen, with a solid build and a dark complexion. He had attitude and definitely walked around like he was Mr. Tough Guy.

"I got this," he said in a gruff tone, getting up and strolling over to the door like he was the head rooster in charge.

Xavier was amazed at the stones on this guy when Hustle yanked the door open and snatched in by the collar some weasel-looking dude wearing a crummy ski coat.

"Why you bumpin' on the door so damn hard fo'?" he screamed at the guy.

Ski Coat was shaking and badly trembling. "Y'all couldn't hear the door."

Hustle ordered Gameboy to take care of Ski Coat.

Xavier just shook his head. He had seen far too many hard dudes before to know how to spot a poser. You know the ones. Overcompensation for the lack of guts.

"I'm up in this piece to make some money, stacked my paper to the ceiling," Hustle said to no one in particular.

Xavier was about to walk back upstairs.

"Hey, new dude," he said to Xavier. He brought his left hand up so Xavier could have a close study of the tiny diamonds of his pinky ring. "Stick around long enough, everybody'll get one."

Another tough guy, Xavier thought. Homeboy was gonna make for an interesting case study. Xavier offered a bogus smile and continued on his way. Before he could get back upstairs to sit down good, the dude Gameboy stumbled in behind him.

"It's Xavier, right?" said Gameboy. Homeboy was probably eighteen, average height, and wore some baggy clothes that were sagging off his body.

Xavier looked at him. "Yeah. Yours is Gameboy, right?"

"That's me," he said like he was proud of the handle. "When I heard that Linus was putting this little team together, I'ma keep it real with you, I wasn't feeling a new guy. Me and that ninja Hustle been working together for some time now."

"I can dig that. I mean, this might be one of the most important jobs here. So I can feel your anxiety, fam. Gotta have somebody you can trust watchin' yo' back, you feel me?"

"What side of town you from, my ninja?"

"Westside."

Gameboy shook his head like he was already up on it. "Yeah, I can tell you one of those Westside ninjas."

"How so?"

"You ninjas got a different attitude."

Xavier figured this was the perfect time to see what made homeboy tick, since they were getting all chummy-

chummy. He cut right into him. "How long have you been on the grind?"

He grabbed his chin between thumb and index. "Maybe about two years, give or take."

The answer messed Xavier up. He thought Gameboy would at least say all his teenage life. Xavier watched a dark-colored SUV ride by. "Why?"

Gameboy smiled. "Nobody ever asked me that before."

"So what you're tryna say is that you don't have any idea."

"I grew up around it. Never saw anything else. Never saw my dad going to work and setting a good example. I thought perfect families like that existed only on TV sitcoms. This is the way it's supposed to be, ain't it?"

Xavier couldn't do anything but shake his head. This dude really didn't have a clue as to why he was putting his life on the line. Xavier could only sum this dude up as being a product of his environment. Unlike Dark, who because of a cracked-out mother was slangin' the stuff to afford the basic necessities for his family.

"Ay, you two geniuses," Hustle said from the door. "Y'all can hold each other's hands and sing Kumbaya later. Gameboy, we got work to finish before Linus Flip comes back talkin' junk."

Xavier had gotten all he needed from Gameboy. The dude Hustle wouldn't be too hard to figure out. The boy was a walking cliché who only saw life one way, and that was getting paid the quick way. The spot would soon be history. Tomorrow would be Xavier's last day of having to come to this death-dealing fleabag. Xavier had done some snooping around, but his findings yielded absolutely nothing. Tomorrow was his last day. Linus was up to something and tomorrow would be the last day to figure it out.

The next day Xavier was back at it, but this time, he was armed with a plan. Since he couldn't figure it out, he'd just make it go away. Xavier was prepared to drop another dime, but this time, on his boy. It would be for Flip's own good. Whatever was causing homeboy's money trouble would have to wait, because this death-dealing drug pit wasn't the answer. Xavier had collected all the data he needed for his essay from the workers. Now was the time to put the brakes on Linus's moneymaking drug spot. He moved over to the window with good intention and used his cell to call the police. Xavier told them everything he knew about the drugs in the crib. Told them about the number of people there and supplied the address and hung up. But he had to be cunning. Xavier knew he couldn't just leave. It would be too obvious—him walking out only to have the cops run in. Hustle wasn't stupid. He would be wise and know that there was some dirt in the game. The whole thing would scream set up. Xavier couldn't have that. All it would take was for this fool to try and piece things together and run with his conspiracy theories back to Flip. Xavier didn't need any beef with his boy. So this thing would have to go down perfect.

It was dark out—seven o'clock in the evening. Fifteen minutes had passed since he'd made the call. The foot traffic was the heaviest he'd ever seen it. Despite this, the two idiots downstairs managed to squeeze in time for NBA 2K15. The sound was up so loud that it seemed like the two boys were right in the same room with him. They sure couldn't hear him if he had to ring the alarm.

Xavier had started to question his actions when the police pulled up out front. The next thing he knew, the entire street came to life. Red and blue lights from police cruisers lit up the area, washing over tattered and torn houses. They seemed to come out of nowhere.

Even though he knew what was up, it felt like the bottom dropped out of Xavier's stomach as he watched bodies in uniform converge on the house. He had to jet out of there. But before he got ghost, for the affect, he screamed downstairs, but the two idiots had the volume high on the television. Xavier was headed to the escape route when he heard the battering ram hit the door. Downstairs, he couldn't hear anything else accept Hustle and Gameboy screaming like girls while the cops barked orders.

He was playing it too close. There was a window in the back room; an abandoned car sat underneath. Xavier had raised the window and carefully placed his butt on the ledge, his feet dangling in the night air. Xavier hadn't seriously taken into account how dangerous this thing could get. As he sat, it dawned on him how stupid he was for putting himself in this perilous predicament.

"Don't do it!" said an officer from somewhere inside the room.

Without hesitation Xavier pushed off and was airborne. Wind was the only sound he heard on the way down. The hood of a crumbling '91 Ford Thunderbird took the brunt of the impact as Xavier buckled and rolled off the car onto the cement. Even though he got up gimpy and grabbing his right knee, Xavier bolted. Dude barely had enough time to get over a few fences and stagger off into the darkness.

27

XAVIER

MONDAY, NOVEMBER 23
11:32 A.M.

As he sat at his desk in English class, Xavier's knee was killing him.

Dude kept on having nightmares last night. Every last one was about him jumping out of a window, but instead of surviving the fall, this time he wasn't so lucky. Xavier continued to divide his attention between Chase and the door. Homeboy was nervous and highly paranoid, not knowing if five-o had a make on his mug. It hadn't crossed his mind that the two boys might snitch on him. It would be his word against theirs, though. He tried to put it out of his mind.

Xavier couldn't concentrate on anything his teacher was saying. Kept on staring at the door and thinking that the same police that had nabbed Hustle and Gameboy yesterday could eventually come for him by using the same tactic. At any minute, Xavier expected Mr. Chase's closed classroom door to be blasted off its hinges and po-po to enter, swarming, and dragging his carcass out in handcuffs. It would be like his plan had come back to bite him in the butt. Although he understood his purpose for being at the spot, the police would probably think it was a complete crock. Nobody operating with a sane mind would enter a drug den that pumped prescription pills into a dying neighborhood to shadow his friend. Keep an eye on him.

Samantha crossed his mind, but as quickly as she appeared, he pushed away the thought. Xavier was far too busy with anxiety to even go there.

Chase walked over to retrieve worksheets on "proper research techniques" from his desk and was back in front of the class, handing them out.

"Today is the deadline on declaring a topic," Chase said as he passed a stack of worksheets out to the first person in the third row. "Pass those back, Mr. Harvey."

"X," Dex said, sitting at the next desk. "Psst, X."

"What, homeboy?" Xavier answered in a whisper.

"Linus Flip been around the school looking for you—attitude and everything. What's up with 'im? We gonna have to go upside his head or what?"

Xavier was straight tripping now. Nobody knew anything about Xavier's phone call to the police . . . or did they?

Mr. Chase was finishing up with the last row. "Dexter Baxter, maybe you should make sure that your topic will hold your attention so that it will hold mine. Perhaps you may like to share your thoughts with the class on how to write the perfect research paper."

Dexter waved Mr. Chase off. "Nah, I think I'll keep those techniques to myself. I'm a pretty stingy guy."

Mr. Chase smiled. "Remember, young people, this paper will count for seventy-five percent of your grade. Do not wait until the last week to start working on this project because the quality will tell off on you."

Damn, Xavier thought. He'd been so busy with Flip's welfare that he'd seriously forgotten to choose a topic for the research paper. This was jacked up. He had to come up with something and quick.

"Mr. Hunter, I would like to see you after class," the teacher said to Xavier. "And for the rest of you, I will be collecting your topics as you head out the door."

There was a lot on Xavier's plate. He wanted to score high on the research paper, go out with a bang. He had to pass Mr. Chase's class. That was a must, period. He'd come too far to let it all slip away because of a crummy research paper. Bullet wound in the shoulder. People had been trying to put him in a body bag since the tenth grade but he was still standing. Dude had gone through hell to get to this point. Not walking across the stage to receive his diploma wasn't even an option. A winning essay would be sweet icing on the cake, though—money, a publishing contract, he couldn't ask for anything better.

Xavier was walking down the hall on the third floor when he came across a huge billboard advertising the Christmas Eve dance program. The piece was a stand-alone in a corner not too far from the girls' lavatory. He knew that there had to be some hatin' going on between the girls in the play. Samantha's gorgeous face stood out and was the only one visible on the poster. The rest were just bodies in the background. The happiness Xavier felt for his ex was genuine. Samantha had worked hard and deserved her dance solo. It definitely looked like his ex-girlfriend was well on her way to fulfilling her dream of becoming a superstar dance choreographer.

"Quit drooling, you bum," Dexter said, walking up behind Xavier. "Too bad. You've lost her forever. Since she doesn't want to be down with your team anymore, would you be mad if I took a run at her?"

Xavier playfully pushed Dexter. "I hate to bust your bubble, homeboy, but you're not even in her league."

Dexter retaliated. "If I recall, you weren't either. You were just a ghetto boy toy to make her rich daddy mad. I'm gonna keep it real with you. They have a name for cats like you: stalker. You stalked the digits out of her. Straight up intimidated the poor little rich girl into going out with you, monkey boy."

Students had started to thin out in the hallway. The two boys had just enough time to get to the lunchroom before the tardy bell rang. They laughed and joked on the way down. Xavier couldn't do anything but smile when he saw Dakota working the far end of the hallway, still handing out flyers to remind everyone that bullying wouldn't be tolerated and had no place in society.

Xavier and Dexter stepped into the lunchroom. An angry Linus Flip didn't waste any time confronting him.

Flip said in a chin-checking type of tone, "Yo, what

happened, dog? Kids telling me you broke and ran without telling them what was going down—left 'em hangin'."

Xavier stepped right in his grill. "Whoa. Check yourself, homeboy, and watch your tone when you talk to me."

Dexter was about to go in on Flip but Xavier waved him silent.

The lunchroom was crowded and noisy. But due to the fact that punches weren't thrown, nobody was really paying any attention.

Linus looked away, as if to taper his anger. "You were supposed to be watchin' their backs. Nothin' like that should've happened. Hustle and Gameboy got knocked. Now I have to find a way to raise some loot to hire an attorney. Instead of getting ahead I've gotten farther in the hole."

The old Xavier would've been straight ripping on dude. Probably would've smacked him twice by now. He'd grown up a lot since then, though, a long way from those old push-yo'-wig-back days.

Xavier said to Linus, "Your boys got popped because they weren't about business. I saw the hook coming, ran downstairs to tell them, but they had that doggone Xbox game up so loud that they couldn't hear. It was too late then. The police knocked down the door and was on us so fast that my only reaction was to run. I ended up jumping out of a second-story window to get away." Xavier didn't feel right deceiving his friend. But it was a necessary evil.

Flip looked like he wanted to cry. "Man, y'all done jacked my stuff up." He wiped the perspiration from his brow. "I needed that bread, fam. Like yesterday. Got bills to pay."

Somehow Xavier wouldn't let himself feel Flip's pain. The way he saw it was that Linus should've been in jail anyway for even running a joint that dealt death. Linus was his homeboy, though. And if it hadn't been for Flip's courage a year ago, Xavier would've been killed. As far as he was concerned Linus was his hero and Xavier would do whatever to keep the boy safe, even if it was from himself.

Linus continued to look distraught. "I can't believe you fools messed this up for me."

Dexter wanted to know, "Do you trust those two knuckleheads not to snitch on you?"

Flip looked at Dex like he didn't have any street sense. "Those two aren't snitches. They're solid. I can vouch for them."

Just hearing *snitch* didn't sit well in Xavier's stomach.

"Needed that money bad, though," Flip whined, "don't know what to do now." He looked like at any minute the tears would start falling. "I'm outta here. Don't know when I'll be back."

Dexter was curious. "What you mean by that, homeboy?"

Linus Flip looked Dexter off. "School is not important for me right now. I gotta get on my dirty."

Xavier and Dexter watched Linus walk away still mumbling to himself.

Dexter was blunt. "Yo, homeboy, what was that about?"

Xavier continued to watch Flip. "A long story, my dude. Flip's overreacting, as usual. Probably been drinking—who knows. But it's all good. Let's go get some lunch."

28

SAMANTHA

THURSDAY, DECEMBER 24
9:35 P.M.

"**Y**oung people," the teacher said, addressing her dance troupe. "Give yourselves a big round of applause. You guys were superb and I'm so proud of each and every one of you."

Everybody within the sound of her voice let off with a rousing ovation.

The dance program "Snowflakes in Wonderland" had been a tremendous success. It had been standing room only in the school auditorium. All the girls had done a tremendous job, but Samantha's dance solo had been flawless and received a standing ovation. The Juilliard rep had shown as promised. Samantha just figured that since the school hadn't given her the okay yet, that, maybe the school was still trying to come to a decision. Whatever.

She'd put the thought out of her mind and had offered a wonderful performance.

Backstage was chaotic. People were everywhere. Parents stood with their little children for photo ops with the dancers. Some of the dancers were standing around in groups, showing off their flowers, laughing, and joking about their performances. There was even a news reporter out covering the event.

Samantha was standing around her parents, one arm filled with two dozen freshly cut long-stem red roses.

Jennifer's folks were with her. They'd brought her roses and were singing her praises.

Sean Desmond stood in the shadows with his goons so as not to draw attention and upstage the dance troupe. If the newshounds found out that the superstar Detroit Tigers rookie was on scene, they'd try to track him down to get a story. Tracy was close by Sean's side, with her jaws tight and hating every moment of Samantha's shine.

"You guys put on a great show," Mr. Fox said to his daughter. "Baby, your dance solo was sensational."

Mrs. Fox was soaking it up, tears in her eyes. "Samantha, your mother is so proud of you." She hugged her. "My little girl has grown up to be a beautiful, talented young woman. God has lined up great things for you. Continue to make us proud, my child."

Samantha hugged her mother and they were both in tears. "You are the best mother in the world and I'm so happy that God placed me with you guys."

Mr. Fox looked like he was a little jealous. "Can an old man get some love too? I mean, I think I had a little something to do with you being here, young lady."

Jennifer walked over. "Samantha, we have to go out and celebrate."

Mrs. Fox said, "Oh yes, we've already made reservations at Samantha's favorite restaurant—my treat."

Sean Desmond slithered over. "I think Samantha and I would like to be alone. I have a helicopter set up to take us to dinner."

His statement totally caught everybody by surprise. The look on her mother's face was priceless.

Mr. Fox was a little caught off guard by Sean's boldness. He was slow to say, "Yes, of course. You young folks have some celebrating to do."

Samantha wanted badly to tell her father that Sean wasn't the nice guy he was trying to portray. The boy was crazy and had made multiple threats against her parents if she didn't go along with his insanity. She was horrified. Samantha didn't know what he was capable of. She was totally alone. Going to the police would all but seal her parents' fate. Plus, Sean was escalating. Whenever they were together, he kept trying to kiss her or touch her, but she wasn't having any of that. So far, she'd managed to fight off his advances. Samantha believed that the only reason Sean hadn't tried anything more was because of loose women like her friend Tracy McIntyre. But he wanted Samantha. His desire chilled her to the bone. The look in his eyes told her that he was running out of patience. She had to do something to end his reign of terror.

Samantha's mother spoke up. "Baby, are you all right with a helicopter ride?"

Samantha didn't even look at Sean. She would've burst

into tears. "Yes, Mother. I'm all right with it. Always wanted to take a ride in a helicopter."

Mrs. Fox had this look on her face like she didn't believe it for one minute.

Samantha walked off with Sean before her mother had a chance to say anything else.

Jennifer said to Samantha's fleeting back, "Don't forget to call me in the morning, girl."

Samantha had a bad feeling in her gut about tonight.

Where was her Xavier?

29

XAVIER

THURSDAY, DECEMBER 24
11:00 P.M.

Despite it being Christmas Eve, Xavier was in his bedroom jotting down a few major points for his essay. Three days spent at the spot had yielded some fascinating findings. There were three young men with individual reasons for risking their freedom to deal illegal prescription pain meds out of a dilapidated colonial. Contrary to mainstream America's narrow, stereotypical view about young black dope dealers, they were human beings who chose the black trade to fill some need in their lives. Dark was the first subject. The boy had expressed to Xavier his desire to finish high school and make something of himself. But that was his dream. His nightmarish decision to risk his life had been driven by the sheer will to step up in the place of his drug-addicted mother and take care of his siblings. This dude exhibited strong leadership potential. Not the type to fall in and follow the crowd. He knew his worth, so therefore he didn't have to use violence to get his respect. But him—Xavier had plans to help. Matter of fact, he'd already spoken with his father about trying to get Dark into the factory. In three months Noah's job would be handing its employees referrals. He had already pulled Dark's coattail about the hook-up. Now, Xavier wasn't condoning the way that Dark made his paper. The homeboy had to do what he had to do. But Xavier just told him to make sure to keep his nose clean until the factory called him in to start testing.

Gameboy was the second subject. The young roller merely fell under the "product of environment" label. When Xavier looked at the boy, he didn't see any strength. No leadership skills. This type of guy was clearly a follower. He looked to be validated by his peers and would go to the extremes to achieve it, even if he had to commit murder. The evil nature of the business was always able to find that "beast" gene and encourage it, turning the most docile hustler into a monster.

The dude Hustle was the third case study. Not much research was required to slap a label on this idiot. The boy was the King Kong of morons and thought that the world should throw major paper at his feet only because he existed. He would do anything to become a rock star in the game. Like step on toes. The kind of cat that would manipulate others into doing dirt for him. Give money to hitters to eliminate the competition. This one was the worst of the worst, an authentic scumbag.

Xavier stood from his desk to stretch his legs. He had wanted to go to the Christmas Eve program to support Samantha. But the essay came first. It was time for him to get on with his life and stop living in the past. The girl had a gorgeous future in front of her. His was somewhat cloudy. The essay paper, though—with a winning paper Xavier could write his own ticket. Book deal. Money for college. There was no more looking in the rearview. The time was now.

The front door opened and Xavier almost went sick at his stomach. Roxanne was singing "Jingle Bells" out of key. She was snort-laughing, slurring, making up her own words, and doing a first-class job of butchering the song.

That eggnog must be killing brain cells, Xavier thought. Earlier she'd sweet-talked Noah into taking her to their plant's Christmas Eve union party, and Xavier bet that Ms. Church Lady was smashed.

"Xavier and Alfonso," Noah called out to them. "Y'all come here for a minute."

He and Roxanne in the same room—this just wasn't going to be good. Alfonso beat him to the front room.

Roxanne's dumb butt had a Santa hat perched atop a blowout Afro and wore what appeared to be a mink jacket with an un-church-lady-like formfitting dress. The dumb bunny had her nerve to be carrying a white sack.

"Ho, ho, ho," Roxanne said, trying to sound like Santa. She was even going so far as trying to use her hands to shake an imaginary Santa Claus belly. "Alfonso, have you been naughty or nice?"

While Alfonso was playing along, Xavier looked at Noah. The old dude's face pleaded with Xavier to humor her.

"You've been good, little boy," she said to Alfonso. Santa-Roxanne went into her white sack and pulled out a medium box wrapped in pretty Christmas paper with a bow on top. "Here you go."

Alfonso snatched the box with kid-like joy and plopped down on the sofa. When he ripped into the wrapping, his eyes and smile looked cartoonish.

"Look, big brother, a brand-new PlayStation!" Alfonso exclaimed, almost unable to contain himself. "Thanks, Santa!"

Noah said to Alfonso, "I deserve some credit too."

Alfonso ran and hugged his father. "Thanks, Dad."

Xavier was growing tired of this foolishness. He yawned out of sarcasm.

Roxanne turned to him. "Santa doesn't need to ask you if you've been naughty or nice, because he knows, just by the bullet hole and your shoulder that you've been a very naughty boy. Oh, but Santa has a gift for even the naughty little boys and girls."

Noah just stood there, hoping that she wouldn't take this thing any further. He was about to say something when she pulled out a small box wrapped in cute paper decorated with snowy Christmas trees. She handed it to Xavier.

He looked at the tiny gift like it had turned into a snake in her hand. The tension was thick and Xavier was wondering if he should take it or not. He only did out of respect for his father. Slowly, carefully, he tore the paper. It was a plain-looking white box. Xavier stole a quick glance at his father before lifting the top. A yellow card the exact same size as a Community Chest card from a Monopoly game lay facedown on a small bed of cotton. Xavier bit his lip out of anger when he plucked the thing from the box and turned it face up.

Roxanne snorted out a laugh. "Merry Christmas! There you go, a Get Out of Jail Free card, gangster. God knows you're going to need it for your future criminal endeavors."

Xavier held up the card and said to Noah, "You gonna let her play me like this?"

Noah's response was weak. "Are you judgin' my son? Remember: Judge not, lest ye be judged."

Roxanne said, "You know the boy ain't gonna be no good."

Xavier's anger grew as he stood there and watched Noah cower before this woman. He wanted to just grab her by her skinny chicken neck and shake her up. But he walked away before he could act on his anger. Dude went into his room and got dressed. He needed to get far away, and catching the bus wasn't going to do it. If he stayed in the house with Roxanne Hudson for another minute, the troll would end up in the hospital and Xavier would wind up sharing a cozy Wayne County jail cell.

He was filled with pure anxiety and grabbed the car keys off the dresser. Xavier hadn't driven since the night he'd been shot. Just the idea of getting behind the wheel filled him with dread. But if he stayed at the crib, he was sure to make tomorrow's headlines.

Xavier moved through the house, heading for the front door.

"Son, where are you going?" Noah asked, grabbing for Xavier's left shoulder. "Can we talk this out?"

Roxanne said, "Let him go."

Noah told her, "Stay out of this."

Alfonso said to Xavier, "Big brother, don't go."

Xavier turned on Noah, flashing the Get Out of Jail Free card. "I don't mind her because she's ignorant. You're supposed to be my dad. Can't you see that she's trying to come between me and you? And you're letting her."

"Son," Noah said, but it was too late.

Xavier was out the door.

30

SAMANTHA

CHRISTMAS MORNING
1:33 A.M.

"You were great dancing out there on the stage, baby girl," Sean Desmond said to Samantha as the two sat in his Rolls-Royce Phantom Drophead coupe. The boy was totally fried, his breath dangerously crossing the line by smelling like dog doodie and liquor. "All I could think about when I saw you out there on that stage moving your body was that I wanted you. We've been dating for a long time, how's about we take it up to the next level."

Samantha thought Sean was delusional if he thought that forcing her into being at his side by threatening her parents was the same as dating. But she was all by herself with him and didn't want to give him any reason to go maniac on her.

Against Samantha's many pleas not to drive while intoxicated, a drunken Sean had ignored her and drove to Belle Isle State Park after the helicopter ride and dinner. They were parked on a secluded road, surrounded by woodland areas—no lamppost on this stretch. Other than the car's interior lighting, it was totally dark. Bone-chilling winds were blowing hard and whipping, whispering like the restless spirits of lost souls. The frozen tree branches clanked together, sounding more like the bones of dancing skeletons.

Samantha was having trouble sitting still. The whole vibe wasn't right and she knew that being alone with a liquored-up Sean could lead to absolute terror. She wanted to call her father and tell him to come get her. But there was no telling what the consequences of her action would be. The death of one, if not both parents, would surely leave her wearing a straitjacket and bouncing off a padded cell in a mental ward at a state hospital. And she wouldn't risk their lives. So she continued to remain calm and play along. Her nerves were riding high in her throat. Sean trying to do something she didn't want was looking like a real possibility. He was so drunk that his head was clumsily flipping from one side to the other. His eyes were bloodshot and highlighted by pure evil. Samantha couldn't look at them, which is why she kept looking for an escape route.

"What's the matter?" Sean reached into the center console and pulled out a few peppermints and a small bottle of eye drops. "Cat got your tongue?" He pulled down his visor and flicked up the cover of the vanity mirror. Those lights instantly activated. Sean dropped the liquid into both eyes and blinked rapidly. He then unwrapped and chewed the mints.

Samantha was trying anything to keep his mind busy. "So where are your two henchmen?"

He crunched the candy. "Gave them the night off. I'm chillin' with my snuggle bunny and don't need any distractions"—he gave Samantha a mischievous look—"if you know what I mean."

That was it. It was time for Samantha to go. "I don't feel comfortable and I'm ready to go home, please," she said to him and carefully watched his reaction.

He got physical with her by grabbing her left shoulder. "You are going to give me what I want tonight!" he shouted, teeth gritted. He shook her. "Stop acting like you're not with it and give it to me."

"Sean, stop!" Samantha screamed, trying to pull away, but he was just too strong. The girl was in a no-win situation. Judging by this dude's muscular shoulders and well-chiseled chest, he could bench press two Smart cars. So he wouldn't have a problem with physically overpowering her if a scuffle broke out. She had to think fast.

With his right hand he was ripping at the neck of her sweater.

"Sean, how are you going to do this?" she said, struggling with him. "We've been friends since we were kids."

Sean's face was contorted with a selfish resolve. The boy wasn't trying to hear nothing. She had to outsmart him. There was no matching his strength. Samantha yelled out, "How can I do anything with you and you been doing it to my friend, Tracy?"

It wasn't her best, but the ruse caused him to release her. Long enough for Samantha to grab her coat and slip out the car door. Her heart was pounding as the wind wrapped her up in its freezing tentacles. She struggled to run while trying to put on her jacket.

"Get back in this car!" Sean roared. He quickly started the engine of the four-hundred-thousand-dollar chariot.

The headlights brightened the scene and picked up Samantha, running down the street and fighting to get her left arm into the sleeve. She hadn't gotten too far when he put the car in drive and slowly started after her, almost like he was stalking her, similar to a lion playing with its food before going for the kill. Sean caught up with her and lightly tapped her legs with the bumper, not to hurt her, but just enough to knock her off balance and send her to the pavement.

Samantha was down but she wouldn't stay that way. Adrenaline was pumping and she was determined that her life wouldn't end like this. She could hear the car door open and it terrified her. Sean had lost his mind and there was no telling what he had planned. He was a professional baseball player known for his brilliant speed. There was no way she was going to beat him in a footrace. Her only chance—she gulped—was to go off the road and take to the woods. Everything outside of the headlights was cloaked in spooky darkness. This was the only way. So Samantha got up and staggered off into the night. She felt along the cold trunks of trees to keep from running into them. How could she have come to this? A couple hours ago she'd been somewhere warm, a place where her phenomenal dancing skills had earned her a standing ovation. Now here she was, running through a wooded area like a screaming white girl in a horror movie trying to get away from some chainsaw-wielding serial killer wearing a hockey mask.

It was so dark out. Samantha had to resist the urge to grab her cell phone and hit the flashlight app to see. But the light would give away her location. As she moved along the frozen leaf litter, touching and feeling, she could hear Sean Desmond somewhere behind her, cussing and screaming for her to come out.

Seconds later, she heard him yell, "I was just playing around with you. Come on back so I can take you home."

She wasn't buying it, though. She kept on moving with no idea where she was headed. It was freezing out. But once she arrived in a safe area, Samantha would call for help.

31

XAVIER

CHRISTMAS MORNING
1:55 A.M.

Though it hadn't come easy, Xavier couldn't believe he was driving again. His stomach was in knots, palms dripped with perspiration, and he frequently checked the rearview and side mirrors to see if he was being tailed, sometimes getting confused and not knowing if he was driving fast enough or slow enough in certain areas. A couple of times he almost pulled over to throw up. He flinched at traffic lights whenever a motorist pulled alongside his new car. Xavier had almost given in to anxiety and parallel parked on the street. The boy had become so overwhelmed by emotion that he was going to get out of the car and start walking.

As he drove through the night in silence, the dude was straight-up steaming. Couldn't believe that his father, a

former dope-game legend, an OG who had spent a decent piece of his life in lockup, didn't have the marbles to stand up to his trout-mouth girlfriend. The disappointment Xavier was experiencing was beyond any that he'd ever felt. After all, he'd been waiting for a long time to have a decent relationship with his father—a long time! And here Roxanne was looking to tear it down overnight. Noah had been living his life by the Bible since he was released from prison.

Shame on him if he can't recognize the serpent slithering in the garden, Xavier thought. Roxanne was a parasite that was looking to get him kicked out of the crib and then move in with her offspring and nest. Alfonso was still an impressionable kid who could be molded and shaped. The boy wouldn't cause any trouble. Would fit into her world perfectly. Roxanne was a total trip. She wasn't slick as she thought. The bimbo had had babies by two trifling men that had never laid eyes on them. The chick wanted a daddy for her boys, plain and simple. And her fake butt didn't want Xavier gumming up the works.

It was Christmas morning and it seemed that drama was the only gift he'd received so far. He still couldn't believe that the lady had gone through all the trouble of wrapping up a "get out of jail free" card to give to him. What respectable grown person would stoop so low as to do something like that? Xavier had to admit that if his mother Ne Ne was out of prison, he'd have turned her loose on Roxanne. Let his old girl go straight Roughneck Santa with brass knuckles on Ms. Hudson and ring the heffa's jingle bells.

He was mentally spent, tired from everything he'd gone through. Didn't know if he had enough to get through to the graduation ceremony. Felt like just walking away from everything and everyone and disappearing for good.

To add matters worse, Xavier's shoulder started stiffening, and pain shot through it. He winced and tried to rub the agony away. Because he hadn't been behind the wheel since the shooting, there hadn't been any way to test the shoulder to see how much it would tolerate the steering wheel. The surgeon had told him that he would more than likely have trouble the rest of his life. But he'd taken that bit of information like a champ, because, after all, anything beat being dead. The good Lord had spared his life, and he was grateful.

With a full tank of gas Xavier had planned to drive as long as he could. Going back to the crib wouldn't be an option. Nobody would have a Merry Christmas if he went back. And that sucked. Before Roxanne's stupidity he'd had a nice little writing flow, too. He couldn't believe that he was out at this time of morning when he should've been home working hard on his essay. Two papers were due in the span of three months, and they both had to be stellar. The pressure was on and there was absolutely no turning back.

Suddenly, something caught his attention in the rearview mirror.

Nah, Xavier thought. *Can't be.* A damn yellow cab was about ten car lengths behind him. Was it his paranoia, or did it seem like lately, yellow cabs were following him? His nerves were on edge. There had been one attempt on his life and he was praying to God that there wouldn't be another.

Xavier's cell phone started ringing. He didn't recognize the number. Never one to shy away from the unknown, he picked up and got the shock of his life.

32

SAMANTHA

CHRISTMAS MORNING
2:20 A.M.

Samantha was cold and scared. The temperature seemed to be dropping and her body was feeling it. Her fingers and toes were tingling. Her teeth were chattering. Acknowledging that she couldn't do anything on her own, Samantha looked up at the dark, starless sky and thanked God for directing her out of that woodland maze. Ten minutes ago she'd emerged somewhere by the zoo. She'd walked over by the aquarium until she could no longer continue and sat down on the edge of a very large fountain. Samantha was completely exhausted. The fear she felt only added to the immense anxiety coursing through her body.

She'd called the one person she could truly trust. And if she had to make another, it wasn't going to happen.

The battery was dead. Besides, her fingers were so cold that she thought they'd burst behind any further movement. Tears wanted to fall as she waited for her ride to pull up, but she held tight. There were dozens upon dozens of people she could've called, but only one name fit the bill.

Samantha climbed into Xavier's car right away. They drove off and didn't waste any time leaving Belle Isle. This was the first time that she could sit and process everything. It was truly hard to believe that the boy she'd grown up with had tried to sexually assault her. The thought of her running through the woods for her life was enough to bring the tears. Samantha put both hands up to her face and cried her eyes out. The stress of everything that Sean Desmond had put her through was coming out. She knew Xavier wanted to ask questions but kept quiet. He knew her. Once she'd let it all out Samantha would be ready to talk.

"I guess you want to know what I was doing at Belle Isle this time of morning," Samantha said tearfully.

Xavier drove up Jefferson Avenue in light traffic with his eyes darting, constantly monitoring the rearview and side mirrors. "Sam, that's your business. You don't have to—"

Samantha threw up a hand. "Please, Xavier, let me talk."

Xavier made a left turn onto the service drive. He then rode the ramp onto I-75 north.

Samantha didn't know if she was in denial. She kept telling herself that it didn't happen. That that monster named Sean Desmond had been a nightmare. She tried to explain, but the painful episode was hard to put into words. As if telling the boy would be a surefire admission of weakness. A few more tears dropped and she wiped them away with the back of her sleeve.

"Sean . . ." she tried to say but broke down into more tears.

The anger on Xavier's face was visible.

Samantha composed herself. "I think he was going to try to rape me."

"Sam, did you call the police and report him?"

"No," she said, almost whispering. "After I got away, you were the first person I called."

"So because you don't wanna rock your daddy's businesses with a scandal, you're gonna let this bum get away?"

"Xavier, please. Do you know how big this scandal will be if I report this? Especially with Sean being who he is. Media will be all over my home and pestering my daddy's business associates. It wouldn't take too long before they start pulling out."

After driving around for fifteen minutes Samantha's hands and toes had warmed up. Her parents had to be going nuts right now. They'd called her twice before her phone had died. And now every phone call would go straight to voice mail. She was way past curfew, and knowing her parents like she did, they'd probably filed a missing persons report by now.

Xavier took 75 to Davison East. He checked the rearview, activated his right turn signal, and took the Woodward exit.

Xavier said, "Sam, you want me to go and whup up on his head?"

Samantha turned to Xavier with a worried look. "He threatened to hurt my parents if I said something to anybody."

"Well, you ain't gotta worry about that anymore, Sam. I got you, you feel me? Nobody's gonna get after you on my watch."

This was the first time Samantha looked into Xavier's face since she'd gotten into the car. He didn't have that usual fire burning inside. It led her to ask, "Xavier, are you all right?"

"Nothing I can't handle, Sam." He let out a deep sigh. "For now, we gotta get this ninja off your back." Xavier headed north on Woodward.

"I'm scared," Samantha admitted. "For my parents."

"Don't worry about nothing, Sam. I'm here, you feel me? We'll work this thing out. Trust me."

In spite of the circumstances, Samantha found herself smiling. She thought she'd never hear Xavier's "you feel me?" catchphrase again. She looked at the street. "Where are we going?"

"Sam, I'm taking you home. Your folks have to be worried to death."

She looked out the window as they passed through Detroit, watching crumbling, dilapidated, spray-paint-covered buildings turn into sparkling, well-kept ones the farther they traveled outside of the city.

"How are you going to explain getting home"—he nodded to the dashboard clock—"at 2:55 to your parents?"

"I'll think of something."

Samantha had missed her intelligent roughneck. Loved

how he took control of the situation and made her feel safe.

"Aren't you going to say I told you so?" Samantha asked.

"No, because Lord knows I've made my fair share of bad decisions over the last three years. None of us are perfect, Sam."

Samantha was happy that Xavier was back in her life, but worried about him at the same time. The boy looked totally exhausted. His eyes were small and red. He had a slouching posture of somebody that needed serious rest. And on top of it all, he kept his eyes glued to the rearview mirror, as if he expected to be ambushed from behind. Samantha felt bad that she was dropping her drama on him. Something clearly was going on inside his head. But she was optimistic. Samantha knew that by working together, they would both find a way out of their individual hells.

33

XAVIER

SATURDAY, DECEMBER 26
4:37 P.M.

Samantha was over at Xavier's crib. They'd been in the basement for a couple hours. She'd lied to her parents about what had happened Christmas morning. Told them that she and Sean had had a disagreement and lost track of time trying to work it out.

"Have you heard from him?" Xavier asked Samantha.

"Not since the other night," said Samantha. "He's been kind of quiet."

"Samantha, tell me everything that happened."

Tears tried to drop a few times as Samantha sat on a couch next to Xavier to recount her painful experience. After she'd explained everything about what had taken place—not even leaving out the part about him hitting her with the car—Xavier vowed not to rest until that baseball-playing punk had been dealt with. Xavier's temper was on bump and he was trying everything within his power to restrain himself from getting after Sean and taking it there. Thank God Roxanne and his father had taken Alfonso and her kids to the movies. There was no way he could've dealt with her garbage right now. He had his hands full with Samantha's situation.

They were leaning over Samantha's iPhone on the coffee table.

Xavier said to her, "Now here's what you're going to say to him."

The next five minutes saw him coaching her on how to handle the phone call she was about to make.

"What if this doesn't work?" Samantha asked, in a voice that shook with nervousness.

Xavier gave her a reassuring glance. "Trust me, Sam. This dude has everything to lose. Stick to the script and you'll be fine, you feel me?"

Samantha took a deep breath and dialed Sean's cell phone number. She put the call on speaker after it started to ring. The phone rang about five times before transferring to voice mail.

She hunched her shoulders. "It's funny. There hasn't been a day gone by that he hasn't answered a call from me. Maybe he thinks I went to the police and now he's hiding."

"Sam, not this guy. He thinks he owns the universe. Hit 'im again."

Samantha was about to place the call, but Sean hit her right back.

"Where are you?" he asked angrily. Being on speaker

had Sean's voice sounding like he was ordering from a drive-through at a burger joint.

Samantha looked like she was about to shrivel under his voice, but Xavier held her hand for support. He nodded for her to be strong.

Samantha took a deep breath. "Never mind where I am. But I'll tell you how this thing is about to go down. If you come near me, my folks, or anybody I love, I swear I'll report what you tried to do to me to the police. My dad has friends in the media and they're just looking for scandal, especially one involving Detroit's little golden boy shortstop."

Sean laughed sinisterly. Like she was bluffing.

Samantha's fear turned to anger upon hearing his arrogance. "You're laughing but I'm not playing. I'll go to the police."

"Nah, you don't have to do that, baby girl. I'll fall back, but where'd you get the balls from all of a sudden— is it because you're back hanging around that ghetto trash? You have me on speaker, so his little weak self must be somewhere around."

Enough was enough. Xavier went off. "Check this here, homeboy," he said aggressively into the speaker. "You come back around Samantha again and you're gonna find out how a baseball feels when I go upside your head with a Louisville Slugger."

Sean said, "Ghetto trash, you saved Samantha from me, but who's going to save you?"

Xavier said, "Ninja, you threatening me?"

"Take it how you want it."

"Stay away from Samantha."

"Or what?"

Xavier snatched the phone up so fast that it startled Samantha. He held the thing with both of his hands, yelling, "Try me if you don't think it'll go down, playboy."

"Oh, please." Sean blew Xavier's threat off.

"Try me, homeboy. I ain't hard to find. You know where I be, you feel me?"

The phone call dropped.

Samantha asked Xavier, "What now?"

"We go to school, graduate, and go on to college— that's what now."

There were footsteps overhead.

"Xavier," Noah called down from the basement door. "Is everything all right down there, son?"

Xavier could hear Roxanne's irritating snort laugh. He didn't want to go upstairs to introduce Samantha to his dad because he knew that there would be a chance of him going ape on Roxanne. He took Samantha up anyway.

"Dad, this is Samantha, the girl I've talked so much about."

Noah shook Samantha's hand. "You are the young lady who has my son's nose open."

"Stop embarrassing me," Xavier said to his father, smiling.

Samantha said, "Nice to meet you, sir. You have a very nice home."

They were standing in the small kitchen getting acquainted when Roxanne barged in.

She popped her lips while looking Samantha up and down. "Pretty girl. Look here, honey, you look like you got a spot of sense. Step away from him before you get caught up in a drive-by."

Xavier said, "Fake Christian, why don't you go and learn how to be a lady. Female dogs have more class than you."

Roxanne went off. "You're a loser who's probably been voted around the school to be more likely to go to prison for life."

Noah stepped in. "That's it, both of you. Roxanne, don't you ever talk to my son like that."

Xavier was surprised by Noah putting his foot down.

Noah continued, "Xavier, you're not gonna talk to grown folks like that. And, Roxanne, where's your moral compass? You know better."

Roxanne had this stupid smile on her face. She called her sons. "Y'all get ready to go. This man has lost his mind talking to me like he's crazy."

Samantha stood in the far corner, shocked.

Roxanne headed toward the door with the boys in tow. She opened it and was hit by a cold breeze. "Noah, I'll be back over to get the things I left in your room."

Xavier watched to see if his old man would punk and cave in. Didn't have to wait too long. Noah took off behind her with his tail tucked firmly between his legs. Xavier could hear him at the front door begging her to come back in the house. His father was whipped. Xavier couldn't do anything but shake his head. It seemed like he couldn't catch a break with either parent's choice of mate. He'd been at odds with his mother's boyfriend Nate and now his father's knucklehead girlfriend. This junk was too much.

He turned to Samantha and said in a frustrated tone, "Welcome to my world."

34

DAKOTA

Dakota had just gotten out of the shower, rubbed on some raspberry body lotion, pulled on some boy shorts and an oversized T-shirt that read *Sometimes it sucks being an angel,* and was now in the bathroom mirror combing and wrapping her hair for bed.

She was proud of her brilliant work ethic. Back in November Dakota had launched a massive campaign at Coleman against bullying. Almost everybody in the school was applauding her efforts. The staff had done a wonderful job of promoting the message and encouraging those students who'd found themselves in the crosshairs of a bully to participate in the event. The program would be held Friday, March eighteenth. It would be an all-day affair and the theme for the occasion was, "Give Bullying a Black Eye."

Dakota had done the research and found out that 77 percent of students admitted to being the victim of one type of bullying or another. These numbers were unacceptable. They meant that goons out there similar to the SNLG girls were giving the business to victims like her. She could feel their pain. Remembering when she'd gained consciousness in the girls' lavatory only to find out that her tormentors had spray-painted her entire head blue, Dakota had vowed to pledge her life to this struggle to bring peace to those who wanted to exercise their right to an education without having to suffer humiliation or embarrassment. She didn't look at it as championing a cause. It was her duty to give a voice to the weak and suffering.

Of course there were always going to be those who stood in the way of progress. She'd been teased and talked about while doing most of the legwork around school herself, talking to students, getting feedback, passing out leaflets, and encouraging victims like her to stand up and be heard. Her activism wasn't just limited to Coleman High; she'd traveled to other Detroit schools and talked to principals and staff members about joining the cause and officially making March eighteenth a day that schools across the city would stand up against bullies.

Xavier had lit a fire underneath her that burned in the pit of her soul to make a difference. She loved him, but not in the normal way a girl would love a sexy, strong guy like him. He was her brother and mentor. Granted, she'd only known him for five months now, but how could you know a person like him and not feel inspired by his resolve to get things done? The boy's life was in constant danger but it never stopped his desire to graduate. Nobody had ever stood up for her like he'd done. Now it was her chance to help somebody else, the old adage of "paying it forward."

It was funny how the haters at school tried to discourage her from putting the event together. She expected those types of people at Coleman. That was a given. But having that type of negativity come from her mother was atrocious. Dakota could remember when she'd first gotten up enough nerve to confide in her mother. Told her everything about how she was bullied and tormented at school by the girl gangbangers. Instead of consoling her only child, she ridiculed her. Called today's kids sissies. Said they didn't make 'em like those in her day anymore. Explained that bullies didn't exist in her day because parents encouraged their children to solve matters with their fists on the playground and not return home until it was settled. The level of insensitivity shown by her ol' girl had brought tears to Dakota's eyes. But she had been careful in letting them drip only after she was out of her mother's sight. Showing any kind of weakness would've brought on her mother's wrath. And truthfully, she'd rather go head up with all of the SNLG girls instead of facing down her mother.

Speaking of her mother, Dakota was glad that the old bird was at work. It meant that she wouldn't have to be nagged. After she'd gotten home from school earlier,

Dakota had done her homework and spent the remain-
der of her time poring over encouraging letters from
well-wishers, tweaking the itinerary for the event, and
trying to hold in tears while reading letters from other
students who'd had the unsettling misfortunes of being
bullied. Her heart bled for each student. She was more
than hopeful that after everything was said and done,
those students would finally get some peace.

She finished up, slipped into her *Sesame Street* Bert and
Ernie slippers, and went about her nightly routine checking
every window and door in their bungalow. Dakota didn't
play when it came to her security. She was always left
alone and there was no telling what maniac was out there
watching. On the news every day there were young girls
her age snatched up by sexual predators and never heard
from again. The thought chilled her to the bone as she
punched in the four-digit code to set the house alarm.
Dakota listened to the mechanical voice count down
while walking back to her bedroom.

There was no night-light. She was a big girl, and big
girls weren't afraid of the dark. She turned out the light
and closed her bedroom door. Once Dakota was snuggled underneath the soft pink comforter she drifted off to
sleep.

At first she thought she was dreaming. *That's it,* she
told herself, slightly waking. The eerie scratchy sounds
were just a bad nightmare. She arrived at a better understanding once she was fully awake. Dakota hadn't been
dreaming at all. Those spooky noises were indeed ema-
nating from outside. Something was out there scratching

against the bricks on the other side of her bedroom wall. She would've been quick to blame it on tree branches— except there weren't any on the property. No bushes either. *Animals. That's what it is,* she thought. Had to be a cat, maybe a dog, rats, mice—anything but the paranormal garbage that was floating through her mind. To calm her soul, Dakota thought, *There are no such things as ghosts.*

Goose bumps hugged her flesh like spandex. Dakota wanted to look out the window but she was too frightened. She hadn't heard noises like these while they'd been living in the house. She pushed herself out of bed and to the window. When she peeked out of the horizontal blinds, the scratching stopped. She breathed a deep sigh of relief—her damn imagination. That joint was running wild. Dakota relaxed and laughed at herself. Between schoolwork and promoting the event, she'd been working too hard. Sometimes the imagination could be played and triggered by exhaustion.

When the doorbell rang, she damn near jumped to the ceiling and hung there by her claws, like a startled cat. It was ten thirty p.m., and nobody was supposed to be out there ringing the bell. But there was no way on God's green earth she was going to open the door. Dakota sat on the end of her bed, her nerves frayed. She didn't know if calling the police would help any. Just last week, a young boy who lived in a bungalow off the corner was shot, and it took the police a half hour to respond. So if five-o had dragged their feet on the shooting, then Dakota would be old and gray before they'd come out to investigate a prowler.

The doorbell mysteriously rang again, and again, and again, and again, and again until the *ding-dong* morphed inside her head into a haunting, bloodcurdling chorus of creepiness. And then just like it started, the noise suddenly stopped. The thought that it might be her mother in distress played on her conscience. Perhaps the old girl had gotten into a car accident and was delirious, suffering from a bad head trauma. And now that the ringing had stopped, that only meant one thing: She was probably lying on her back unconscious in front of the door.

Dakota mustered the courage to slowly open her bedroom door. Out in the hall, she took careful steps toward the front door. The truth was that she didn't know the danger existing on the other side. Could be her mother, but on the other hand, it could be some psycho-freaky nutcase killer. Just in case, Dakota opened the coat closet and pulled out a baseball bat. She held the thing down by her knees as she disarmed the house alarm. At the front window, she took her free hand and moved back the vertical blinds. The view overlooked the front porch. No porch light. And though it was dark out, she could see there was nobody standing at the front door.

Somebody stopped to terrorize the wrong house, she thought. *Then they figured out that they had made an error and left.* But something was out there. She looked closer. Dakota could see it, but what was it? To find out she would need to be brave and open up the front door. The cold chill inside her gut told her not to, but her inquisitive nature needed to know. With the bat slung over her right shoulder, she twisted the doorknob until it opened. This was a time she wished that the little neighborhood gangsta rats hadn't shot out the streetlights. Though the door was open, she couldn't see anything until she slowly cracked the screen door. There it was— down on the welcome mat.

Dakota slowly and cautiously stooped down to pick up a skinny glass vase that held two roses, some type of envelope affixed to it by a single piece of tape. She warily looked around before closing both the screen and heavy doors. Back inside, and under house lighting, Dakota's discovery made her flesh crawl. The flowers were roses, black ones. She'd seen in many mobster movies that the recipient of black roses always died behind a hail of bullets shortly after delivery. And if the flowers weren't enough of a warning, the card inside the envelope spelled it out. The cursive writing was bad, barely legible, but she could still make it out: *Stop the bully awareness event or die!*

Dakota's blood turned cold at the threat. Tears fell. It was all good, though. The threat probably would've worked before she'd met Xavier. His strength and courage and fearlessness were enough for her to push this aside and continue the course. Dr. Martin Luther King Jr. hadn't let threats deter him from having a dream and acting on it. It was because of him and those like him that minorities now had freedoms. Dakota wasn't comparing herself to the brilliant civil rights leader, but the goal was the same. She wasn't going to stop until all those being bullied were able to enjoy one thing: peace. Do or die— she would make a difference.

35

SAMANTHA

Samantha, Xavier, and Dexter were chilling at the food court inside Twelve Oaks Mall. The place was brightly lit, enormous, and housed a hundred and eighty retail stores. Over the holiday Xavier and Samantha had started spending time with each other. No boyfriend or girlfriend stuff, just friends who loved one another. And to Samantha it really felt good being around him. Felt good to laugh and joke with his crazy butt. For the first time in a long time she felt safe. Xavier's father was really nice too. Samantha seemed to fit right in with his family, with the exception of Roxanne Hudson. The chick was an amazing piece of insanity. She had Noah wrapped around her little finger.

Being at the mall, Xavier and Samantha were breaking

all of their rules. With the danger they faced, both had pinky sworn to limit their public activities. To stay indoors until their problems had been resolved. It was scary because she hadn't heard from Sean since that day in Xavier's basement when the two had gotten after each other over the phone. Sean was a maniac who got whatever he went after. The boy didn't give up that easily, and that's what was worrying her.

But the biggest problem was her doggone daddy. When his BFF had stopped showing, her father had become difficult, drilling her with question after question about Sean's whereabouts. The old man wouldn't let up. He was grilling her right now on the phone. She had to get up and walk away so that Dexter and Xavier wouldn't hear him trippin'.

"I can't believe you're going to let that boy slip away from you," Mr. Fox said.

Samantha was beyond frustrated with his line of questioning. "Daddy, when are you going to let me handle my own business? I'm seventeen, and I believe I'm old enough to make decisions for myself. I'm sure you think that Sean is a great guy, but he doesn't work for me."

Her father wouldn't give up. "Don't you want a man who can take care of you? Give you the world, like I have done? You are my little girl and I only want what's best."

Her dad would be kicking down Sean's door and trying to go upside his head if he knew what the creep had done to his "little girl." Samantha still couldn't bring herself to tell her father that his BFF was a complete fraud, a lunatic who wasn't fit to wear a Detroit Tigers uniform.

Samantha looked at the foot traffic in the mall. People

were coming and going, some carrying bags and others window-shopping. Dexter was going to town on some McDonald's grub. Xavier was too busy scanning the crowd to be focused on the Chinese food in front of him.

"All I'm saying, sweetheart," her father said sincerely, "is Sean Desmond is good for you."

"Daddy, please. You mean he's good for you."

"And what does that mean, young lady?"

"Skybox at Ford Field, courtside tickets to watch the Detroit Pistons play, need I go on."

"You know your daddy can buy his own skybox. Matter of fact, I get company tickets to see the Pistons play, but I give them to the rest of my partners. Sean is a cool guy and I like hanging out with my son-in-law."

No, he didn't just go there, she thought. "The son you always wanted?"

"I didn't mean it like that, pumpkin. Your daddy loves you and wants the best."

"You've already said that. Daddy, I have to go."

"If you're not with Sean, who is it that you seem in a rush to get back to?"

"Friends, Daddy."

"I don't like it, pumpkin. Don't mess anything up with Sean."

"Bye, Daddy." Samantha ended the call. She didn't know what she was going to do with him. Despite the immense pressure he was applying, Samantha had to continue playing the part. Not letting him in on the truth about Sean. Her father held resources. His prominent status around town had earned him friends in very high places. Sean Desmond wouldn't have a chance with him in a legal battle. What would be the endgame, though? Sean would surely retaliate with his goons, and they were twenty times deadlier than any business suit her father had on his team. Ozzie and Cash's courtroom was the street, and muscle like that would turn this thing real ugly.

Before she walked back over to the table, Samantha made sure to chase away any emotion in her face left over from the conversation.

"Sam," Xavier said, suspiciously scanning those seated around them and others walking past the food court. "You good?"

Samantha said to Xavier, "Just my dad. I'm fine."

Xavier relaxed and smiled. "Your dad? Shoot, no, you're not *fine*. That man will worry the shine off a bowling ball. What his tight-cheeks self want anyway?"

Samantha sat down and pursed her lips. "My father thinks he knows what's best for me."

Dexter said to Xavier with a mouthful of food, spitting all over the place, "Dude, you gonna finish that shrimp fried rice and boneless chicken?"

Xavier screwed up his face. "I was, homeboy, but your spit just took care of that," he said, pushing his food over to Dexter.

"Two Big Macs, a double cheeseburger, a ten-piece Mc-Nuggets, a supersized fries, and chocolate milkshake," said Samantha, "Dexter, you can't still be hungry?"

Xavier wiped his fingers with a napkin. "If I was his dad I'd rather clothe than feed him. I swear the boy has the appetite of an escaped circus gorilla."

"Whatever," said Dexter, packing his mouth with shrimp

fried rice, "y'all just haters. Some people just can't accept the fact that I'm a growing boy."

"You're growing something all right," said Xavier.

Samantha just sat there, smiling.

Dexter chased his food with a swallow of milkshake. "Homegirl, if you smile any harder, your lips gonna crack and bleed."

Xavier said, "Why are you smiling like that, Sam?"

Samantha giggled. "I miss you guys. The camaraderie we used to share. I'm glad y'all are back in my life."

"You trying to make my eyes leak, heffa," said Xavier. He leaned over and kissed Samantha on the jaw.

Dexter shoved a forkful of boneless chicken into his mouth, swallowed, and slurped some shake. "See, that's what you two miss—that nasty stuff right there. Don't nobody want to see that hideous display of infection—I mean affection, especially while I'm eating Chinese."

Xavier ignored Dexter. "You didn't tell your old man that you were hanging out with me, did you?"

"And give him high blood pressure, no. As far as he knows, I'm out with friends."

Dexter said to Samantha, "You're slick."

Samantha said, "I told the truth. I am out with friends."

Xavier added, "Call Mr. Tight Cheeks back and let him know who you're hanging out with and see if the medics don't be over there trying to revive him."

Dexter cracked up. " 'Mr. Tight Cheeks'—you're a fool, X."

"I know you're not talking, Xavier," Samantha said

sarcastically, "with all the drama that your stepmama is causing in your house. Aside from the fact that your mama Ne Ne tried to kidnap me, Roxanne makes her look like one of Jesus's disciples."

Everybody laughed.

Dexter said, "Xavier has been telling me about his new mama. Why don't y'all show her a crucifix and if she backs away, stake her ass through the heart."

"Punk, she's not my mama, frogboy," Xavier said. He looked at Samantha. "Sam, where is your driver, the big black Lurch," Xavier wanted to know.

"I told him that I was fine and that I didn't need him to come in."

"I'm surprised he went for it." Xavier looked at the two of them. "Y'all ready to go?"

They cleared off the table and left. It was time for Samantha to get her shop on.

36

XAVIER

SATURDAY, JANUARY 9
7:00 P.M.

The two boys walked behind Samantha, playfully talking junk to one another, as she nosed around in front of different store window displays.

"Anyway," said Dexter. "X, have you started the research for your paper yet?"

"You're late, homeboy. Started in December."

"What's your topic?"

The mall was crowded. People were everywhere, but Xavier made sure to keep his eyes on Samantha. That coward Sean Desmond had taken her through a terrifying ordeal. Cats like him didn't go away easily. Not when the worm's ego was involved.

Xavier said to Dexter, "I'm doing my research paper

on black comedians from the seventies and the eighties. What are you doing yours on?"

"MJ, fool."

"Which MJ?"

"There's only one," said Dexter with a goofy look on his face.

Xavier just shook his head and laughed. "Jackson or Jordan?"

"Jordan, of course. Ain't much into the other guy."

"What? Your head get rolled over by a car tire as a baby? Michael Jackson was the truth."

"Well, not in my world. I don't do Jackson, so there is only one MJ, and in my opinion Jordan is the one."

Xavier noticed that Samantha was getting too far ahead. He yelled to her, "Sam, not too far, knucklehead."

Samantha was too much of a lady to scream back. So she just pointed to bebe and mouthed to Xavier that she was going inside.

Xavier continued to survey the sea of faces.

Dexter said, "Dog, what's up with yo' situation?"

Xavier looked down at his right shoulder. "All I can say, homeboy, is that I'm gonna continue to go to school. Hopefully I live to graduate. But I can't stay in the crib and be scared. They can try to holler at me there."

"True, true," said Dexter, "you think they're gonna try again?"

Xavier had no idea if the creep who'd blasted him in the shoulder would come back for seconds. It didn't matter because Xavier wasn't ducking, nor was he hiding. He was a straight-up soldier and nobody walking on two legs struck fear in his heart.

"I'm more concerned about Sam."

Dexter asked, "What you mean?"

Xavier swore Dexter to secrecy. Told him everything that had gone down that night Samantha called him to pick her up.

"Straight up," said Dexter, unbelieving. "That busta needs his head whupped on for that."

"Yeah, but don't say anything. Sam's already been through enough."

"Come on, guy. Y'all family. What I look like telling the business to some ninja in the street."

They finally stepped up to bebe. Samantha was toward the back of the store with the phone up to her ear and looking through a rack of jeans. Foot Locker was right next door.

"X," Dexter said, pointing at Foot Locker, "they got those gray and red Jordan 13s joints."

"You got a raffle ticket?"

"Skip that. My homeboy works in there. We probably can get da hookup. Let's go in."

There was a look of concern on Xavier's face. "Did you just hear anything I said? I'm not leaving Sam alone."

"Man, all these people in this mall, nothing gonna happen to her. Besides, we'll be right next door," Dexter persisted.

Xavier hesitated. He thought about it and arrived at the conclusion that he was being overprotective. He gave Samantha one last look before they stepped next door.

The two teens had only been in Foot Locker fifteen minutes when Xavier heard a commotion out front. Voices were raised and one of them sounded like Samantha's. When Xavier finally made it out, his anger was instant. A small crowd had gathered, and Ozzie and that ninja Cash were up in Samantha's face like little women, talking junk. Samantha wasn't backing down, though. She had her finger damn near touching the bridge of Cash's nose, giving it right back to them.

"Trust me, we don't mean you no drama, mama. We're not following you or anything. Our meeting is straight up coincidental." Ozzie raised his Champs Sports shopping bags. "But the homeboy Sean Desmond did tell us if we ran into you to make sure that you were tight, and to see if you needed anything. But we can see that you're co-pacetic."

"Although you're not protected like we would protect you," Cash said with an evil smirk on his face.

Xavier walked over and pushed Samantha safely behind him. "What's the problem, homeboy?" he asked Ozzie, letting the scowl on his face serve as a warning.

Dexter stepped up like he was ready to scrap.

Ozzie said to Xavier, "You again? Dude, you just won't go away, will you? Didn't we serve you up at the skating rink? I knew Cash should've did you in front of the school that day."

"We can fix that right now," Cash said, dropping his Footaction bags. "I'm about to stick my sneaker so far up yo' butt I'ma give your tongue athlete's foot."

"You say you want to scrap, what you still talking crap for?" Dexter asked Cash, his fists down by his sides.

Cash tried to move on Dexter, but Xavier killed all that noise when he fired on ol' boy, catching the clown on the left temple with a vicious right jab. Cash dropped to the floor without offering a sound. After Ozzie saw his boy get done up, it looked like he was reaching into his jacket for something, but promptly withdrew the hand when security came running in their direction. Ozzie picked his homeboy up and they staggered away in the opposite direction.

Xavier and his crew weren't trying to stick around either. He grabbed Samantha and the three used the crowd to camouflage their getaway.

Back at the crib, Xavier went straight to his bedroom. Had some work to do inside. He'd found trying to multi-task two assignments was pretty troubling. The feeling that he'd bitten off more than he could chew came to mind a few times. That excuse could kick rocks. Xavier needed to put together a dope essay if he expected to collect the loot from the writing contest winnings. His knuckles were swollen and left him shaking his head. But the truth was as painful as his injured hand. God had given him a gift for helping people. He couldn't ignore it. Seemed like it was a blessing and a curse. Somehow helpless souls always found him, sought him out, and he protected them. Xavier often felt good about helping others, but trouble was never too far behind, sometimes putting him in the position where he was forced to defend himself. More than likely it had led to him getting blasted in the shoulder. Today was just one of those instances. Billy Hawkins also told him that he had a special gift for helping others. Xavier wasn't trying to be funny, but God could've kept the gift and given him a Corvette instead.

He sat down at his desk, trying to focus on his research. It was no use, though. Dude was still too pumped up on adrenaline. That little scuffle he'd had with Sean Desmond's goons a few hours ago was far from over. Cats like them never got over a butt whipping. They were the losers who always went home to get the gat and came back to prove their manhood by killing and causing tragedy. But if he had to smack up Cash again to protect Samantha, then it would go down.

Xavier made sure Dexter had gotten home safely. He didn't have to worry about Samantha because her driver was on the job. The guy was enormous, and anybody crazy enough to muscle up to his big butt needed to be put to sleep.

An hour later Xavier had settled down. He jumped on the Internet to research famous black comedians from the seventies and eighties. Pen in hand, Xavier was about to start taking notes when he heard the front door open and Noah called his name. He would've heard Roxanne by now if she was with him. Thank God.

Xavier walked into the living room, working his injured hand. His dad was taking off his coat. Xavier's swollen hand drew Noah's attention.

"What's wrong with your hand?" Noah asked.

Xavier was about to open his mouth but his father beat him to it.

"Don't tell me you've been fighting."

Xavier took a seat on the couch, slowly opening and closing the hand. "Yeah, it was a slight dustup."

Noah took his son's hand and examined it. "Pretty banged up. You mind telling me what happened?"

Over the next ten minutes Xavier explained his side of the story.

"The Detroit Tigers shortstop, Sean Desmond?" his old man asked again.

"Yup."

"If the story is true, don't you think she should be reporting this to the police?"

Xavier continued to work the hand. "Samantha's father is rich and he has a lot of business associates—"

"She's afraid that a scandal would hurt his business."

Xavier slowly said, "Bingo."

"Son, Samantha's a nice girl, but don't you think that's her problem?"

Xavier knew his dad wouldn't understand. "I just made it my problem."

"Jesus, Mary, and Joseph. Do I have to remind you that you were nearly killed four months ago? But the Lord saw fit for you to remain here."

Xavier shot straight from the hip. "Why can't the Lord tell you that your girlfriend is trying to come between us?"

Noah rubbed a hand across his beard. "You're being blasphemous. Stick to the subject."

"Pop, you're such a hypocrite. You throw Jesus at me and Alfonso whenever we mess up, but what about your girlfriend Roxanne? You allow her to get away with those little stupid cracks about me—matter of fact, you let her give me that Get Out of Jail Free card and didn't even say anything. What was up with that?"

Noah didn't quite know how to answer the question. "Xavier, I'm afraid you don't understand."

"Yeah, Pop, I think I do. But don't worry about it.

Alfonso and I are used to this type of treatment. Ne Ne put her boyfriend before us. Now you're doing the same thing—I can dig it. Same ol' game, just a different parent."

Noah ran a hand down the back of his neck. "Don't forget your place, son."

Xavier stood up, slowly working the hand. "I know my place, Dad. And if it's left up to your girlfriend it'll be outside of this house." He shook his head at his dad and walked back into his bedroom.

How somebody could have so much biblical knowledge and fail so miserably in recognizing the evil serpent that was slithering in the family garden with the intention to destroy it was beyond him. It didn't matter, though. There was once a time where his old man didn't exist. And mentally it wasn't a thing for Xavier to go back to that time.

37

XAVIER

Doug summoned Xavier to his office right before lunch. There was a surprise waiting for him. Dakota was there with tears in her eyes. She hugged Xavier as soon as he walked through the door.

"What's wrong, munchkin?" Xavier asked Dakota.

Doug was sitting at his desk. There was a vase with two black roses sitting in front of him. "Looks like somebody's trying to frighten her into calling off the event," Doug said, handing Xavier an envelope with some type of Hallmark card inside.

Xavier read the card.

Dakota said, through tears, "Nobody's going to stop me from doing what I have to do. I just wanted somebody to know what's going on." She shivered. "You know . . . if something was to happen."

Xavier handed the card back to Doug. "Don't worry about that, munchkin. You gonna be just fine."

Doug took the card and chucked it on his desk. He had this "I'm too old for this crap" look on his face. He took his ball cap off and ran a hand over his head. "Listen, Mr. Hunter, I know you don't have any faith—and I know this from the mess you got into trying to protect students a couple years ago—in my security team. I don't have to but I brought you here to let you know of this threat. Don't need you running around the school playing detective. I got this. The principal has been alerted, a few of my cop buddies will keep an eye on her house, and I've launched a full investigation into the matter."

Xavier grinned. "Trust me, Doug. I have far too much going on. This time I'm leaving it to the professionals."

Doug looked at Dakota. "Young lady, don't worry. We will get to the bottom of this. My hat is off to you. You have schools across the city trying to copy your anti-bullying campaign. You should be proud of yourself. Don't let anybody scare you away from helping others."

Xavier said to Dakota, "From now on I will be picking you up and taking you home from school." Xavier looked at Doug and then back to Dakota. "We're all in this thing with you."

Tears—Dakota couldn't stop them. "Thank you, Mr. Banks. I really appreciate the support. I'm putting all I have into my efforts at ridding schools of bullying."

"That's right, Ms. Taylor," said Doug, "nobody likes a bully"—he picked up the card from his desk—"especially these kinds." Doug glanced at Xavier. "Ms. Taylor, can me and Mr. Hunter have a moment alone?" He thought for a second. "Oh yeah, Ms. Taylor, Principal Skinner would like to have a word with you."

Doug handed Dakota some Kleenex.

She wiped her eyes and blew her nose and hugged Xavier. "Thank you, big brother." She looked at Doug. "Don't worry. I won't."

Xavier kissed her on the forehead. "Anytime, munchkin. Remember, I'll be picking you up and taking you home, so get at me in the south lobby after your classes."

After Dakota left, Doug said to Xavier, "We haven't talked in a long time, Mr. Hunter. That means you've been keeping yourself out of trouble, I'm assuming?"

Xavier knew what Doug was doing. Homeboy wasn't born yesterday. He was being nosy.

"I haven't been bringing any trouble to your school," Xavier said, folding his arms across his chest.

"Glad to hear it. How is your arm?"

Xavier's smile was of suspicion. "It's my shoulder. Look, we've known each other too long to beat around the bush. What you up to?"

"I'm worried about you. You have five months to go before your graduation. I would have to say that when you told me that you weren't going to another school after all the trouble a year ago, I have to be honest, I didn't think you would make it this far."

"Gee, Mr. Banks, thank you for the vote of confidence."

"I'm not trying to be funny, Mr. Hunter, but men like Slick Eddie—they are dangerous people who have resources to hire very dangerous men. But you have an angel on your shoulder."

Xavier was losing patience. "Is there a point to all this?"

"Okay. Maybe it's nothing, but a few of my officers observed a suspicious-looking rusty, ancient Ford Econoline van sitting on the outer edges of student parking last Friday. They didn't get a good look at the driver because when they went to approach, he drove off."

A cold feeling crept through Xavier's gut. Sounded like the hitman who'd chased him through the school his junior year. The dude was charcoal black, big ears, and had an affinity for wearing a dark-colored Rocawear hoodie. Oftentimes Xavier had referred to the hitman as Tall and Husky. And he had indeed been sent by Slick Eddie, even had the nerve to call Xavier on his cell phone at the end of his tenth-grade year to tell him that he was a dead man walking. For all Xavier knew, Tall and Husky could've been responsible for blasting him in the shoulder. Junk just got real.

Doug reared back in the chair and clasped his hands behind his head. "Like I said, maybe nothing. Then again it could be something. I don't know. Just watch your back." Doug scratched his right ear. "By the way, your boy Linus Flip, what happened to him?"

Xavier rolled his shoulders. "Don't know. Told me that he was in trouble and needed some money. Said school was secondary. He'd come back when he handled his business."

"Doesn't sound right, but okay."

Xavier walked out of Doug's office before he could ask any more questions.

Billy Hawkins had been weighing heavy on his mind. He'd tried his friend and mentor on the cell joint, but the old dude never picked up. Traveled to his house a couple times, rang the doorbell—nothing! It was like the geezer had just disappeared. It wasn't like him either. This only added to Xavier's worries. Too much was already riding on his shoulders. He just wanted to throw up his hands and run off screaming until he ran straight to Alaska somewhere. One thing was for certain, though: If he survived the foolishness to get through to graduation, Xavier was going to attend college far, far away—maybe Russia.

38

DAKOTA

Dakota was feeling some kind of way about sitting in front of the principal's desk. Skinner's secretary had let her in and told the girl that the principal would be with her after he'd finished meeting with some parents. Not knowing what this was about made nervous perspiration form on her nose and left her hands feeling cold and clammy.

Dakota looked around the office. Nice big green plants sat on the floor by the window, while smaller ones sat on a shelf. This is where it all had started. When she'd first pitched Skinner her idea. Matter of fact, he'd loved the idea so much that he was the one who'd come up with the slogan: "Give Bullying a Black Eye." He'd been the one to suggest the date. Skinner had also given her every available resource to make this thing happen.

The door opened and Skinner walked in wearing a plain navy blue suit and leather shoes.

He took a seat behind his desk, opening the bottom button of his suit jacket to get comfortable. "I have some pretty exciting news for you, young lady."

Dakota perked up.

Principal Skinner looked excited. "Our little campaign to stop bullying has not only caught on around the city with other schools, it seems that the media has gotten wind of it." He tried to compose himself before he blew a gasket with excitement. "They will be here to cover the event. We're going to hold an assembly. Some very prominent leaders, ranging from businesses to religious institutions will be speaking about the evils of bullying. This thing is going to be big, so please get some sleep the night before. You are the little cog in the machine that started this wonderful endeavor and I am so proud of you."

The tears flowed for the ninth grader. Skinner handed Dakota some Kleenex.

She was overwhelmed by sheer joy. When she started on this journey, there was no way she could ever imagine that the lights would burn this bright. With more tears in too few words, Dakota shook her head as if to say "thank you" and walked out of the office.

39

SAMANTHA

Xavier and Samantha went out to enjoy a relaxing Valentine's Day evening. Despite the real danger that plagued them both, a movie and dinner was a welcome change of pace. So to not run into Sean Desmond and his two minions, the couple traveled out to a TGI Friday's in Brighton, Michigan, to decompress and unwind. The AMC theater was just up the street. The movie started at eight thirty, which gave them plenty of time to grab a bite.

The restaurant was noisy and animated with movement. As the hostess sat couple after couple, waitresses hustled in and out of the kitchen placing orders. Thank God Samantha and Xavier had gotten to Friday's when they did. The line was out the door now with a two-hour wait.

"How's the shoulder?" Samantha asked.

Xavier looked around. Before the shooting the boy was perfectly at home in large crowds, but now they made him super nervous. "It hurts sometimes, especially when it's cold. The doctors say that I might have to live with the pain the rest of my life."

"I'm sorry, Xavier. You have your faults, but you deserved better."

Samantha was dressed in black—expensive jeans, suede thigh-high boots, and a form-fitting top with *bebe* spelled out in glittery silver rhinestones across the breast. Her gorgeous mink swing jacket sat neatly in one of the extra chairs at the table.

She quietly glanced around the dining area. "OMG, I can't believe how crowded this place is," she said.

Xavier wasn't listening because he was too busy staring hypnotically at Samantha's lips as she delightfully pronounced every syllable.

"Xavier, did you hear me?"

He playfully snapped out of it. "Huh—did you say something?" he asked with a slick, mischievous grin on his face. Xavier had on black Levi's, a sweet gray jacket with black trim and *Detroit* across the chest in red lettering, a nice Detroit Red Wings patch just above the lettering, and a ball cap hosting that very same team logo. On his feet—red and gray Nike Air Max 95s.

Xavier and Samantha sat at a table for four in the back of the restaurant by an emergency exit. He'd talked her out of sitting at a booth by explaining the disadvantages. Sitting there presented many blind spots. Couldn't tell who was sitting behind you because the backs were too high to see over. The blind spots created too many bad angles—angles that presented the advantage to the hitter. It was better to sit at freestanding tables out in the open. Having a 360-degree view took the element of surprise from the attacker. And dining next to an emergency door was simply a no-brainer.

"Okay, Mr. CIA Agent, who are you and what have you done with my friend Xavier Hunter?" Samantha put a hand over her mouth and giggled.

"No. Serious. I'm here to keep you safe."

"Where did you learn all of this stuff from?"

Xavier looked around before giving his answer. "Books. A couple of courses on security and surveillance. Did a stint over in Iraq—"

"Xavier," Samantha said making that "tell the truth" face.

Xavier put his head down and laughed. "Okay. You got me. Movies—tons of spy movies, especially *The Bourne Identity* with Matt Damon."

"And I'm supposed to feel safe because my friend loves Matt Damon."

"Stop twisting my words—didn't say I loved anybody. Just liked the movie."

"So you learned some moves from a clever actor playing a spy. I feel much better."

"That's funny, I didn't hear you criticizing the moves that kept you safe at Twelve Oaks about a month ago."

Samantha playfully slapped one of Xavier's hands. "No, darling, that was my little roughneck who kept me safe."

Xavier laughed. "I can't believe you're sleeping on my skills."

"Okay, Jason Bourne, on our way here, did you happen to pay attention to the yellow cab that looked like it was following us on the freeway?"

Xavier looked like he was spooked. "So I'm not crazy. You saw it too?"

"Yes. I thought it was following us until it kept on riding by on the freeway as we came up on our exit."

"Sam, I know I'm not crazy, but I've been seeing yellow cabs lately."

Samantha cracked that gorgeous smile. "Have you been seeing little green men from Mars too?"

"Sam, I'm serious," Xavier said, like he was desperate for someone to believe him.

A cute slender white waitress with Belinda on her name tag stepped up to the table and took the drink orders—two sodas. Once Belinda returned with the drinks, she took their orders and left.

Xavier continued to carefully scan the crowd for potential threats.

Samantha slurped her Coca-Cola through a straw. "Hey, I figured since you and that girl Dakota Taylor is cool, what's going on with her? She looks a little stressed out."

Xavier swallowed down some Sprite. "This stays between me and you."

Samantha looked like she was insulted. "When have I told anybody your business?"

"Anyway, she's been receiving death threats, warning her not to go through with the anti-bullying event. She's also been receiving weird phone calls—and just last month somebody left black roses on her doorstep."

Samantha was a square, but even she knew the significance of that. "Wow. Is she still willing to go through with it?"

Xavier nodded. "Yup. I told her never let anybody scare you out of doing you."

"Typical hero."

"Whatever, punk."

"I have your punk."

Xavier smiled. "She rides to school with me and I take her home."

Xavier's generous spirit for helping others in distress was one of the biggest reasons in a huge list of them that made her fall in love with him. "Aren't you concerned about spreading yourself a little thin? How are the research paper and the essay coming along?"

"I'm good. I'm through with the third draft on my essay and almost done with the research paper."

Samantha sucked down some drink. "I'm excited for you. I can't believe your English teacher was nice enough to give you an opportunity like that. You definitely have the writing skills, Xavier. Why don't you give me a little sneak preview on what the essay is about?"

"Nope. If I did that I would have to"—he used the index finger of his right hand to drag it across his throat—"kill you."

They both cracked up. The rest of dinner was filled with laughter and delightful conversation. Samantha had no idea how deeply she'd missed Xavier. Just being out on a special day like Valentine's Day brought some semblance of normalcy back to her life. She knew that Sean was bound to try something ugly. Her life had been going swell over the past month. Ozzie and Cash had been quiet, a little too quiet for her taste. There was no way they were going to let Xavier slide with smashing one of them. Samantha had been around those two long enough to know that their taste for revenge was otherworldly. She felt guilty dragging Xavier into her mess. What if he got hurt? Could she look at herself in the mirror?

What about her old man? He still hadn't a clue about the real Sean Desmond. As far as her father knew, the boy was a saint. And if he knew that she was hanging out with Xavier instead of her girl Jennifer on Valentine's Day, he'd have a fit. Samantha hated lying to her parents. But it was better than telling the truth and having to listen to him preaching a sermon about how Sean would make a fine husband. Besides, being with Xavier was worth the risk. It reignited all those feelings about him that she thought were dead. Samantha simply loved these feelings and didn't want the night to end. But she knew the night had to end eventually.

As the two walked out of auditorium twelve and blended in with the crowd, people moved across the plush red carpets, passed enormous movie posters along the corridor, and spilled out into the lobby. The fragrance of fresh, hot buttered popcorn was alluring. And even though they were leaving, Samantha wanted to get a bag to go. If she hadn't decided to grab some kernels before leaving, they would've missed a real live, hot, steamy erotica performance that was taking place smack dab amongst the crowd in the middle of the lobby. And it was starring Roxanne Hudson . . . Xavier's father's girlfriend.

40

XAVIER

SUNDAY, FEBRUARY 14
10:45 P.M.

Xavier and Samantha just stood there with their mouths hanging open in disbelief. Even though they were far off, Xavier was 100 percent sure that it was her. He could tell that raggedy weave from anywhere.

But there they were, Roxanne and some big, black unknown man, nestled in amongst the crowd, and going at it heavy, like a liquored-up teenage couple at a prom after-party. Xavier couldn't believe his luck. Talking about a gift from God. Xavier felt bad not being able to offer up the proper amount of sorrow that his old man would feel once he laid the info on him. But his father's feelings would have to wait. This chick had to be outed, and now. Noah couldn't do it. He'd been blinded by the booty. Too weak for this Jezebel and clearly not in charge of his right mind. It left Xavier with the all-too-familiar task of stepping up to save his family.

Samantha asked Xavier, "Are you sure that's your father's girlfriend?"

"It's the weave—looks like two Texas tumbleweeds mating on a dusty prairie. If I live to be a hundred, I might forget her face, but never that hair of hers."

"Look at them," Samantha said in disgust, "all out in public like this. I guess they don't care about these people looking at them."

"Roxanne is all about the attention."

Samantha asked him, "Are you going to let your dad know about this?"

Xavier smiled wickedly. "I'm going to do better than that. If I step to him without any proof he'll probably blow me off, as if I was lying on her."

"Now what?"

Xavier got out his cell phone and jostled his way through the crowd, readying the camera app. He walked right up, aimed his phone, and said, "Ms. Hudson."

The flash went off in her face when she broke the liplock and turned in Xavier's direction.

"Xavier," Roxanne said in startled surprise, "what are you doing here?"

Xavier gazed up at the big black dude with cartoonish pink lips and then back to her. "The question is what are you doing here, and with him?"

She broke her connection with the guy and nervously started fixing her clothes and finger-combing her tangled weave.

The big black dude seemed to be annoyed. "Who is

this, Roxanne?" dude asked in a deep baritone voice. He said to Xavier, "Why did you just snap me and my wife's picture?"

"Your wife?"

"My wife." Homeboy pointed a short thumb at his chest like he was proud.

Xavier couldn't do anything but smile. He was enjoying Roxanne's anxiety. But he wasn't done. This chick was married and dating his father—all while working on getting him kicked out of the house. He was about to lower the boom on her cheating behind.

"Mr. Hudson, is it?" asked Xavier.

The big man said, "Yes. It is. Now you want to tell me who you are?"

This was the part where Xavier expected Roxanne to wet herself. She was nervously moving her feet back and forward, like she really had to go to the bathroom. Xavier relished the power he had over her. All of those nights where she had talked that slick stuff to him and reduced his character to nothing. Painting her version of his future where he would turn out to be the lowest scum on earth, a chain-snatching petty criminal. Now the shoe was on the other foot, and it was fun to watch her squirm. Xavier wanted to laugh in her face as she pathetically pleaded with her eyes for him not to drop a dime. He wanted to take it there. Tell on her butt and watch the explosion of a marriage. It'd be good for her. Xavier knew that his father loved Roxanne and the old dude was going to be crushed. But try as he might, Xavier couldn't bring himself to pull the trigger.

Xavier told Mr. Hudson, "My name is Spencer Hoffman and I was an underprivileged inner-city youth until a chance encounter with your wife, Mrs. Hudson, outside a liquor store I'd noticed that she frequented before work. I was hungry and I'm sorry to say, sir, I'd set it up to steal your wife's purse. But thank God it never progressed to that point because she talked to me and made me understand that I had to get back into school. Mrs. Hudson even gave me twenty dollars to get something to eat. And it's because of her I stand here a changed man and about to graduate high school. And that's why I took the picture, because I'll always have something to remember her by."

The big dude looked at his wife with a smile on his face. He hugged her. "Baby, you are an angel. And I am so happy that God has blessed me with you." They walked off.

Roxanne was looking back as if to thank him for not saying anything. But Xavier was serious when he mouthed, "Stay away from my father!" and held up his cell phone like the picture was evidence.

Xavier walked back over to Samantha.

"I heard the whole thing," she said. "Xavier, you are wonderful."

"Well, I try to be."

Samantha kissed him and they walked off, holding hands.

It was 1:16 a.m. when Xavier pulled into his driveway. Dude was completely exhausted. He couldn't believe that he'd busted Roxanne. But the kicker was that the chick was married. How trifling. His old man was probably in the house asleep. Xavier planned to let him stay that way until morning, and then he would drop the bomb. The day's events with Samantha had his head spinning. The way things had gone down between them at the beginning of this school year, he'd thought their relationship had been a done deal. Everything was different now. They had even talked about maybe getting back together later on. His world seemed, for the first time, to be traveling in the right direction. His luck was changing and he had two papers that were sure to score high.

Xavier got out of the car and walked to the side door. That's when he felt cold steel pressed against the back of his head. The coolness of the shooting iron was ice cold against his skin.

Damn, Xavier cursed. The two stood in complete darkness. He could've strangled his pops. Noah had been procrastinating and dragging his feet about putting up a security spotlight on the side of the crib.

"Don't turn around." The voice was low and threatening.

Xavier froze instantly. He could've kicked himself for dropping his guard. And it wasn't all the trouble in his world that caused him to do so. The love of his life was back and he'd been seriously overjoyed with the potential to have a great future with Samantha. The potential for happiness had been enough to distract him and cause him to drop his guard. Now the Grim Reaper was at his back to collect payment for his past misdeeds.

The voice said, "Be cool and nothing happens to your people inside. I need for you to get back in your car. Me and you are about to take a ride, playboy."

Xavier was dead and he knew it. But he needed to

know. "Slick Eddie sent you?" he asked, already knowing the answer.

"You know it," the hitman answered. "You might've gotten lucky when I tried to take you out a couple months ago, but somehow you survived. I was impressed."

The wind started howling, like souls beckoning him to the grave.

"So that was you who shot me?"

"Yup."

"One more question."

"Ninja, this ain't *Jeopardy*. But since you about to die I think I can accommodate you."

"It's been you stalking me since Slick Eddie and Romello were locked up? You're the big-eared guy wearing the Rocawear hoodie? I'm not dying without knowing your real name, you feel me?"

The guy pressed the muzzle aggressively into the back of Xavier's head. "You got jokes. I don't make it a habit, but like I told you before, I can accommodate you. Name's Dirk Frazier. Enough talking, let's go."

With a name like Dirk Frazier, no wonder he's violent, Xavier thought.

Dirk Frazier took the weapon down and planted the muzzle in the small of Xavier's back. The dude pushed as if to relay to Xavier to get moving.

They had the car door open and Dirk said, "You're gonna drive. I'ma get in the passenger side. Do what I tell you because if you don't, I'll come back here and kill your family."

This was the first time that Xavier had seen the killer's

face. Yup. It was him all right, the charcoal-black, big-eared rascal, and dude was still wearing that Rocawear hoodie. Xavier shook his head. This was it. Throughout the years of them trying to punch his ticket, this was the day, February fourteenth. He wouldn't put up any resistance. This would be his last act of unselfishness. Xavier wanted his dad to raise his brother to be a better man than both of them. Alfonso deserved a shot at greatness. And at the same time, Xavier thought about his greatness, a greatness that would go unfulfilled. It was a damn shame about how much work had gone into perfecting the research paper and essay.

"Don't try anything," Dirk said, "I'm gonna walk around and get to the other side."

Xavier sat there in the cold, eyes closed, head down, praying.

A minute later, a highly familiar voice said, "Youngster."

Xavier slowly opened his eyes and saw . . . Billy Hawkins, his friend and mentor. He had to pinch himself to make sure this moment wasn't some hallucination.

"What—how, who," Xavier mumbled. He opened his eyes wide. It was Billy all right. Big black winter coat, hospital scrubs pants, and combat boots, laced tightly all the way up.

"No time for that," Billy said, vigorously massaging the knuckles on his right hand. "You should be all right from now on."

When Xavier exited the car, Dirk lay unconscious on his back on the cold, hard cement behind the car. Xavier watched suspiciously as Billy slowly trotted down the street and came back driving a yellow cab.

"So, you're the one," Xavier asked.

Billy told him, getting out of the cab, "I don't have time for no jaw-jacking. Let me get him in the trunk."

Xavier was about to help but Billy stopped him.

"I don't need you involved. Take your tail in the house, young'un." Billy smiled at Xavier. "Remember, you ain't seen nothing."

He did as he was told, not even looking back when he heard the trunk open and close. As soon as he put his key in the side door lock, Xavier heard the taxicab burn rubber and then take off.

The next morning Xavier got up to the sounds of gospel music and the fresh fragrance of bacon, pancakes, and eggs. He climbed out of bed, yawning and stretching. Anxiety had its way with him last night. The boy twisted and turned until he finally went to sleep.

It was six o'clock Monday morning. President's day. With everything he'd gone through last night, Xavier was glad it was a three-day weekend. He would have time to chill.

Xavier rubbed his eyes and walked into the kitchen. His father was working over the stove, wearing pajama bottoms and a robe slightly open, showing his bare chest. Xavier leaned against the wall by the basement door.

He mentally braced himself. "Pop, I have something to tell you."

His father took a few pancakes off the griddle with the

spatula. There was no expression on his face. "No need to, son. Roxanne called me before you got home last night and told me everything."

"You all right?"

Noah broke open a few eggs and started scrambling them in a bowl. "I'm fine."

To Xavier, short answers like that meant the opposite. He wasn't fine. Far from looking it.

"You sure, Pop? You want to talk?"

"Are you going out today?" his dad asked him.

"Nah. I'm too mentally exhausted."

"Okay. Why don't you see if your brother is good and ready for breakfast?"

Xavier hesitated and considered telling his dad about what Billy had done last night. But he decided he'd better. "You know Billy—"

Noah beat him to it. "He called me this morning and told me everything."

Whatever it was the old man had done, Xavier didn't want to hear any details. He was about to get ready to walk out of the kitchen.

"Slick Eddie won't be bothering you again. Did a little research earlier this morning and found out he's at the prison that I did time at. Got some people in there."

Xavier waited on his father to continue but he didn't. The boy wasn't a dummy. His father had been a real bad man in a life before prison. And it was apparent that the old man still held powerful connections on the inside.

Noah continued, "In case you were wondering, Billy explained to me that you and Alfonso are like his kids. Said that when y'all hurt, he hurts. He also said that you seemed to be hiding something, maybe the reason why you were shot. When it happened to you, he vowed to find out why. So he got himself a cab job. That way he could keep an eye on you."

"I used to see a cab following me. I thought I was losing my mind."

"He just wanted to protect you. I owe him my life for keepin' my oldest son safe." He looked at Xavier through eyes of seriousness. "You are never to talk about what happened last night with anyone. Billy had friends that took care of the hitman. Let's just say that the guy was roughly persuaded to leave town or die. The guy wasn't a dummy, he left town."

"How will he assure that the dude won't come back?" Xavier wanted to know.

"Somehow, Billy found out where his family lives. Y'all be safe son. I'm proud of the man that you are becoming." Noah smiled. "Go and see your mother soon."

When the landline rang, Noah answered. After a series of questions, he smiled and gestured with the receiver. "Looks like she beat you to it, your mother is on the phone, son."

Xavier smiled. "How?"

"I wrote her." He grinned back at Xavier.

Xavier took the cordless and ran into his bedroom.

Everything was starting to look up.

41

DAKOTA

THURSDAY, MARCH 17
11:46 P.M.

Dakota couldn't sleep. This was the main reason that she was in the kitchen fixing herself some warm milk. The concoction was something her mom used to give her when she was younger and couldn't fall asleep.

She stood wearing an oversized T-shirt, stretch pants, and fuzzy bunny slippers, warming a coffee mug of milk in the microwave. Dakota was anxious. She was having pregame jitters—tomorrow was the big day for schools across the city to stand up against bullies, and she was feeling a bit nervous. Tons of work had gone into getting other high schools on board and on the same page. Tomorrow had to go off flawlessly. There was no time for do-overs. This was it. Some said it couldn't be done—

uniting high schools across the city to stand up for one common cause—but thank God, Dakota had pulled it off.

Despite the negative, sarcastic comments that had been made by some of her classmates, she was proud of herself. Standing up for a belief took guts. And to accomplish this goal without the support of her mother was bittersweet. It hurt Dakota when her mother told her that she was embarrassed by her daughter's cowardice. Said not to be looking for her to come to that school and support any of her daughter's foolishness. Commented that no child of hers would ever consider crying to others about raising awareness. Elaborated further that any real daughter of hers would go and beat the hell out of those who considered themselves too big and bad.

Her old girl would not stand in her way. She loved her mother, but she felt that God had given her this calling. So therefore nobody would get in her way of helping others. It was also cool about the support that she'd been receiving from Xavier. Her adopted big brother had inadvertently set the bar for any boy who would come around her sniffing for a commitment. If they weren't on Xavier's level, then they would have to get to steppin'.

The microwave bell sounded. Dakota took her steamy, hot mug and was about to go back to her room when the doorbell rang. She took a deep breath and set the coffee mug on the kitchen table. Dakota had half expected this. That's why she wasn't scared. The Internet had been invaluable to her study on past powerful leaders who had fallen to an assassin's bullet. They all had one thing in common: at some point or another, they knew that their campaign would end in bloodshed. Of course this gave her no comfort, but she was a soldier. And soldiers were the ultimate symbolism for protection. Stood to reason she wasn't scared of what was on the other side of her front door.

The time for fear was over. It was a brand-new day, a time in which she could no longer afford to be terrified of those cowards who portrayed themselves as strong. Maybe she could talk some sense into those who had come to harm her tonight.

The doorbell rang again. She wasn't afraid. No future in it. Dakota had to take a stand. Her movement depended on it. In the coat closet Dakota shed her slippers and pulled on some sneakers. Her main objective would be to reason with them. Let them know that there were other ways of solving differences. But she wasn't a fool. If talks broke down and she had to get physical, then it would be best to have on sneakers. Something comfortable and light to throw punches in.

In the living room she clicked the camera app on her cell and pressed Record. After holding back the blinds and setting the device on the window ledge, she focused on the front yard.

Dakota stood resting with her hand on the doorknob when somebody knocked on the door. She guessed that they'd grown impatient. This stuff had to stop tonight. Her mother wasn't much of a praying woman. Matter of fact, her mom didn't believe in too many things. Left Dakota wondering where she'd picked up on a praying spirit. She offered up a little prayer. When she was done, she clicked on the porch light and opened the door. They were waiting for her. With the exception of Bangs, every last one of the SNLG girls was out front.

Mouse, the new leader, stepped forth out of the darkness.

She said to Dakota, "You should have heeded our warning and put the clamps on your little event. As we stated in the card, you either stop or die."

Dakota spoke in a strong voice. "Well, y'all gotta do what you gotta do, because there is no way I'm shutting down anything."

The diabolical smirk on Mouse's face said that she wouldn't have it any other way.

"Suit yourself," said Mouse as she balled up her fists.

42

XAVIER

Xavier sat in Mr. Chase's classroom still trying to figure out what had happened to Dakota. He'd gone by this morning to pick her up and there was no answer. It was so unlike her not to answer his phone call, either. He'd taken a look around the house, and nothing was out of place. The windows were intact. Doors were fine. Maybe she'd gone off with her mother somewhere. He'd hated to leave without answers, but Xavier hadn't wanted to be late for school.

Mr. Chase walked his tall self to the front of the room. The teacher was wearing khaki pants, a short-sleeve shirt made of blue jean material, and handcrafted Native American moccasins. He said, "Class, do you know what day it is?"

A boy sitting two desks in front of Xavier answered, "Today is the first day of spring."

Mr. Chase cracked a smile. "I asked for the day and not the season, Mr. Richard Arnold."

"Moron," Dexter said to Richard, laughing.

Xavier shook his head at Dexter. "We turn in research papers today," he said to Mr. Chase.

"Gold star for Mr. Hunter," Mr. Chase said. "This is the make-or-break assignment. I hope you guys have brought your A games. Don't want to see anybody have to repeat this course."

There was a rustling sound as the students retrieved their papers.

Xavier grabbed his, looked over at Dexter, and whispered, "I guess he was talkin' about you having to repeat the course, huh, homeboy?"

Dexter spoke in a low tone to Xavier. "The devil is a lie. I'm gettin' that hunnit on my joint and breeze this course, you feel me? How much paper you got on a bet?"

"Everybody pass their papers to the front of the row," said the teacher.

Dexter continued talking. "I gotta holler at you at lunch."

"You got it," said Xavier.

At the end of the class Mr. Chase wanted to see Xavier.

Xavier told Dexter he'd catch up and stopped by the teacher's desk. He went into his folder and pulled out his essay. "Here it is, Mr. Chase," he said, handing the paper over. "I want you to know that I busted my butt on this paper. Don't know if it will win the contest or not, but I put everything I had into it."

Mr. Chase took the essay and smiled. "It's called optimism, Mr. Hunter. Personally, I would not have chosen you if I didn't think you were up for the challenge. I'm sure I will receive great pleasure in reading your research paper and this essay." He flipped some pages. "Be in touch with you, Mr. Hunter."

Xavier walked out of the classroom thinking that that essay had better win, being that he'd almost gone to jail gathering research for it. The stakes were high and a potential writing career was on the line. Given the positive direction in which his life was now headed, Xavier felt invincible. Like nothing could stop him. And with no Slick Eddie standing on the runway to big dreams, Xavier had been cleared for takeoff.

On the way downstairs to the lunchroom, Xavier tried Dakota's cell phone. It went straight to voice mail. He hadn't seen her anywhere on campus either. The posters promoting anti-bullying were flying all around the building, but so far, the captain of the event had been a no-show.

Xavier took a couple of deep breaths before walking into the cafeteria. His nerves were an irritating ball of TNT in his stomach. Dude was definitely afraid if somebody stepped to him the wrong way, he'd detonate.

It was a bit noisier than usual, but Xavier paid it no mind and moved in the direction of their lunch table. When he got there Dexter was sitting and staring intensely at a cell phone. The boy looked up with a very disturbed expression on his mug.

He handed Xavier the cell joint. "I think you should look at this, homeboy."

Xavier took the phone and noticed that Dexter had streamed some Fox 2 News clip that he already had set up to roll.

"Just push the Play arrow," Dexter instructed.

Xavier went off. "Homeboy, I didn't grow up in the Stone Age. Don't need any instructional video, so chill out, you feel me?"

"What is wrong with you?"

With his free hand Xavier pinched the bridge of his nose and let out a long sigh. "My bad, fam. Just have a lot on my mind."

"Don't worry about it, homeboy. I ain't sweatin' you. On the real, though, you need to watch that clip."

The clip showed the inside of a bank. It hadn't been rolling a couple seconds when Linus Flip walked into the frame and stuck a gat to the temple of a short, light-skinned female bank teller. There was no sound, but Xavier didn't need any to understand what Flip was demanding of the lady. Dude didn't even have on a mask—grill was in full view of the cameras. Whatever money troubles he was having had led him into this desperate act of stupidity. Xavier watched, shaking his head, as the terrified teller filled up the bag with the content of her drawer and shoved it to him. The clip ended with a dark-complexioned male security guard shooting and wounding a fleeing Flip in the left leg.

"Damn," Xavier said, taking a seat. He couldn't believe it. The dude that had been holding him down for two straight years was probably going to prison with a healthy double-digit sentence hanging over his head. There was no way Xavier could help his homeboy. Dude was straight up on his own now.

Bigstick walked up. "What are the long faces about, fam?" he asked the two boys.

Xavier just handed over the phone. "Press Play, homeboy, and see for yourself."

Bigstick took the phone and did as instructed. The clip had the same effect on him as it did Xavier. "Man," said Bigstick, "I can't believe Flip went out like that. Is he on something?"

Xavier told him, "Not that I know of. He kept telling me he owed some loot to somebody, but the conversation never went further."

Bigstick handed the phone back to Xavier. "That must've been some mean pressure the boy was under to make him do something"—he pointed at the cell phone—"like that."

Dexter stepped in. "Not only that, dude got plugged in the leg. It's a wrap for ol' boy."

As the three sat there trying to make some sense of why Flip went all stickup kid with it at the bank, the south door was snatched open and in rushed Samantha and Tiffany. Both were out of breath when they arrived at the table.

Samantha said, breathing heavy, "Da-Da-Dakota."

Xavier's blood ran cold at the mentioning of his protégé's name, but he stayed composed. "Calm down, Sam," he instructed.

She tried to take a deep breath but nothing would come out.

Tiffany spoke up. "Dakota's up on the roof of the

school and threatening to jump. We tried to talk her down but she wouldn't listen."

Xavier didn't have to hear anything else. He pushed Tiffany out of the way and almost trucked a skinny guy who had the sad misfortune of walking in the door as Xavier was barreling out.

Xavier was the first one to the rooftop. Once he opened the door, there she was, with her back to him, standing near the edge and looking down. His mind was a funnel cloud of emotions. He had never been involved in something like this before. Didn't have the slightest idea what to say. It was no telling how close she was to jumping, so Xavier had to handle this thing just right. There would be no second chance.

Xavier was out on the roof when he heard a squadron of footsteps echoing up the stairwell behind him. He twisted his head to see Doug and a number of others.

Doug's face held overwhelming concern. He whispered to Xavier, "Don't. The police are on the way."

Xavier ignored him and softly called out to Dakota, "Munchkin, what are you doing?"

Dakota just stood there as if she was a gargoyle statue perched on the rooftop of a Catholic church.

Xavier looked around. Nothing but ventilation systems were out there. The tar on the rooftop was slick, slippery—each step toward her was taken with caution. He stayed still. Didn't want to startle her.

Xavier had too much distance on Doug, so instead of yelling, Doug lightly clapped his hands to get the teen's attention. When Xavier looked back, Doug slowly shook his head as if to say, "Don't."

Xavier understood Doug's concern. The security officer wanted to wait for someone with the proper training to handle tense situations like this one. But they'd be scraping what was left of his munchkin off the pavement below before the police crisis intervention team could get off their butts at the doughnut counter to respond.

"Munchkin, can I ask you a question?" Xavier said softly.

Dakota didn't flinch, nor did she acknowledge him.

It was freezing out and he wasn't wearing a jacket. But Xavier couldn't feel it because his adrenaline was pumping. "You have to talk to me, munchkin. That's the only way I can help."

Doug got Xavier's attention again by softly clapping his hands together and holding up a cell phone. The distance prevented Xavier from seeing clearly. He backed up without taking his eyes off Dakota. What he saw on the screen was enough to make him want to seek out all the participants and start snatching spines out through noses.

Doug told him, "Students are looking at this clip. It's gone viral on YouTube."

Extreme anger had Xavier grinding his teeth together as he watched nine girls pulverize Dakota. Three of them he recognized. Mouse was acting as the leader and directing others to stomp a defenseless Dakota. This wasn't the time for his rage. Xavier had to get a handle on his emotions. But God help those who did this to her.

Doug's walkie-talkie crackled. He removed it and listened. He clicked it and said, "Copy." He looked at Xavier. "The police are en route. They just picked up every last girl in that clip. Let them—"

Xavier wasn't buying it. He took the phone with him and stepped back out onto the rooftop.

"Munchkin, the police have just picked up every last SNLG member," Xavier explained to her. "Please talk to me."

The wind picked up and Xavier was praying that it wouldn't blow her over the edge. He had his head turned around and was looking at Doug when Dakota finally spoke.

"Just think, all of this started because I looked at somebody in my first week of school," she said, sounding like she was mumbling. Like she was speaking through swollen lips. "It's funny you can't even look at anybody today without them misinterpreting it as disrespect. When I looked at Bangs I had every intention of speaking . . . you know, being friendly." She burst into tears.

Her tears triggered a few out of his eyes. The girl felt like she was totally alone in this world. And mentally that was the worst place to be, especially standing out on the ledge of a roof. "What can I say, munchkin? There are some real jacked-up people in this world, you feel me? But that's not on you. It's their shortcoming."

Dakota finally looked up and turned her face to the side. If Xavier could've burst into raging flames from anger, the entire rooftop would've been ablaze. From what he could see, the right side of her face was badly bruised—black eye, swollen lips, and it looked like her nose could've been broken.

"I'm tired, big brother. My mother doesn't care about me—I might as well be dead. Every time I look up, those girls are jumping on me. I'm tired, big brother. If I do this, at least it will put a spotlight on the cause."

The wind blew, whistling, blowing locks of Dakota's hair.

Xavier looked back and saw the police and paramedics. The boys in blue beckoned for him to let them take over, but Xavier looked them off and continued to plead.

"Please, munchkin, let's talk about this. You've come too far. Look at what you've accomplished. Everybody, every school is trying to model this day you created. The media is up here to do a story on you and this event you put together—please, munchkin, don't do this."

She didn't say anything. Just kept looking over the edge.

"Munchkin, if you do this, what message are you sending to those suffering from being bullied? This is not the way. Show those bullies that you are strong. Fight back by helping others with this cause. So many victims will benefit from the event you've put together."

She paused for a second. "Do you ever get tired?"

"Yes, I get tired, but when I do, I think of ways that I can make somebody else's life better. Munchkin, we're down here to serve and help each other out. I was shot in the shoulder but it didn't stop me. You know that."

She turned her face to the side again, but this time there was a smile. "Big brother, if I don't do this, can me, you, and Samantha go to IHOP and have pancakes?"

Xavier let out the breath that he'd been holding. "Sure, munchkin. Anything you want. Just come in from the edge."

The paramedics walked over, threw a blanket around her shoulders, and escorted her down the stairs. Amidst a thunderous ovation, Xavier walked through the crowded stairwell, being patted on the back by staff and students as he stayed close to Dakota.

43

SAMANTHA

SUNDAY, MARCH 20
10:34 A.M.

"**S**on, you showed a brilliant exhibition of courage on that school rooftop," Mr. Fox said to Xavier. "Personally, I would've waited on the professionals to arrive and do their job, but that's just me. I wouldn't have had the guts to do what you did." Mr. Fox was wearing a navy blue business suit and expensive Italian shoes.

Two days after Dakota Taylor had single-handedly opened the eyes of a sleeping nation on how truly bad bullying had become in its schools, Samantha had been blown out of her socks when her dad asked her to set up a meeting with Xavier over breakfast. Apparently, the heroism the boy displayed in front of the cameras had been enough to alter her dad's negative, narrow-minded view of him. They were dining at an exclusive breakfast club in the heart of downtown Birmingham.

Xavier politely smiled. "Douglas Banks, our head of security, wanted me to wait for the police crisis intervention team, but, sir, I wasn't afforded the time."

Mrs. Fox was dressed casually in jeans, cute black leather shoes, and a beautiful blouse that showed off nice spring colors. She looked across the table at Noah. "You must be very proud of your son, Mr. Hunter," she said.

Noah was dressed in tan slacks, brown leather loafers, button-up, and a necktie in those same colors. "God is good, and all the time. How else could that rooftop miracle have happened? I'm extremely proud of my son."

Samantha said, "Amen." She was dressed like her mother. "Dakota's story was big headline news. National. It gave me goose bumps when I saw the cell phone footage of the rooftop on *HLN*. Xavier, I couldn't believe how composed you were. I would've been shaking like a leaf on a tree experiencing an earthquake under those circumstances." She winked at Xavier. He was sitting to her left.

"The young lady Dakota Taylor showed tremendous bravery to face down those girl gangbangers in her front yard," said Mr. Fox, then sipped on his orange juice.

"She knew that she could bring attention to this problem if she recorded herself under attack," said Samantha. "And after taking a beating like that, having the strength to go back in the house and upload the whole thing to YouTube was beyond strong. Mom, I don't think I could've done that."

Alfonso was sitting on his father's right-hand side.

Dude wasn't saying anything. He was merely chowing down on a stack of buttermilk pancakes.

Mrs. Fox sipped coffee from a mug. "Xavier, we all heard your Fox 2 News interview. You are a very humble person." She rolled her eyes at her husband. "I knew that there was something special about you from our very first meeting in Principal Skinner's office. And of course, we've all heard some of the critics say that you should've waited for the professionals. What made you think that you could pull it off?"

"Mrs. Fox," said Xavier, looking around at every face at the table, "like I've been telling news reporters, it wasn't really anything special. I love Dakota as a very good friend. Everything that came out of my mouth in that moment was from my heart. I spoke love from my heart, you feel me?"

Samantha loved herself some Xavier—a complex bad boy, good guy, intelligent nerd all rolled into a handsome, LL Cool J knockoff was her only way to sum him up. The original. Would never be another. And the boy had never been afraid to be himself. Kept it real. And that gangster "you feel me?" catchphrase of his seriously did things to her head. At this point she didn't care what her folks thought. She grabbed Xavier, hugged him, and kissed him on the jaw.

"I love you," said Samantha. "You are a blessing to all of our lives."

"It's important for me to say that Dakota will be receiving counseling. Her mother was never there for her and in the end she felt alone and vulnerable. She's a strong girl and I'll be right there by her side to help her recover, but she's taught us all something very valuable"—Xavier looked at his father—"and that's never take family for granted. Because in an instant, it could all be taken away."

Noah looked like he was getting ready to cry. "I'm afraid you've shown your father some things about being a man. And I'll never get tired of saying that I love you, son. We will always put God first, and long as I live our family will stand united and continue to love the way we should."

Samantha was enjoying herself. Unlike that made-for-reality TV drama that had happened when she'd tried to mix their families before at that Italian restaurant, this time it was much more pleasant and with the right combination of folks. She was also pleased to know that Sean Desmond was a thing of the past. Her threat to go to the media and expose him for the dirt-bag that he was had worked like a charm. There were no more phone calls from him. And the only time she saw the scumbag was during an after-game interview for the Tigers' preseason—and she'd turned the channel. Didn't make any sense to tell her father. Get him all upset and for what? Samantha had it covered. She'd handled her business with him well. She was 1,000 percent sure that Sean Desmond wouldn't cause any more trouble for her. He'd better stay in his lane if he knew what was good for him.

Noah's emotional confession prompted Mr. Fox to stand and raise his glass of orange juice. "I propose a toast."

Everybody followed suit, standing and raising their glasses.

Mr. Fox examined everybody's face at the table. "Here's to Dakota Taylor. May she continue on her road to recovery so she can get back to work and champion the cause of the victims of bullying in schools across the country."

Everybody drank, but Mr. Fox wasn't finished.

"I have one more toast." He looked at Xavier. "Can you forgive this foolish old man? Too busy being a parent and trying to keep the wrong element away from my daughter, my eyes were closed to the wonderful, thoughtful, and loving person that you are. Here's to you and my daughter graduating and becoming great pillars of our society." He sipped his OJ.

Everybody followed up in unison with "Hear, hear."

Alfonso put his glass down and ran to hug his brother. "I love you, big brother."

Xavier held him tightly. "I love you too, little brother."

44

XAVIER

TUESDAY, JUNE 21
10:44 A.M.

It was the day before graduation. Xavier had one more loose end to tie up. He and Alfonso had gotten up early this morning and hopped a bus to Muskegon, Michigan. They were now sitting at a table in a huge room. People sat in chairs and at tables all over the place. Looking back on his conversation with Noah before they'd left, Xavier was glad he'd chosen to go alone. Noah had tried to convince his oldest that he should be there, but this was something that he and Alfonso had to do by themselves. Xavier had to admit, there were more butterflies in his stomach than there'd been on the school rooftop that day.

Xavier checked his watch. He had a few minutes, so he didn't mind Alfonso grabbing a few z's with his head down on the table. The bus ride up had taken two hours and fifty minutes. His little brother was wiped out.

As Xavier looked around at the faces belonging to a colorful assortment of ethnicities, he couldn't help but to reflect back on his life. Statistics said that a young black male like himself would be dead or in jail, selling drugs or walking around the ghetto and sticking people up to feed a drug addiction. So far, he'd defied the odds. He recognized what others had failed to—that God gave everybody a brain—and he was showing mainstream America that he knew how to use his.

Billy had finally gotten in touch with Xavier. Said this was his week to have the baby. He also told Xavier that if the boy didn't want any trouble, Xavier had better include him in the graduation ceremony. Didn't care if he was some big-time hero, Billy brought him back down to earth by letting Xavier know that heroes could get their skulls busted too. Billy's comedy was always appreciated. He'd promised old man a ticket to the ceremony.

There was movement up front. A heavy steel door swung open and this big black Sasquatch-looking guard led out a line of women dressed in orange and green jumpsuits. Xavier shook Alfonso awake just in time to see Ne Ne walking, with a huge grin on her face, in their direction. Alfonso jumped up and met her with a bear hug before she could get to the table. His mother looked great. Her skin looked lighter and she appeared to have shed fifteen pounds. Xavier had noticed that all of the black women prisoners sported cornrows. Probably weren't any real beauticians in the joint, so the braids had to be easier to maintain.

With tears in her eyes, his mother hugged her oldest son.

The first thing out of Ne Ne's mouth was, "I love you both."

"We love you too," said Xavier, as the family stood together in a group embrace.

"We have a lot of catching up to do," she said to Xavier. And then this wasn't a shocker—"Y'all daddy let y'all come up here alone?"

Xavier just shook his head and smiled.

"It was good you talked a girl down from the roof—but where is my gorgeous baby daddy at?" Ne Ne asked.

Xavier laughed and shook his head again. With Ne Ne, some things would never change.

EPILOGUE

Xavier pulled into the parking lot with a carload, parked, and turned off the ignition.

Xavier asked Samantha, "I need to know if we are boyfriend and girlfriend?"

Samantha said, "Xavier, I think that can wait. Let's go in."

"I'm not spending any money on a jump-off," he told Samantha.

There was laughing in the car.

Samantha took the joke good-naturedly. "You wanna be my baby daddy?" she said in a horrible attempt at a home-girl impersonation.

"Samantha, I'm serious," he said to her.

Dexter said from the backseat, "For goodness' sake, will you put that man out of his misery and tell him that you will be his wifey so I can go eat."

Samantha kissed Xavier. "Okay, if you feed me in there, I'll consider you for my boyfriend."

"Sam," Xavier said with a look of frustration on his face.

Samantha said, "Okay, okay, you're my man. Now can we go eat?"

He told Samantha, "Don't y'all embarrass me in this place, you feel me?" He looked at Dexter in the backseat. "Homeboy, I'ma need you to act like you have a couple of drops of table manners and not like you've been raised by a clan of hyenas."

Dakota cracked up laughing. She was in the backseat next to Dexter. Xavier didn't care; he blazed her too.

"And you," he said to her, "I don't care anything about your fame. Don't let me catch you in there signing autographs. It's our time to eat and enjoy each other. So tell your little fans to beat it."

Samantha giggled. "Y'all, don't let this ogre bother you. Since we've graduated and about to start college, he's gotten bitter in his old age."

Dexter said, "I'm hip. He's letting winning that little essay competition go to his dome. Since he's about to be a big-time street-lit author, homeboy thinks that he can push people around."

Xavier said, "Let me correct you for the fifteen hundredth time, Mr. I Barely Got By on the Skin of My Teeth in Mr. Chase's Classroom. I did not win that competition. I guess they didn't think that an essay dealing with"—he made air quotes—"'the real reasons why young black brothers resort to the hustle game' just wasn't compelling enough for mainstream America."

Dexter said mockingly, "Blah, blah, blah—fool, they still thought enough of you as a talented writer and gave your blockhead a book deal." He reached for the door handle. "So if you are finished, I'm going to go in there and spend some of yo' big-time advance money on stuffin' my face, you dig?"

Samantha said, twisting in the front seat and giving Dexter a high five, "That's telling him."

Dakota finally spoke up. "Samantha, you have your nerve. You were accepted to Juilliard and kept it a secret until a week ago."

Samantha smirked. "And, Dakota Taylor, how does it feel with every school in the city wanting you to come and speak to their students when school starts back? You keep that mess up and Oprah Winfrey will bring her show back just so that she could interview you."

They almost blew the roof off Xavier's car with laughter.

Xavier got out and opened Dakota's door. "You ready to go in here?"

Dakota looked at the storefront. "Yes. I've been waiting on this a long time."

When they were all out of the car, Xavier held Samantha's hand and put an arm around Dakota's shoulders.

He told them, "Let's go in and have breakfast."

Dexter held the door open and let them walk into IHOP.

Don't miss Amir Abrams's

Diva Rules

On sale now!

Diva Rules

Diva Rule #1: Keep it flossy-glossy. Always step out camera ready.

Diva Rule #2: Keep it cute. Never, ever, fight over a boy. No matter how much you like him.

Diva Rule #3: Serve 'em grace 'n' face. Politeness with a smile goes a long way. *Please and thank you* seals the deal in every situation.

Diva Rule #4: Read 'em for filth. *Snap, snap!* Never, ever, look for trouble. But if trouble comes strutting your way, give 'em a tongue-lashing before a beat-down.

Diva Rule #5: Keep a BWB—Boo With Benefits—on speed dial. Every diva should always have a rotation of cuties at her beck 'n' call.

Diva Rule #6: Love 'em 'n' leave 'em. Never, ever, get too attached to a boy. All that letting a boy be your life is a no-no. Getting cuckoo-nutty over a boy is for the ratchet! A diva has no time for that.

Diva Rule #7: Never kiss 'n' tell. Always keep 'em guessing.

Diva Rule #8: Say hi to your haters. Let 'em hate. Someone's gotta do it.

Diva Rule #9: Never let another chick steal your shine. You are your only competition.

Diva Rule #10: When in doubt, always refer back to rules number one through nine.

1

Diva check . . .
Hey, hey now! It's diva roll call . . . Are you present?
Rude, check . . .
Bitchy, check . . .
Spoiled, check . . .
Selfish, check . . .
Overdramatic, check, check . . .

Scrrrrreeeech! Hold up. That is *not* what *this* diva is about. No, *hunni*! Being a diva is all about attitude, boo. It's about bein' fierce. Fabulous. And always fly. It's about servin' it up 'n' keepin' the haters on their toes. And the rules are simple.

So, let's try this again.

Fiona's my name. Turning boys out is my game. Fashion's my life. Being fabulous is my mission. And staying fly is a must. Oh, and trust. I serve it up lovely. Period, point blank. At five seven, a buck twenty-five with my creamy, smooth complexion, blond rings of shoulder-length curls, and mesmerizing green eyes, I'm that chick all the cutie-boos stay tryna see about. I'm that chick with the small waist and big, bouncy booty that all the boys love to see me shake, bounce, 'n' clap. I'm that hot chick that the tricks 'n' hoes at my school—McPherson High—love to hate; yet hate that they can't ever be me.

Like I always tell 'em, "Don't be mad, boo. I know I give you life. Thank me for giving you something to live for."

Conceited?

No, hun. Never that.

Confident?

Yes, sweetie. Always that.

No, boo. I don't *think* I'm the hottest thing since Beyoncé's "Drunk in Love" video. I'm convinced I am. Big difference. *Snap, snap!* Don't get it twisted.

Now who's ready for roll call?

Always fly, check . . .

Always fabulous, check . . .

Always workin' the room, check . . .

Always snappin' necks, check, check . . .

Always poppin' the hips 'n' turnin' it up, check, check . . .

Wait. Wait. Wait. Let's rewind this segment *alllll* the way back for a sec. Yes, I keeps it cute, all day, every day, okay? And, yes, I know how to turn it up when I need to. I'm from the hood, boo. Born 'n' bred. But that doesn't mean I have to *be* hood. No, honey-boo. I'm too classy for that. Trust. But know this. If I have to let the hood out on you 'n' introduce you to the other side of me, it ain't gonna be cute. So don't bring it 'n' I won't have to sling it.